LIGHT UNTAMED

BONNIE GILL

SOUL MATE PUBLISHING

New York

LIGHT UNTAMED

Copyright©2018

BONNIE GILL

Cover Design by Fiona Jayde

Published in the United States of America by
Soul Mate Publishing
P.O. Box 24
Macedon, New York, 14502

ISBN: 978-1-68291-820-3

ebook ISBN: 978-1-68291-778-7

www.SoulMatePublishing.com

To Mom & Dad

Thank you for being there.

Acknowledgments

Sincere thanks and love to the following:

The readers who asked for Pepper and Ottar's story. I hope you enjoy their journey.

Dion, Nicole, Jessica, Brenda, Becky, Jane, and my parents, your support and encouragement allowed me to follow my dreams and believe in myself. I can never thank you enough.

God, who has carried me through some tough times and gave me strength when needed.

Paula Millhouse my fabulous critique partner, your critiques and insights helped me grow as a writer. This story would have never made it without you. I can't thank you enough.

Terry Spear my mentor, your friendship means more to me than I can ever express. You are an inspiration and a true professional.

Kerry, Mary, Marybeth, Susie, Ellen, Karen, Kim, Beth, and Chris, you guys have stuck by me since grade school. You're more like sisters and I thank you for your love.

My editor Cheryl Yeko and Soul Mate Publishing, for sticking with me.

Fiona Jayde, for creating the most awesome cover.

Chapter 1

Pepper Peterson stabbed the damp soil with a screwdriver, then placed the tampon stick into the hole. "I need more ammunition," she called out to her bestie in the dark.

Abby brought over an unopened box of womanly necessities. "I'm not opening it. *Nah uh*. How come you're so dead set on doing this?"

Pepper peeled away the plastic wrapper. Her friend refused to open tampon boxes ever since an evil Genie popped out of one and cursed her to become the Jersey Devil every time she got her period. They broke the spell, but she didn't blame Abby for having the phobia.

"Because Keith stood me up for Charlotte. Look, you can see them watching television." She pointed to the six-inch crack in the curtains covering the big picture window of the small blue home. Two people sat on the couch, their heads close. "I have to teach him there are consequences for being a rat bastard."

Keith had broken their date, saying he'd be out of town for work. *Liar.* She planted another tampon in the ground. Perfect for mushrooming, the old fashion tampons perched on a stick applicator instead of the plastic push kind, standing tall with the string flapping in the evening breeze.

A slight October chill nipped at the back of her exposed neck, causing her to shiver. "The cotton will absorb the night's dew and expand, causing it to mushroom. That's why this technique was named Mushrooming. In the morning, he'll see our message spelled out in the yard." She couldn't wait. "Hey, does River still have those surveillance cameras?"

She'd love to see Keith's face when he saw the full-bloomed tampons.

"They're at the police station. Maybe we could break in and get one?"

Her bestie never shied away from Pepper's escapades, even though she was set to marry the Sherriff in a couple weeks.

Abby and River had a great relationship. Maybe someday she'd find someone who would love her unconditionally like her friend did.

Fat chance.

Most men bailed on her after they met her large herd of rescued pups. She could only imagine what they'd do if they found out about her family's secret.

"Car," Abby called out.

They darted next door into the empty field and ducked down behind the three-foot tall weeds. When the tail lights of the vehicle faded into the night, they strolled toward Keith's lawn.

"Come on, we're almost done," Pepper said.

"Where on earth did you find these old things?" Abby asked.

"My aunt had purchased a buttload, and I have another full carton in the attic. She must have found a great deal, or maybe they fell off a truck. Who knows." A total packrat, her Aunt had enough cases of toilet paper stashed in the house to last her years. Her heart still ached even though her Aunt died years ago.

"I can't let Keith get away with standing me up. Or other guys will think it's okay to bail on me for another woman. It only takes one time of slacking and they get reprogramed. Men are like dogs, you can't give them an inch. They need constant discipline." She'd learned her lesson early on with her dog rescue.

"I hate to say this," Abby said, "but you have a reputation for dumping your men after the second or third date. Don't you think he beat you to the breakup?" She handed Pepper another tampon.

I have a reputation? News to her. Okay, maybe she did tend to break things off after a few dates. Big deal. If she got the yuckies for them, she wasn't going to waste her time or theirs. She could tell if it wasn't a good fit after a few dates. "I don't think it's fair to string them along. Besides, he didn't break up with me. He postponed our date and lied."

Abby hummed as she placed the tampons into the ground. They'd both dressed in black from head to toe for the mission. After sticking the last tampon in the yard they stepped back to admire their artwork. LOSER was spelled out across his lawn, the letters perfectly executed so there'd be no mistaking the message.

Grinning, Pepper snapped a few photos with her phone as headlights flared in the distance.

"Car," Abby called out again.

They darted to the vacant lot and ducked down behind the brush. The car slowed as it passed by Keith's house. A street light in front of his property made the tampons glow in the dark like a scarlet letter.

"Umm, Pepper," Abby said in a shaky voice.

"I'm right here." She crept over to her friend in the damp weeds.

"I think we have to call River."

Oh no. "What in heaven's name for?" Could her friend be chickening out? River would totally make them remove all the tampons.

Abby pointed to her left. "There's a dead body. I almost touched it." She danced around, flinging her hands about. "Ewww."

A large man lay face down on the ground. Bending over, Pepper grabbed his wrist. No pulse. His skin cold to the touch. Her heart pumped faster and almost jumped to her throat. *Ick.* Now she'd touched a dead person. Dropping his arm, she wiped her hands on her pants. *Cooties!*

"Who is it?" Abby took a step away.

"Heck if I know." He wore tan pants and a dark shirt, but she couldn't see his face. His legs were sprawled and bent at odd angles. She breathed in the clean pine scent of the night's crisp air. At least he didn't smell dead.

Abby pulled out her phone and dialed River, informing him about the body. "We're on Main Street two blocks north of town, between Keith's house and the Taxidermy place." She paused. "Okay. See you in a few."

"What did he say?" Pepper asked.

"He said we have to stay put until he gets here." Abby looked over at Keith's yard. "I don't think River's going to be very happy with me."

Pepper glanced over her shoulder at the tampons. They were starting to puff out already. It was a glorious sight. She smiled, giddy with pride.

Freaking mission accomplished.

"Aww Abby-do, River won't care. He loves you. Besides, he knows we do crazy stuff all the time. You'd think he'd be used to it by now."

Not long after the call, red and blue lights flashed from down the street. They walked toward the road to meet him.

River pulled the squad car over, stepping from his vehicle. "Are you girls all right?" His blond curls swayed in the wind, his deep blue eyes creasing with concern. He gathered Abby in his arms and hugged her tight.

"Oh my gosh. I've never been so scared in my life," Abby replied.

Pepper rolled her eyes. Apparently, her friend was going to milk this as much as she could.

River kissed Abby's cheek and squeezed her again. He glanced up at Pepper over Abby's head. "Are you okay?"

"I'm fine. I checked for a pulse, but his body is ice cold." She wrapped her arms around her middle, totally freaked out. They didn't know how the guy died.

River looked over at Keith's yard and shook his head. "What did you two do this time?" A smile snuck from his lips.

Pepper shrugged. "Come on, River, we were just having a little fun. No harm done."

An ambulance parked behind River's car. The paramedics unloaded.

"Where's the body?" River asked.

Pepper pointed to the spot. "Over there."

Nothing could make her go back and see the dead guy. Besides, they probably contaminated the area with their DNA or something. Haber Cove was a small town, and not much of anything happened around there.

If he was murdered, a homicide would be a big deal.

~ ~ ~

Pepper couldn't have asked for better luck. Reporters swarmed the area, flashes from photographers popping to her right and left. River had taped off the dead body, so the reporters concentrated on Keith's yard instead, and the mushrooming tampons. Now everyone would know he was a no-good cheating loser.

Pepper pumped her fist in triumph.

The reporters gathered around, sticking their microphones in her face. "Can you tell us about what took place here tonight?"

"No comment," Pepper replied. Funny, she always wanted to say that to a reporter.

"What were you doing when you found the body?"

"No comment." She had this. They wouldn't break her.

"Does this resident have anything to do with the dead body?"

"I have no idea if he was involved," she said innocently enough, managing to put just enough question into her tone to make the vultures take notice.

Frowning, Keith stepped outside and scanned his yard. A minute later Charlotte exited the house, eyes widening as she slapped a hand over her mouth. The reporters ran over and bombarded him with questions. He scratched his head, then curled his lip at Pepper.

Pepper smiled her biggest smile while waving to him.

Serves you right, dirtbag.

The paramedics left, and the coroner arrived. River strolled away from the site where they'd found the body, and a half dozen microphones were shoved in his face.

A blond reporter asked, "Sherriff, was this a murder?"

"I'll give you a full report after the autopsy. Time to go home, everyone." He signaled to Abby for them to follow him to his police car. Her friend sat in the passenger seat while Pepper took a seat in the back. She sucked in the new car smell and waited.

River got in but didn't start the vehicle. "All right, ladies. You have a lot of explaining to do."

Abby turned to River, her mouth clamped shut. It looked like Pepper would have to take over. Which was fine. At least she could control the conversation.

"We were only having a little fun. Keith cheated on me, so I decided to teach him a lesson."

"Really? Isn't this a little childish even for you two? Abby, we're getting married in a couple of weeks. Don't you think it's time to put an end to this kind of shenanigans?"

Abby narrowed her eyes. "Keith had it coming. No one disrespects my friend and gets away with it."

Way to go Abby-nator. *That's my girl.* "Come on River, we didn't damage his property or anything. It was only a little prank."

"How did you two even get here?"

"My car is a couple blocks over. Who's the body?" Pepper asked.

"It's Louie, and he was murdered."

Louie Appleton owned the town taxidermy shop next to Keith's house. The creep hunted animals and mounted their heads on plaques. Really, what kind of person does that? Not that Pepper had wanted him dead or anything. "Holy cow. How'd he die?"

"I'm afraid I'll have to call Ottar in on this one. It doesn't look like an ordinary homicide."

Pepper swallowed hard. The only reason River would call Ottar was if a Cryptid was responsible. Cryptids were mythical beasts like Big Foot or the Loch Ness Monster. The last time she'd seen Ottar he'd hauled away a man-eating gnome. The barbarian Aussie loved to aggravate her any chance he got. "Do you think the gnome escaped?"

"No, this is something completely different. I don't need to remind you that this is confidential. I'm only telling you two because I don't want you walking around by yourselves. I'll drive you to your vehicle, then you're both to go straight home. Got it?"

They both nodded.

A sinking feeling settled in the pit of Pepper's stomach. It was only a week away from Halloween. How would she be able to carry out her family's obligation with Ottar snooping around?

Chapter 2

"Oh hell no. I'm not going anywhere near those two crazy broads." Ottar sat back in his chair and drained the rest of his beer, then twirled his empty bottle on the Formica table.

He glanced at the people sitting at the dark bar over his boss's shoulder. The lights from a neon sign illuminated a pool table where a hot blonde and a redhead shot some stick. What he wouldn't give to be knocking balls around with a couple of babes instead of being briefed on his next mission by Houston, a monumental dickhead. The man sat there all smug with his crew cut and navy suit, looking like a typical government official.

"In the past years our satellites recorded a hot spot on this property." His boss unfolded a map of New Jersey and pointed directly to Pepper's address. An address Ottar avoided like rabid crocodiles for the past two months.

The last time he'd visited Haber Cove had been a nightmare. Not to mention his friend and fellow coworker was marrying one—Abby—who happened to be Pepper's best friend and co-conspirator.

Houston leaned over the table. "I need you to check this area and report back to me," he said in an authoritarian tone. "You're ours and we can make you do anything we want." He tapped Ottar on his wrist to remind him of the microchip implant.

Ottar jerked his arm back, repulsed by the jackass's clammy hand.

Damn, they had him by the balls. L.A.M.P.S., Legends and Myth Police Squad, the agency for whom he worked, could force him to do almost anything. As a teen, he'd been sentenced to prison for life in Australia for killing a tribe of Aborigines. Only he hadn't killed anyone, the Drop Bears were the culprits. L.A.M.P.S. pulled some strings to get him transferred to America. In exchange he was to work for L.A.M.P.S.

He couldn't remember the block of time when it happened, and it drove him batshit nuts.

"We know River's wedding is in a couple of weeks. His hands are full. Besides, we heard you're the best man." Houston gave him a closed mouth platypus smile. Some days he hated working for the plunker. Well most days. But he did enjoy hunting monsters. Maybe he could chuck a sickie and call in?

Ottar had a million and one excuses he'd made up to avoid the whole ceremony—mainly Pepper. He'd never turned down an assignment in almost fifteen years. Not that he could anyways. He signaled the waitress for another two stubbies.

This did peak his curiosity a little. "So what kind of hot spot are we talking?"

"There are several more around the country, but this one, this is the largest. They only pop up on Halloween night, and then again the next morning for a brief period."

A long sigh escaped Ottar's lips and he leaned back in his chair. "Wouldn't this be under the paranormal department?"

L.A.M.P.S. had several different sections. He was an area manager of the Cryptid unit. They hunted monsters like Moth Man and the Jersey Devil. The Paranormal unit took care of ghosts and demons and such. Lastly, the alien unit dealt with ETs and UFOs.

"All our paranormal agents are tied up this Halloween.

It's their busiest time of the year. Besides, we have no idea what this is." Houston studied Ottar's face.

Ottar schooled his expression and tried to look uninterested. He wanted to avoid Pepper.

A waitress with huge knockers brought Ottar his beers and he took a long drink. "Could the heat signature be a large bonfire?"

Houston chuckled. "This is much larger than a campfire. Although I'm not ruling out witchcraft."

The last time he was there Pepper and Abby danced around naked while chanting, and their spell backfired into a stampede of possums. He couldn't help the smile that spread across his face. Pepper dancing in the moonlight naked was a sight to behold. Too bad she was nuttier than a pecan tree. "If you remember, my report indicated they were trying to break the curse on Abby. They botched the spell and had no idea what they were doing."

Since that night, he'd thought about her every single day. Her long legs, blond hair, and those pouty, naughty lips. What if they did know witchcraft and Pepper had placed an attraction spell on him? His heartbeat picked up.

"All the more reason to check on them." Houston steepled his pointer fingers. "River is too close to these women. I need someone who will get to the bottom of this. You're our man."

"I'll check it out. Any certain time the heat signature shows up?"

"It's usually after dark, but before midnight on Halloween. Who knows, maybe after this assignment we could talk about removing that microchip."

Ha! The wanker had promised the same thing for the past five years. "That would be a nice change." He minded his manners. One day he'd go all berserker on Houston and show him what he really thought.

"Get it done." Houston rose from his chair and threw down a couple of twenties on the table. "I want a full report by November first."

Ottar nodded, and watched him walk past the sheilas playing pool, then out the door. He finished his beers, but the cool liquid hadn't quenched his dry mouth. Did Houston realize what Pepper did to him? That firm, round hop-on-me arse. Her kooky vegan beliefs and her never ending love for varmints and other scurrying animals. Crikey, he was getting a stiffy thinking about her.

The odd warm feeling came back to his stomach. Happened every time he thought about the woman. The only explanation, she was indeed a witch and placed a lust spell on him.

His phone vibrated. River's number appeared.

"Ottar here."

"Can you come early? I think we've got another Crytpid loose."

"What's up?"

"Abby and Pepper found a body tonight. An adult male with both Achilles tendons clipped and bite marks on his neck. The guy bled out, but there was no blood at the scene. And, listen to this, he was a taxidermist." River let out a long breath.

"You think it could be Jackalopes?" Damn, he'd heard about these little ferocious creatures, but never hunted them. His pulse sped up. They usually kept to the West.

"That's what I'm thinking. I'm sorry to ask you to come early but I have a lot going on."

"No worries, mate. I'll be out there tomorrow."

~ ~ ~

The next morning, Pepper and Abby worked together at Pepper's Perky Pets pet shop. Pepper popped her bat-shaped vegan Halloween dog treats into the oven, clanking the baking pans on the racks. She'd had rented out the storefront next to her pet store and converted it into a small, but efficient, kitchen. This year she'd have a couple hundred treats ready for purchase for when the townspeople dressed up their poochies and stopped by. Her internet store sold them by the thousands. She could barely keep up with the orders. The nutty smell of peanut butter and oatmeal wafted through the room.

"I think we should make plans for Halloween night. River will be on patrol most of the evening," Abby said.

"I have plans." There was no way she would let Abby be involved in her activities that night. No doubt she'd blab to River.

"You do not. Let's watch scary movies and eat popcorn. Or we can go to the Halloween shindig they're having in town." Abby rolled out some cookie dough.

"No really. I have something I have to do."

"What?" Abby brushed her hands on her pants, leaving white flour splotches all over the deep blue denim material.

"I'd really rather not say right now. It's a commitment." Best to keep it as vague as possible. She couldn't afford the risk of River sticking his nose where it didn't belong.

"Ottar is going to help River investigate Louie's murder. He's meeting River this morning."

Pepper's throat suddenly became too tight to swallow. Keeping her secret was hard enough without Ottar poking his nose into her business. No matter what, though, she had to perform her task. She wouldn't fail her family's obligation.

"So what?" Her voice squeaked a little.

"So maybe he'll fix your dinosaur statue. Isn't that what you wanted?" Abby raised a brow at her.

Yes. The stupid man shot her life-size dinosaur's eye out with a huge tranquilizer dart. If he was so great at his job, you'd think he could tell the difference from a Flintstone statue and a monster. "Of course, I want him to fix it."

"Good, then it's settled." Abby pressed the pumpkin cookie cutter into the dough.

"What's settled?"

"I'm making him repair your dinosaur as soon as he gets in, otherwise I'll un-invite him to the wedding."

"I highly doubt you or anyone else can 'make' that man do anything, Abby-bridezilla." She'd figure out how to distract him Halloween night.

The cookies cooled and they'd decorated them with pup friendly icing, wrapping each one in a cellophane bag. Pepper picked out black ribbon with little candy corns painted on it and tied a bow on the baggy. She held it up for Abby to see.

"Oh, they're adorable. Can I have one for Hercules and Kazoo?" Hercules was River's Mastiff and Kazoo was Abby's three-pound Chihuahua-dachshund mix. The two dogs became best of friends when River and Abby started dating.

"Of course. Take as many as you want." Abby sat at her counter and a wave of exhaustion washed over her. She took two of the ghost- and bat-shaped cookies and put them by her purse.

"Uh oh." Abby placed her hand over Pepper's. "You have that burdened look on your face. What's really going on?"

Chapter 3

Ottar walked into the Haber Cover Police department and dropped his duffle bag next to the door. "Oi, anyone here?" The small building had a couple of desks in the reception room, a bathroom, and two jail cells in the back. His boots clumped on the dull green tile that had seen better days.

River walked out of the bathroom drying his hands. "Hey, Ottar. Good to see you." He gave Ottar a quick man-hug. "I haven't received the report from the Coroner yet."

"I was headed here anyways. Houston wants me to tie up a few loose ends in the gnome case." A bunch of kangaroo crap. He'd keep River in the dark until he knew exactly what Pepper had festering on her land. Besides, Abby might also be involved. River was super protective about his wife-to-be.

"Well, I'm glad you came. Would you like to stay at our house tonight?"

"That would be great." Ottar picked up his olive-green backpack and slung the dead weight over his shoulder. They left for River's house.

Once they arrived, River grabbed his arm and pulled him inside the brick ranch he called home. "Can you believe I'm getting married next weekend?"

Yes. River had done nothing but make goo-goo eyes at Abby since he'd met her. She was the reason he'd left L.A.M.P.S. Ottar's hands fisted. River was a damn good agent, now playing Sheriff to a teeny town. What a waste. "Are you getting nervous?"

"Na. Abby is the one for me. The past few months have

been great. I hope you brought the supplies to fix Pepper's dinosaur. Every single time I see her, she asks about it."

The insane woman was obsessed with that hunk of resin. "Of course." The original artist of the statue died so he commissioned a glass artist to blow a new eye. He'd snuck over to Pepper's property and snapped a few pictures of the remaining eye and took measurements so they'd match it.

"Great. You know, I think deep down she kind of likes you."

Hah. Joke of the year. They were like gas and fire. Fine alone, but when they got together explosions happened. Sure, she was hot. With her long bouncy blond hair and those brilliant blue eyes. She was also annoying as a prickly hedgehog stuck in his shorts. "Thanks, but I'll pass." He plopped down on the tan overstuffed couch and crossed his ankles on the coffee table. "That woman is trouble. I hate to say it, but your wife-to-be is her bestie, so if I were you I'd get used to it."

River shrugged. "They're full of life."

"What were they doing when they found the body?"

River raked his hand over the top of his head, and Ottar fought back a smirk. Poor bastard was in for a lifetime of rigmarole with those women.

"They were mushrooming someone's yard."

"What the bloody hell is mushrooming?" Were they hunting for fungus or taking psychedelic mushrooms for their witchy incantations?

"It's not what you think."

"I'm thinking whatever it is, it's not good by the look on your face." Pepper and Abby would put poor River in his grave.

"They were sticking tampons in some guy's yard. When the dew hit them, they puffed out like mushrooms. The word *Loser* was in full bloom across his front lawn."

Ottar grinned. "What did the poor bloke do to deserve their wrath?"

"He broke his date with Pepper for another woman."

Ottar swallowed. Then swallowed again. "Pepper has a boyfriend?" he growled. For some insane reason, he wanted to find this man and beat the bloody piss out of him.

"Pepper has a lot of boyfriends, they really never last."

"Why?"

"I have no idea. Why don't you put your bag in the spare room?"

Ottar picked up his backpack and headed to the room where he'd stayed the last time he visited only it didn't look familiar. The room was an explosion of pink. Pink and dark pink striped walls surrounded a white canopy bed that vomited pink froo-froo lacy ruffles over itself. A cold clammy sweat broke out on his forehead. "What the hell?"

River cleared his throat behind him. "Sorry. Abby decorated."

"It looks like a panty shop exploded in here." He shook his head as he dropped his duffle onto the bed crowded with about a hundred frilly lace pillows. "Your woman is out of control." Ottar glanced up at the dainty chandelier and gritted his teeth. He sucked in a deep breath through his nose. Big mistake. Bubblegum scent! He coughed, trying to expel the sugary thick aroma curled inside his lungs.

"Abby always wanted a girly room."

"This is a nightmare. I don't think I can stay in here. I might lose my manhood. The swimmers will go belly up."

"Negative. The other bedroom is being used for storage. Abby plans on decorating it after the wedding. You have no choice, pal." River's smile turned devious.

Sure he had a choice. "I can always sleep outside, mate." Which seemed to be the only option now.

"Or . . . You can shack up at Pepper's house. She has three vacant bedrooms."

True, but Pepper would drive him absolutely bonkers with her vegan lifestyle and all those animals surrounding her. Still, he considered his options. What he wouldn't give to catch her naked again?

He'd never forget the goddess image of the woman when she danced in the moonlight, or when she rode her horse naked through the woods. With her long blond hair trailing in the wind behind her and those glorious pointers bouncing to the rhythm of the horse's gallops, she'd bewitched him for sure. She'd pulled the Lady Godiva stunt to distract him when Abby turned into the Jersey Devil. Clever sneaky woman. "I'll pass."

"Close your eyes and you won't even notice the pink while you sleep."

Was he kidding? "I doubt that."

"I have to patrol the town. If you need anything, call me." River gave him a nod and chuckled as he left the room.

The kitchen's pastel orange walls and blue accents made the room homey. The stainless-steel appliances sparkled. He grabbed a beer, sat at the wooden table, and took a long swig. He'd need a few frosties before he dealt with Pepper and her statue. Tipping the bottle, the cold liquid ran down his throat. His cell phone vibrated in his pocket.

"Hey, Ottar, it's Roman." Roman McClure was Holly's oldest brother. Their dad was one of the founders of L.A.M.P.S., and Roman was one hell of a Cryptid hunter.

"What's up?"

"I need you to convince River to come back to L.A.M.P.S. Cryptids are popping up all over the map."

"River is freelancing. I'm sure he'll step in when needed."

"We've had five hunters leave the organization in the past six months. I think something fishy is going on. L.A.M.P.S. is not what it used to be."

"I think his wife-to-be had a lot to do with his decision." Ottar swallowed another drink of his beer.

"Do me a favor and get him back to full time." He ended the call.

Roman was a huge Irish bastard, with dark hair and green eyes. Why would Roman ask him to get River back, instead of Houston? Usually, the dickhead took care of personnel issues.

He grabbed his backpack and headed out the door. Maybe Pepper wouldn't be there. Then again, maybe he'd catch her naked.

~ ~ ~

Owning a business was tough and dealing with animal adoptions was even tougher. Pepper held her ground and refused a family who wanted to adopt a puppy. The family wasn't bad or mean, but they didn't understand puppies couldn't be left alone for ten hours while they were at work.

To train a puppy properly, he'd have to be taken outside at least every five hours. It also wasn't fair to leave a pup in his cage alone for so long.

"Oi, hey." A distinct Aussie voice called out from her yard.

Startled, she stepped back and peered up at her beloved dinosaur statue. Ottar perched on the curved neck of her Brachiosaurus sculpture. His chiseled face almost beautiful, as wild brown hair fanned in the breeze like the mane of a ferocious animal. A leather strap wrapped around his left bicep, and a tribal tattoo encircled his right.

Pepper wanted to trace her tongue over every swirl and shape inked on his beautiful, bulging muscles.

No. No. No. What the heck was she thinking?

He was *so* not her type. She'd officially gone insane. The stress of the day must have fried her brain, scorching her common sense to ash.

She gave him a little wave and continued toward her house.

"Hey. I'm repairing your dinosaur." He pointed to the busted eye.

What did he want, a freaking trophy? "I see that. Thank you."

She didn't want to deal with him right now. She'd been daydreaming all day about soaking in a hot soapy bath, while sipping on a big glass of red wine.

Alone. Without him.

Opening her front door, she stepped into her house.

Her four dogs bounded to her with tails wagging. "How's my babies?" Barney the St Bernard, and Betty the Great Pyrenees, banged their large bushy tails against her legs. Dino the Sheltie, and Bam Bam, a Golden Retriever, spun in circles with excitement. It was good to be home.

Betty rubbed her fluffy face on Pepper's thigh. She'd rescued Betty from the pound, along with eight of her puppies. Pepper found homes for the pups but decided to keep Betty. She placed a kiss on the top of her furry head.

She loved being at work, having built her business from a little hobby into a dream. Today had been rough, but mostly her job was very rewarding.

She flipped through her mail and came across a letter addressed to her with no return address. Letters cut from a newspaper formed words in the letter. How creepy was that?

Pepper.

You are a spoiled bitch. I'm going to kill you.

From,

Wouldn't you like to know?

A cold sweat broke out on her brow. Why would someone want to kill her? She flipped over the envelope. The postmark read two days ago. So, it wasn't Keith getting back at her for the tampons she'd left in his yard.

A knock on the door sounded, and she nearly jumped out of her skin.

"Can I use your dunny?" Ottar stood on the other side of the screen wearing his usual cargo shorts and a tight T-shirt. The light material clung to his abs, showing every ridge and valley of stomach cobblestones. Dark auburn hair hit past his shoulders with a few small braids intertwined. His deep brown eyes sparkled full of mischief and knowledge—but underneath the surface, a void or sadness swirled in the depths. *Interesting.*

She cleared the lump from her throat and motioned him inside. "Wow, I'm surprised you didn't wiz on a tree."

"I'm tryin' here." He held his palms up by his sides.

"I appreciate it." She placed the letter on the end table with the other mail.

Her pups circled around his legs with their tails wagging and tongues slurping.

"Sit," he said.

The four pups sat on their behinds, gave him an attentive gaze, and waited for another command. *Traitors.* He patted their heads on the way to the restroom.

She didn't trust him. He was a L.A.M.P.S. agent, and that made him nosy. He did make her feel a little safer though, considering the death threat. Who on Earth would want to kill her?

She sat on the overstuffed gold sofa and waited for him to finish.

"Thanks. I'll get back to work." He wiped his brow with his forearm.

Darn. She couldn't be rude, bad manners weren't in her genes. "Would you like something to drink? A beer?"

His eyes lit up and his smile revealed two adorable dimples. Why the heck was she thinking about his good looks? His hunter occupation made him a threat, and she didn't need him snooping around when she carried out her important task.

"Oi, yeah. I could go for a tinny."

"A tinny?" What in the world?

He shrugged. "Sorry. A can of beer would do the trick."

"Ottar, I know you're from Australia and all, but you don't talk like the others from there." She grabbed a can from the fridge. The dogs followed her back into the front room.

"I grew up in the outback, or the bush. My grandfather raised me far from the city." He took a long swig of his beer. With each gulp, his Adams apple slid up and down his large sexy throat. "You're from New Jersey, but you're accent switches from eastern to southern when you want something."

"Maybe I lived in Texas for a while?"

"Stop telling porkies. I know you've lived here all your life."

That bastard must have done his research on her. "It's none of your business."

He nodded one nod. "River asked me to stay at his house."

"I thought he might." Poor Abby would have to put up with two men until after the wedding.

"Can I camp out on your land instead?" He tilted his head and waited for her to say something.

"No way. The last time you stayed here you barbecued one of my rabbits." Lord knows what he would eat next time.

"It wasn't *your* rabbit. It was a *wild* rabbit. And I didn't know you were so attached to them. I promise I won't eat any of your critters while I'm here. I'm kind of desperate. Abby Barbiefied her spare room. I won't be able to sleep in there."

Serves him right. He burned his bridge here. "River has a backyard."

"He lives on a postage stamp."

"My answer is still no." She crossed her arms and shook her head to finalize her answer.

Ottar's expression showed a flare of hurt, then went neutral. "Thanks for the beer." He chugged the rest of his can, hung his head, and walked out the door.

There was no way he would make her feel guilty. No way. He killed one of her bunnies. Not to mention he shot her dinosaur statue. He was trigger happy, and a maniac. Sure, today he was civil, and it must have hurt him to be on his best behavior, but she wasn't budging. His showing up early would throw a wrench in her well-oiled wheel of life.

Halloween was almost here and the one time of year when her family duties called. A commitment she intended to honor. She'd reconsidered and would call Abby to help. Could her friend keep her secret? Also, she wanted to tell her about the letter.

She dialed her number.

Abby's sweet voice answered. "Hello."

Pepper peeked out the window. Ottar banged on the damaged eye with his hammer, while dangling from the dinosaur statue's head. His muscles tensed with each swing of the tool.

"Hey, Abby. Ottar's here."

"I hope he's repairing your statue." Abby let out a snort.

"Yes, but that's not why I'm calling. Someone wants to kill me. I need your help."

Chapter 4

Ottar balanced on the head of the Flintstone dinosaur statue and studied Pepper through her kitchen window. The crazy woman would never let him live down eating the rabbit and shooting her stupid statue. Too bad Pepper wouldn't give him permission to stay on her land. It just upped the game. He'd stop at nothing to find out about the heat signature on her property.

He looked down at his wrist and rubbed the slight lump of the tracking device. Never had he failed a mission, and he wouldn't now.

Four furry dogs barked at him while he clung to the statue's head. They circled the dinosaur with their tails wagging at full speed. He liked Pepper's misfit pups.

The crunch of tires on gravel grabbed his attention. A police car pulled in the driveway. River and Abby slammed their doors and bounded to Pepper's house. They didn't once look over at him.

What the bloody hell was going on?

Eager to find out, he shimmied down the brachiosaurs' neck and followed them inside.

Pepper's hands trembled while she held a sheet of paper.

"Are you okay, Pepper?" Abby asked.

She held out the note, nibbling on her plump bottom lip. Ottar wouldn't mind taking a taste of her soft pink mouth.

River read the note and looked up at her. "Do you have any idea who could have sent this to you?"

"No. I mean some people get upset if I reject their adoption applications." Pepper rubbed her temples.

"I'll need a full list of everyone you've turned down. And, anyone else that you may have angered."

Odd. "What's going on?" Ottar asked.

Abby slammed her hands on her hips. "Pepper received a death threat from some psycho."

"Do you think it could be a prank?" Pepper asked in a soft sweet voice.

"Let me see." Ottar held out his hand.

River passed the paper to him. He read the short letter. His arms and legs heated up first, then the blaze moved through his body to his head. He wanted to punch someone. "Are you sure you haven't provoked anyone?"

"Don't blame her. She's the victim," Abby piped in.

Pepper shifted from foot to foot. "I'm sure. We've been really good lately. Except last night we mushroomed Keith's yard, but the envelope is postmarked two days ago."

Sure enough, she was correct.

"She shouldn't be alone. I think I should stay with Pepper," Abby said.

"I'll be all right. You don't have to stay here."

"Abby, I don't think that's a good idea. You may get hurt. How about Ottar?" River nodded to him.

Perfect. He'd keep her safe and investigate the hot spot. Good ole River pulled through for him.

Pepper shook her head. "I don't want to inconvenience anyone."

"It's no trouble at all. I told ya, I can't sleep in the pink room."

Abby flinched.

"Sorry, Abby. It's too girly for me."

Pepper twirled a long golden lock of her hair. She paused a moment and then said, "There will be no killing of any animals or birds on my property. In fact, you will only eat what you buy in the grocery store while you're here."

She wagged her finger at him. "No hunting on my land or anywhere else. And, don't leave any socks laying around, Bam Bam likes to eat them. Do you understand?"

Bingo. "I'll be on my best behavior."

She shrugged. "Okay, I guess he could stay. But, only until we catch who sent the letter." She narrowed her eyes at him like she'd might regret her decision.

If she was hiding anything, he'd damn well find out. And maybe see a little boob in the meantime.

Chapter 5

Pepper checked her watch and stared at her bathroom door. "Come on, Abby-diva, she called out. "We need to leave. Now. The Halloween festivities started twenty minutes ago." What was taking her so long?

Abby popped out of the bathroom. "I love this costume."

Pepper had planned the whole night and their ninja costumes were part of the scheme. She hoped it wouldn't be too obvious. The black faux leather pants and hoodies would conceal them, so they could slip from the party without notice.

She loved Halloween. Every year the town barricaded Main street and threw a big holiday shindig. The carnival games, food booths, and plenty of beer in the beer garden always drew a big crowd. No one would ever miss them.

Ottar chose to lurk in her house for three days straight. How long did it take to repair a hole in a fake dinosaur's head? She didn't want him to rush and do a sloppy job, but come on, three days?

Okay, she realized the real reason he hung around because of the pesky death threat note. But since no attempts had been made on her life, it was most likely a prank. Or maybe Ottar wrote the note as a way to spy on her. She wouldn't put it past the sneaky hunter.

They both checked their costumes in the full-length mirror. She grabbed her black hoodie out of the closet. "You make a sexy ninja, Abby."

"Do you think so? I'm hoping to reap some benefits

from River after dressing in this get up. He'd better not work late tonight."

"Oh, I bet you'll get lucky. River loves you."

Abby stuck her lip out, fiddling with her tin foil throwing stars. "I asked him if I could use his real weapons, but he said no."

"We don't need their equipment. We look awesome without it." And they did.

"River should be waiting for us by the apple booth at five o'clock." Abby slipped a sly smile. "I bet Ottar will tag along."

No doubt about that. Ottar was either working on her dinosaur, with River, or sneaking around her property. For some reason, she did feel safer with him there. She wondered what "Loose ends" he had to tie up? With two agents working on the same case, they should've been able to wrap it up and place a pretty bow on top. Oh well, not her concern. "I don't care if he's there tonight."

"Oh my gosh. River and I see the way you two look at each other. Like you want to rip each other's clothes off."

She often wondered what he'd look like without them. Fair is fair, he'd seen her naked. Pepper gave a slight shrug. "I really don't care about Ottar. He's good looking, but he's an ass." A total barbarian. So *not* for her. "You haven't said anything to River or made him suspicious about tonight, have you?"

"Nope. I totally nailed this secret squirrel stuff. What time do we leave the festival?"

"I need to be home after dusk, the earlier the better though." Her aunt always stressed the importance of her task. If she blew this mission the whole good and evil balance of the world could be in jeopardy.

"Okay. We can do this," Abby said.

Pepper removed her blow-up doll, Bob, from the front of her pickup truck and placed him in the back seat sitting up. Her aunt suggested she get a car buddy when she started driving so she wouldn't get carjacked. Not that they had a carjacking problem in Haber Cove. But, she'd grown used to having her blow-up companion ride along with her. "Come on Abby," she called out.

Abby joined her in the truck and they drove downtown to the Halloween festival.

River and Ottar waited for them by the apple orchard tent. Stacks of spikey hay bales and bunches of corn stalks decorated Main Street. Several bees buzzed around the sweet aroma of the red ripe apples piled in barrels. If Pepper wasn't so preoccupied with tonight's activities she would've bought a bushel. She reached up and stroked the golden dog whistle around her neck. Whatever it took, she'd carry out her important duties tonight.

~ ~ ~

Ottar paced back and forth. In the past three days nothing peculiar happened at Pepper's ranch. He intentionally dragged out the repairs on her beloved dinosaur statue so he could monitor her activity, while watching for any threats. He'd installed cameras to spy on her and hoped she wouldn't find them.

Although last time she'd been pissed, and Pepper was super-hot when angry. His blood heated, remembering how her blue eyes flared, and a seductive little curl lifted her upper lip.

"What are they dressed as?" he asked River.

"Abby said they were going as ninjas."

His eyebrow rose. A sexy one no doubt.

River's phone rang, and he walked over to the side of the deli.

Two ninjas clad in black sauntered down the street, one much smaller than the other. Abby's legs moved in double-time to keep up with Pepper's long thin limbs. They were both painted in soft black leather. Oh yes, he'd been right. Pepper made a smoking hot ninja. Ottar quashed the smile fighting to spread across his face.

"Hey, Ottar," Abby said. She poked Pepper.

Pepper nodded to him.

"Hey," he replied.

"Where's River?" Abby asked.

"He got a call and went over there." He pointed to River who didn't look very happy.

River walked over to them. "Someone called in another murder."

Chapter 6

Ottar and River pulled into the parking lot of the Taxidermy shop. Old barn wood covered the building and the gray cement stairs led to a dingy brown door. Ottar stood on the step and waited for River to enter. While it killed him not to take lead in the investigation, he let his friend do his job.

This was Sheriff River's town. He'd respect that, even though taking a backseat went against his nature. See, he could play nice. River had proved himself a good friend over the years and his competency as an agent.

Ottar paced, waiting for River to wave him in. He peeked through the windows. Deer heads stared back at him with lifeless eyes, along with dead fish, all mounted on wooden plaques on the wall. This cheeky fellow loved to display his trophies.

"Hey." River poked his head out the door. "Looks like you're going to have to take over on this case."

Ottar's blood pumped extra fast through his veins. "You mean as a L.A.M.P.S. agent? You know you can rejoin the agency. We're shorthanded now that you decided to play house with Abby."

"Nope. We already discussed that." River's face paled. "C'mon, you need to check this out."

Ottar followed him into the store. A woman lay sprawled out on the floor, her shirt and pants, bloody and ripped. "Oi, holy crocodile crap." He knelt to inspect the body. Bite marks riddled both her ankles, deep and torn. He pointed to bites the size of a quarter covering her neck. "That's not normal."

"This is the wife of the man we found a few days ago. They both owned this taxidermy shop." River pulled back the victim's hair and exposed her neck even more. "These wounds are the same as the other victim's."

"Bloody hell. They chewed clear through her carotid artery. The woman bled out."

River cleared his throat. "But there's hardly any blood around the body. What does it look like to you?"

"Something small killed her and they hunt in packs." He studied the tracks of tiny muddy footprints around the body. "Look. It has four toes and a pad in the middle. Those tracks are similar to common rabbits. The lack of blood means whatever murdered her drank her dry." Ottar glanced up at River with his lips pressed tightly together. "It's consistent with the other Jackalope attacks we have on file."

"You should see the display in the back room."

Ottar followed River into the back room of the shop. A large, but ancient, white porcelain stove covered half the workspace. Several trophy Jackalope heads hung on the wall. "Take one down."

River took down a stuffed rabbit head with antlers mounted on a plaque. "The first time I saw them, I thought they were fake."

Ottar pulled out his large knife and cut the fur on the back of the head. "These jackarses killed real Jackalopes. Where the hell did they find them?"

"That's the million-dollar question." River turned and headed toward the door. "I need to secure the scene. Can you finish with the body?"

"Oi. Let me get a few pictures and samples to send to headquarters and I'll call the cleaner. Didn't you search the premises after the first murder?"

River bit the bottom of his lip and exhaled through his nose. "Of course I did. She refused to let me into this back room though. She was mourning her husband and said nothing back here would help. I figured she was ashamed about the store being messy or something. You know how weird women get about that stuff."

Ottar collected saliva and a few stray hairs left on the body. It appeared the little beasts sliced her Achilles tendon with their teeth so the victim fell, then they zeroed in on the carotid artery. Or they could have jumped up to her neck. Hell. She must have screamed her damn head off when they attacked.

He didn't know much about Jackalopes. They were supposed to be mythical but the evidence in the past proved the little buggers were real. Swallowing hard, Ottar finished collecting samples. He'd seen a lot of gore, but he'd never get used to it.

He texted the cleaner. The organization often flew cleaners in by helicopter if the person was in another state. He covered the body with a tarp River had left by the back door.

After looking around for a while, he noticed a door off the hallway and pushed on it. The door creaked open to reveal a stairway down to a basement.

The sawdust and rodent stench became stronger as he descended. He covered his nose and breathed through his mouth.

Several stacked wire cages and hay were on one side. Behind them, cardboard postal boxes cluttered the corner. One of the boxes sat on the floor next to the stairs, addressed and ready to mail. He pulled out his knife, slicing it open. Under the packing lay a Jackalope trophy head. "Damn it," he said under his breath. They bred the beasties and killed them, then sold the mounts for a hefty price. "We've got a pack of vigilante Jackalopes on the loose."

Stepping closer to the cages, he observed the twisted, open wire doors. Had the little rascals broken out? Ten cages big enough to hold four or five of them each, stood empty.

They could be looking for fifty Jackalopes. Ottar did the math in his head. Knowing the explosive rate at which rabbits reproduced they could have one hell of a Cryptid disaster on their hands. Crikey. A drop of sweat dripped down the side of his face. With a large colony of pissed off Jackalopes on the loose, the whole damn town could be wiped out.

Chapter 7

"You named your Hellhounds after the Beverly Hillbillies?" Abby asked once they were back at Pepper's property.

"What can I say? The names and personalities fit." Pepper loved her old sitcoms.

When her mom left had her for long stretches, sometimes days, the television personalities became her friends. At first she'd hoped her mother would come home and tell her how sorry she was to be gone so long, and maybe tell her "I love you." But there'd been no apologies or loving words.

Pepper still knew every episode of her favorite shows and watched them when she got lonely.

She led Abby to the storm cellar behind the barn. "It's not far."

"I've been in your cellar before and haven't seen any gate to hell."

"That's because you weren't looking for it." She lifted the heavy metal storm door and headed down the stairs. "Click on your flashlight."

Abby's light bounced off the walls and shined right into Pepper's face.

She pushed Abby's hand to the side. "Shine it on the back wall."

"Okay. Okay." Her friend panned the light across the concrete wall and stopped on the corner.

Pepper took the lead into the shelter. After both had made it down safely she scanned the small area. To the normal person it looked like a refuge for a wicked storm, but Pepper knew better. Behind a loose stone was the lever to open the gates to the underworld.

"Stand behind me. It gets hot when the gates open. The pups are usually pretty friendly, but they can get protective of me. They've never met you." She'd never seen an aggressive bone in their bodies, but then again, she'd never had anyone tag along before. She'd hate for Abby to get hurt. In fact, she'd never forgive herself. But the hounds were like over grown puppies around her and she didn't think they would do anything to harm her bestie.

Abby slid in back of Pepper. "I'm ready. Release the hounds."

Pepper smiled. This was why she loved Abby like a sister. She'd accompany her in all of her kooky plans, no matter how strange. Her presence was like a blanket of comfort wrapped around her, making her feel warm and snuggly.

She pulled down the cold, rusty lever. The wall moaned. Stones shifted and moved at a slow pace. Both took a giant step back behind the cover of the wall. Yellow flames whooshed from the opening. Sweat beaded on her forehead.

The crackling inferno danced in the space, but soon died out, revealing a huge black iron gate from the floor to ceiling. Behind it, an unending dark corridor, leading to the pits of Hell. It should have bothered her that the underworld was in her backyard, but it didn't. Her hounds guarded the entrance, and nothing could breach the boundaries.

Five tiny beasts, black and fuzzy, rose from their sitting positions and jumped excitedly against the gate. The hounds resembled small Pomeranian pups.

Joy and adrenalin flowed through her heart. Pepper grinned. She loved these cute dogs. She petted their warm wet noses through the fence.

"These are the ferocious Hellhounds?" Abby stepped up to the gate and showed no fear.

"Don't be fooled, these little guys have superpowers. They can grow to be the size of rhinos. They also can go invisible."

"But they're Pomeranians." Abby bent down and cocked her head at them.

"Exactly. Have you ever owned one? This breed is not submissive and are notoriously stubborn. They also have tons of energy and love to bark. Poms aren't for everyone, especially families with small children."

"What happens next?"

"I open the gate and they run off into the night to complete their job."

"What exactly is their job?"

"They mark the damned to be taken to hell throughout the year." At least that's what her aunt told her.

"Who's the damned?"

"Murderers and rapists. Bad guys and gals who do evil things."

"Oh." Abby swallowed hard and took a step back. "These tiny cuties are going to track down criminals?"

"They'll grow when I release them."

"Do they come back on their own?"

"No. I have to call them back with a magic whistle." She pulled the slender ruby encrusted gold whistle from her chest where it hung on a chain.

"Cool. Can I blow it when it's time?"

"I don't know. See that one with pink nail polish?"

"You painted its nails pink?"

"Yep. That's Ellie Mae. She liked it. They're really smart." She scratched the pup behind her pointed ears.

"I bet this one is Granny." Abby pointed to the smallest dog with gray hairs sprouting from her black head.

"Yes. She takes her paw and smacks the others when they get rambunctious." Granny was a feisty old bitty. "She keeps everyone in line."

"Okay. So the one that just ran into the wall has to be Jethro."

"You got it. And that one over there, the one looking all alpha, is Jeb."

Abby shook her head as if she couldn't fit all this information in her brain. "What about the one in the corner growling?"

"That's Mr. Drysdale. He's a crabby one." Pepper maneuvered her hand through the bars with a vegan dog snack. "Who wants a cookie?"

All five dogs bounded up to the gate. Plumes of gray smoke puffed out their little nostrils, filling the area with a thick sulfur scent. "Take them nice." She waited for the hounds to line up by the fence.

Ellie Mae's long purple tongue slurped her hand, leaving gooey saliva on her knuckles.

Pepper laughed. "You goof." She stroked the small dog's fluffy black hair. "I'm happy to see you, too. I missed you."

"Can I give them one?" Abby asked, with a wide-eyed look.

"You know they can sense fear."

"Who said I was afraid?"

Pepper smiled. "You sure?"

Abby nodded fast.

"Okay. You can give Jethro one. He's over there with his head caught in the bars." She handed Abby a fire-hydrant-shaped treat.

"Hey, Jethro. You're just a little black doggy that smells weird." She held out the cookie.

Jethro howled and snatched the treat from her hand.

Abby jumped back from the bars.

"Jethro. That's no way to behave." She tsked tsked him. "Sorry, Abs. He's a little touched in the head, if you know what I mean."

Granny walloped Jethro across the muzzle.

"Thank you, Granny. Hey, Jeb, do you want your cookie or not?" The largest of the Pomeranians strolled up to the gate. He couldn't have weighed more than eight-pounds. He looked back at all the other hounds and then sat back on his rear. A coal colored nose poked between the iron fence, and he opened his mouth wide.

"Here you go." She placed a treat in his mouth.

The five tiny black dogs bounced around and nipped at each other in play. They took turns jumping on the gate with their brimstone breath stinking up the storm shelter. She didn't care if they were from hell and marked the damned, or even that they could turn invisible. They were still dogs and she would treat them with all the love and respect she showed every animal.

"Can I give them another treat?" Abby held out her hand.

"I guess so. They seem to like you." She handed her friend a ghost-shaped doggie cookie.

"Who wants a treat?" Jethro and Ellie Mae lunged for Abby's hand. Their purple tongues lapped across her wrist. She cackled and giggled. "I need another cookie."

"Mind your manners." Pepper scolded the naughty pups. "Sit."

All five Hellhounds sat back on their haunches and waited for her to give the next command. At least they were obedient when they wanted to be.

"Good puppies." Pepper rewarded each one with a treat. "It's time for you to do your job." She turned to Abby. "Let's see how they react to you when I let them out." Lifting the squeaky gate latch, all five bounded for her. They bounced on their hind legs and pawed at her ankles like a bunch of excited puppies.

Abby bent down and scratched the smallest one behind the ears. Granny responded by rubbing her snout on her fingers. "Wow. They're like regular dogs. I bet Kazoo would love to have one as a big brother."

Kazoo, Abby's three-pound Chihuahua dachshund mix, thought he was a hundred-pound Doberman.

"I don't think the Sheriff would appreciate it." River would absolutely kill Pepper if he found out about the Hellhounds. Then he'd try to capture one, if not all the hounds, for L.A.M.P.S. Pepper knew he freelanced when they called him and needed extra help.

"Yeah. I think you're right. Hercules would probably get his feelings hurt, too." Abby pouted her lip. Hercules was an over emotional big baby of a dog who slobbered, but you couldn't help but love him.

"Okay, time for you guys to go to work. When you come back I'll bring some more cookies for you."

The dogs stepped back and their images blurred. They grew to the size of Rhinoceroses, and suddenly the storm shelter was cramped. They bounded toward her. Large purple tongues slurped hot saliva all over her face. Pepper pushed up and patted one on the butt. "Get going, you don't have much time.

They looked down at her. Their long tongues hung from their huge mouths, and white teeth shone with brilliant contrast to their ebony bodies. Ten bright red glowing eyes studied her and waited.

"I release you. Come back before morning."

The huge pile of dogs landed on her, lavishing her with love and affection. Large curled fluffy tails whipped back and forth, beating against her body. Pepper laughed and tried to wrestle herself free. "Go on, you troublemakers. We're counting on you." The pack of Hellhounds bounded out of the storm shelter to hunt down and mark the souls of the damned.

Chapter 8

Ottar searched the field behind the Taxidermy shop, but only found tiny footprints and Jackalope poop. The animals disappeared long ago, and now that darkness had settled in, tracking the little buggers would prove difficult at best. Tall dry grass strands whipped at his shins as he walked through the field. His phone vibrated.

His boss's number appeared on the screen. The dickhead checked up on him all the time, and it drove Ottar batshit crazy. "Hey, Houston."

"How come you're not on Pepper's property?" *Shit, the hot spot.*

Ottar scratched his wrist where Houston had implanted his microchip. Stupid bloody tracking device. He should have known his boss would track his whereabouts. "We have a situation going on here."

"The large heat signature showed up again. You better have a good explanation for why you're ignoring my orders."

"Something came up."

"What do you mean something came up?" His voice was so tense Ottar thought he might snap.

"It seems we have a herd of Jackalopes on the loose. They've already killed two civilians." He filled Houston in on all the information.

"Well, that's just fantastic." Sarcasm bled through his words.

"The beasties are gone so I'm headed over to Pepper's now."

"You better get over there pronto! I can't believe you blew this. We may have to wait another year before we can figure this out." Houston sounded like he was stomping around while he was talking.

"I'll get to the bottom of it. I've never failed you before, and I'm not gonna start now." Ottar hung up the phone and kicked a nearby tree. Houston never ceased to jump on his last nerve. He found River in front of the taxidermist shop. He wished he could be in two places at once.

"River, I have to leave now."

"What the hell is more important than a fresh Cryptid case?"

"I'll be back."

"Look, I'm getting married in a week. I don't have time for this shit."

"Bloody hell, mate. I'm on it. I have other cases, too." He wished he could tell River about Pepper, and Houston's suspicions, but he knew better. Also, River's precious Abby was most likely involved in whatever was going on, and he was determined to find out first.

"What the hell is more important than killer vampire Jackalopes?" River yelled.

He'd have to use a different angle. "How about checking the safety of your wife to be?"

~ ~ ~

Pepper took her time walking back to the house with Abby. Barney the St. Bernard darted out of the barn with the rest of the pack, to greet them. She adopted Barney when his family left him at the Humane Society because he drooled all over their new furniture. She couldn't imagine disposing of a family member for a new couch. It wasn't like he started drooling overnight. She scratched his behind. Barney wiggled his butt under her fingers.

"Can I see the magic whistle?" Abby asked.

"Sure, when we get inside."

"I'm so glad you shared this secret with me. After the whole Jersey Devil fiasco, I thought I was the only one that had to deal with freaky stuff. I want to know the whole story. How it started and how you got elected to be the caretaker of the notorious Hellhounds."

Where to start? "I guess it started way back before my relatives came to America. They lived in England and worked as caretakers of the Hellhounds. My family was cursed, kind of like yours. Anywho, I only know that when my great-great-great-grandmother settled here, she was called upon. I think a gargoyle visited her."

Abby's mouth dropped open. "A gargoyle? That's so cool."

"Yeah, well, I guess it scared the crap out of her, but the women in my family must take on this role. They pass it down to another animal lover in the family. The caretaker chooses a female who can handle the responsibility." She considered the job was more of an honor than a curse. She truly enjoyed spending time with her hillbilly Hellhound pups.

"How did you get elected?" Abby walked double time to keep up with her.

"My aunt said she always knew I would be the one." Her aunt raised her as her own after her mom overdosed on painkillers. If only she could have saved her mom.

"I think she made the right choice."

"Thanks, Abby-doodle."

The wooden porch stairs creaked with each step. She would have to replace a few boards soon. They stepped through the small entryway in her old farmhouse. The soft yellow décor in the front room and old worn couch added a touch of her aunt's warmth to the home.

"So how did your family get the whistle?"

"The gargoyle gave it to my great-great-great-grandmother," Pepper replied, enjoying Abby's enthusiasm with her family's story.

"I can't wait to blow it." Abby rubbed her hands together. "Let me see it."

Pepper patted around her neck in search of the sturdy but delicate chain. The muscles in her throat clenched, and the moisture in her mouth disappeared. Gone. Her whistle was gone. How would she call the Hellhounds home? More importantly, what were the consequences if they didn't return to hell on time?

Chapter 9

"Let's check the forest," Pepper said to Abby while they set out on a search for the whistle.

"How can we find invisible dogs? Not to mention, it's still dark. We won't be able to see a thing out there." Her friend kept in step next to her.

"Either we'll hear them or smell them. Besides they may not choose to turn invisible tonight," Pepper said. "It's complicated."

"True. What are we going to do when River and Ottar come over?"

"We can say that we're looking for some stray dogs we heard in the woods."

Abby let out a long deep breath. "You think they'll believe us?"

Pepper wiped her hair from her face. "Probably not but it's worth a try. Come on." She pulled on Abby's arm in the direction the hounds took.

Thank goodness they had a flashlight. The darkness of the forest engulfed her. Several times she almost walked into a limb. Skittering of leaves across the damp earth sent creepies up her spine.

She breathed in the piney fresh air. "The sulfur scent is dissipating. Do you smell it anymore?"

"Nope. Where do we go from here? Should we look for the whistle instead?" Abby asked.

"I think the pups took it when they tackled me. Let's go back. Maybe they'll return to the cellar by nature." It was too much to hope for, but right now hope was all she had. She should have known that one day they would take advantage of her, the little rascals.

"Uh oh, it looks like they're here," Abby added.

Peppers heart picked up. "Really? They returned on their own?"

"Not the hounds, the guys." Abby pointed to the car headlights lighting up the night.

Double darn. They walked over to the driveway where River's squad car was parked.

"Why are you two out in the woods. Do you know how dangerous it is?" River scolded. "There's a murdering beast on the loose."

Déjà vu. River and Ottar never failed to catch them when they were trying to hide something.

"We were looking for some stray dogs. We heard them barking," Pepper added.

Ottar jabbed his index finger toward her, an accusing glare in his dark brown eyes. "You and Abby are up to no good again."

"I have no idea what you are talking about." How the hell *could* he know? Oh, man, the last thing she'd wanted was for L.A.M.P.S. to find her Hellhounds.

"Why would you go traipsing through the forest at night? Do you sheilas have a pack of wallabies loose in the upstairs paddock or something?"

"What the heck are you talking about?" Really, the man needed to stop using those stupid Aussie phrases.

"Crazy. It means that you're nuts."

Pepper rolled her eyes at him. "I told you, we heard some stray dogs out there. It's not safe for them, especially on Halloween. People are cruel." She walked toward her barn and stopped in front of the door. Barney raced up to her and rolled over on his back. She rubbed his soft belly. His tail swished back and forth on the grass. He rose to his feet and licked her fake leather pants.

Ottar frowned. "You and Abby weren't performing another spell, were you?"

Pepper tried to look dumbified. "What would give you that idea?"

"Oh, nothing really." He paused. "Except I smell sulfur."

"You do?" River sniffed the air.

"What?" How the heck would he know such a thing? Unless . . . "Are you guys spying on us again?"

He stretched his neck and rolled his shoulders. "Um no?"

"Ottar whatever your last name is, I can't believe you're doing this again. Shame on you." That stinking Aussie needed to go back Down Under. "I better not find out you wired cameras in my trees." Her gaze scanned the branches above her.

"My last name is Jones. Tell me what you *did* and maybe I can help you."

Well, this was just ducky. "I didn't. Do. Anything."

A smirky, smart-assed smile spread across his lips. "Okay. Know this. I will be on you like blow flies on croc-shit."

"And I will citizen's arrest you for stalking me."

River and Abby watched her and Ottar banter back-and-forth as if they were watching a volleyball match. Pepper frowned at them.

"Woman, you can't do anything to me that hasn't been done before. You are up to something, and I'm going to catch you doing whatever your hiding." His eyes blazed with a passion, and she had to admit, it turned her on. But she couldn't let him know that.

"Blah, blah blah." She tossed him a hand and walked into the barn. No time to waste arguing. Duties called her. Grabbing the pitchfork, she stabbed the hay and threw it to Wilma and Fred, her horses.

Ottar followed her and stood in the corner which suited her just fine. Maybe she'd make him a dunce hat. Abby and River came inside too.

"What exactly killed the taxidermist?" she asked.

"That's classified." Ottar pushed from against the wall and strolled toward the door.

This sucked. Of course he wouldn't tell her. She'd have Abby find out what they were hunting from River. She shot a glance to her friend. Her Hellhounds couldn't possibly have killed the taxidermist because the timeline was all wrong. Besides, they'd never killed before. They weren't allowed to hurt people—only mark them for justice. Then how come she had a bad feeling in the pit of her stomach?

Ottar turned to face her. "You know if you weren't such a pain in my ass, you'd be kind of cute."

He thought she was cute? She gave him her exaggerated eyeroll and turned her back to him. Great, not only did she have to deal with finding her Hellhounds and whistle, she'd now have to deal with Ottar's snarky sexy ass. Not to mention, his ability to blow her case wide open.

Chapter 10

Ottar's heartbeat slowed as soon as he stormed from the barn. The woman was a danger to mankind. He'd have to keep an eye on her twenty-four-seven. He chuckled. At least Pepper was entertaining. Watching her without strangling her would be most challenging. Her Flintstone dog pack patrolled the property and always alerted her when someone was near. Which would work to his benefit.

River and Abby said their goodbyes and Pepper went inside the house. He stepped into the woods about two hundred yards from the barn. The foliage concealed him out here. He breathed in the fresh crisp fall air filled with dried leaves and cedars. Shrugging, he pulled out his sleeping bag from his backpack and unrolled it.

Twinkling stars dotted the inky black sky. Free from walls and city noise, a calmness swept through his chest. He missed the rugged terrain in Australia. The old saying that home is where your heart is rang true. L.A.M.P.S. had ripped out his heart and tossed it away for the beasties to gnaw. The familiar chirping of crickets and hooting of owls sang a familiar song as he faded to sleep on his bed under the pines.

Ottar cracked one eye open, then the other, shifting in his sleeping bag. Peeking through the tree canopy, sunrise painted the sky in soft pinks and purples.

Shimmying out of his sleeping bag, the stench of urine engulfed his nose.

What the hell? His upper lip curled in disgust at the cold wet spot staining the dark material on his pantleg. "Damn it."

Not a little spot either. How in the hell had he not noticed an animal getting close enough to pee on him? Searching for tracks, he stomped around his campsite but found no evidence of the guilty animal.

He kicked a tree and called River. "Oi," he muttered when his friend answered.

River grunted. "Do you know what time it is?"

"Some animal peed on me while I was sleeping," Ottar grumbled.

River laughed. "Holy shit. That's the funniest thing I've heard in a long time."

"Sure, laugh it up, mate. You're lucky it didn't happen to you. The puddle was rather large. I looked for tracks but didn't see anything."

"Well, that will teach you to sleep outside. Come on over. I'll leave the door open so you can shower. Or do you want me to pick you up?"

"What's up?" a sleepy female voice said in the background.

"Nothing, Abby. Some large animal peed on Ottar. Go back to sleep."

"Hey, I'd appreciate if you didn't spread this around." Ottar gnashed his teeth together. Funny how lightly his friend was treating this. Didn't he realize this was crucial?

"Come on over and we'll talk about it. I'm up now." River hung up the phone.

Ottar rolled up his wet sleeping bag and stuffed it into a plastic bag, then packed up the rest of his gear. The sun peeked through the clouds to give the woods a soft orange glow.

Before he set out to River's house, he checked the large brown barn. Both of Pepper's horses were tucked into their stalls, so they weren't the culprits. Soft whinnies and pa-rumphs indicated they sensed him but didn't feel danger. After searching the area for her dogs, he remembered she kept them inside at night.

Relieved, he headed back into the woods toward River's place. Twenty minutes later, Ottar entered River's house and held the bag up to his friend's nose. "Take a sniff."

River slapped it away. "I don't need to smell it, dumbass. I'll take your word for it."

"It smells like urine, but it also has a smoky aroma."

River stepped away to wash his hands in the kitchen sink. "Why don't you wring it out and get a sample?" He let loose a smart-arse grin.

What a plunker. "The largest mammal in these woods is a deer. This isn't deer pee. It smells more like dog urine. A rather large dog or some kind of canine Cryptid."

"How the hell can you tell what kind of pee that is by smelling it?"

"It's not cat pee. This doesn't have a distinct ammonia odor. I have a feeling it has to do with Pepper's stray dogs. When I lived in the bush, I had to depend on all my senses."

Ever since River moved in with Abby, Ottar had assured himself Abby wouldn't cloud River's judgment. Now he wasn't so sure.

Abby strolled into the kitchen and grabbed a coffee cup from the cabinet. "Hey, Ottar. Tough night?" The smile on her face hinted she might burst out laughing. She bit her bottom lip and composed herself though. "Want a cup of coffee?" She held out a yellow cup with Pepper's Perky Pets blue logo on it.

He shook his head no.

River raised one eyebrow at his fiancé. "Ottar was trying to get me to smell the pee on his sleeping bag. He thinks it could be dog pee. Do you want to tell us about the stray dogs you and Pepper were chasing?"

Abby shrugged, took a swig of coffee, and sat down at the table. "I don't know what kind of dogs they were. You'd have to ask Pepper. I only heard them." She sat back in her chair, at ease.

Ottar studied her eyes. Maybe she was getting better at lying? "How big were the dogs?"

"How would I know? We'd only heard them. I'm not a dog expert." She sipped from her cup.

"You shouldn't go around chasing stray dogs. They could be rapid," River said over his shoulder while topping off his coffee.

"I highly doubt that. Not to change the subject, but could whatever peed on Ottar be the same cryptid that killed the taxidermist?"

"No, too big," River blurted out.

Ottar shot imaginary hunting knives from his eyes at River. He didn't want Abby to run and tell Pepper. The tree hugging, nature loving woman would get herself killed protecting the jackalopes. He picked up his wet sleeping bag and stuffed it in the large front loader washing machine.

"Let me add the soap," Abby said behind him. "Men tend to think more is better when it couldn't be further from the truth especially dealing with these new washers."

"She's very protective of her new appliances," River added.

Women. Ottar signaled for her to carry on with a hand roll.

"Do you think we're dealing with another type of Cryptid?" River asked.

Abby snapped her attention to them.

Just what he needed. Nosy troublesome sheilas. He nodded at River to go outside and then gave Abby an it's-none-of-your-business look.

Outdoors seemed to clear the urine odor that clogged his brain. "I think these two were looking for something other than stray dogs. I don't care if you're marrying Abby in a week, or not. These women are trouble."

Chapter 11

Pepper's stomach knotted and the pounding in her head wouldn't subside. Why did those blasted Hellhounds steal her whistle? She was too lenient with them. After all they were from hell. She should have known they'd display some devilish behavior sooner or later.

"There's no sign of them." Abby trailed her through the woods. "Do you think we should check the gates again?"

Pepper had checked several times to see if they'd come home. It was as if they'd disappeared. "We can look again in a little while."

If Ottar got wind of this, he'd track her hounds down for the government agency so they could perform experiments on them. She'd do everything in her power to keep Ottar away from her hellish pups. "You haven't told River, have you?"

"Are you kidding me? No. But I have a feeling he suspects something. He asked a lot of questions about why we were so worried about stray dogs. One of them must have peed on Ottar last night. I won't be able to keep up the lie if we don't find them soon."

"They peed on Ottar?" Strange.

"Yes, he slept on your property and woke up in a puddle. He found his sleeping bag was soaked with dog urine, like one of them lifted their leg on him." She hesitated, and her eyes grew wider. "Do you think that's how they mark the souls of the damned for hell?"

True, dogs lifted their legs on things they wanted to claim as their territory. Could Abby be right? Her throat tightened.

Ottar was a total pain in the rear end, but she didn't want him sent to hell.

"You like him, don't you? I think he likes you too," Abby said.

She liked the way the gold in his eyes seemed to glisten when he got upset. Or the way each muscle contracted when he moved. She also liked that he honestly cared someone had sent her that threatening letter. She changed the subject fast. "Do you think River would let me borrow his four-wheeler?"

Abby called River and he said yes.

They headed to the police station.

"Can you work in the pet store today while I continue my search?" Pepper asked.

Abby's gray eyes revealed disappointment. "I guess so. Are you going to be okay out there alone?" Abby was much smaller than her, but her size never deterred her when she was on a mission.

"Of course I will. You know I go into the woods by myself all the time. Besides, my little pack of hellish hoodlums would never hurt me." Her heart warmed. She was truly blessed to have a friend like Abby.

"Are you sure? I mean, you don't have the whistle anymore so I'm betting you don't have any control over them." The last part of her sentence was quieter, as if she was afraid to say it. "What if you get hurt?"

"You worry too much," Pepper said.

When they arrived at the small brick police station, River was bent over the four-wheeler. Gasoline vapors wafted on the wind as he filled the tank for her excursion.

Abby ran over to her groom-to-be and laid a big kiss on his cheek. "Hi ya, honey poo."

"I really appreciate the use of the vehicle." Pepper held her hand out to him.

River grabbed her hand and tugged her closer for a hug. "You're almost like a sister to me. What's with the handshake?"

"Sorry. I guess I'm anxious to get on with my search." She fake grinned at him.

River patted the leather seat. "The ATV is ready to go. Do you know how to drive it?"

"I sure do." She jumped on and turned the key. After putting it in gear, she waved. "See ya'll," she said with her fake southern drawl. She loved to talk with a southern accent ever since she'd visited Texas because she liked the way it sounded. Unfortunately, sometimes her Jersey accent would override her sweet southern voice.

Speeding off toward the woods that surrounded the police station, the pine scented air blew in her face.

If I were a Hellhound, where would I go?

~ ~ ~

Ottar stalked through the woods and hid behind the trees as Pepper approached on a four-wheeler, calling out, "Granny, Jethro, Ellie Mae."

Had she already named the stray dogs? He ducked behind a large bush as she zoomed past, tendrils of blond hair trailing behind her in the wind. Her blue eyes blazed with determination. His instincts told him Pepper wasn't hunting for your average stray dog. Keeping his distance, and hiding behind the pines, he followed her.

She pulled over next to the stream in the same area where he and River caught Abby—when she turned into the Jersey Devil. *Oi, wait just a damn minute.* Did Pepper change into a beast like her best friend? He quashed the thought.

His left wrist itched where Houston had inserted the microchip. The device moved with his scratch. It was time to have a new one installed.

They replaced the chip every two years. The bloody wanker didn't trust him after all this time. The funny thing was, he couldn't remember a block of time after they'd arrested him.

All he remembered was hunting for a Drop Bear, a large ferocious koala looking beast, and then talking to Houston about working for L.A.M.P.S.

Supposedly, that Drop Bear killed a whole Aborigines Tribe in Australia, a tribe he was friends with, and the authorities blamed him for the deaths.

L.A.M.P.S. offered him a way out of prison, so of course he went to work for Houston.

Ottar shook his head. No time to take a sprint through memory lane.

"Mr. Drysdale, Jed," Pepper called out.

The woman picked weird names for her pets. She bent over the stream and dunked a scarf in the water. After wringing it out, she pulled up her long blond hair and wiped it along the back of her neck. She swished it along her chest, water droplets dripped down the smooth pale skin above her round breasts.

He swallowed hard. *Come on, lift your shirt and cool off those perky heated nipples.*

Where the hell did that come from? The damn spell she'd cast on him, that's where. He intended to confront her about removing the love spell before he went insane. Whenever he was around her he felt a pull. A weird, strange pull. A pull he could only explain as attraction. It was like she was the Earth and he was the moon. He wanted to be closer to her. Hell, he wanted to orbit around her. He'd never felt the draw around any other sheila before, no matter how hot they were.

Which meant it *had* to be a spell.

Damn troublesome woman.

He took a step back and a twig snapped under his left foot.

Pepper swung her head around and she locked her gaze onto him.

He cringed. How could he be so stupid?

"I don't believe it. You're spying on me." Her deep blue eyes swam with fury.

Ottar shrugged. He didn't have to explain anything to her, let alone feel guilty for doing his job. After all he'd been through with her and Abby, he had a right to keep an eye on the suspicious women. Still, something inside of him wanted to cool Pepper's anger. "Of course, I'm keeping an eye on you. There are dangerous Cryptids out here. They killed two people. And remember that threatening note?"

The crease wrinkling her sexy forehead relaxed. She glanced around at the pines and oak trees in the woods. Then her gaze locked his. "What am I supposed to be afraid of? What kind of Cryptid are we talking about?"

"Sorry, no can tell. That's confidential information. You should've had your brain wiped after the whole Jersey Devil escapade. You're lucky River went to bat for you." He wasn't going to tell her that he'd also recommended leaving her memory intact. Only because he wanted to make sure she remembered the spell she placed on him, so she could remove it.

"They better not erase my memory. I'd sue them." She crossed her slender arms over her flat stomach and drummed her graceful fingers on her bicep.

No one sued the secret government agency, because on paper, they didn't exist. They were essentially ghosts who hunted mythical creatures.

"What kind of dogs are you looking for?"

She rocked back and forth on her feet, then shrugged. "I don't know. We heard a bunch of them barking in the forest last night. I think they're small." She uncrossed her arms and twisted the scarf in her hands. Her bottom lip quivered and she raked her teeth across it.

Damn, he didn't want to upset her. His chest tightened as if a large clamp wrapped around him and squeezed.

He stepped closer. Not wanting to spook her, he slowly placed his arm around her shoulder.

"What are you doing?"

His gut twisted like a snake coiled around its prey. For some reason, he wanted to make this better for her. A stupid urge compelled him to comfort her. *Bloody hell.*

The pink highlighting her cheekbones brought out the deep blue in her eyes. She batted her lashes. Those lashes fluttered and taunted him to kiss them. Without thinking, he dropped his arm from her shoulders and placed his hand on her back. Pulling her closer, her minty breath tickled his chin when she exhaled.

He placed a light kiss on each of her soft eyelids.

Her lashes fluttered, and she licked her lips. She wiggled in his grasp, then went still.

He couldn't hold back any longer. He kissed her. Her mouth was hot and wet and tasted of dark chocolate. Wrapping his other arm around her waist, he drew her closer. She smelled of fresh sunshine and a hint of hay.

Ottar plunged his tongue between her lips. With slow strokes, he swished his tongue against hers. She responded and kissed him back. Her heart thumped against his chest which shot his adrenaline pumping. His Johnson grew hard in his pants.

She opened her eyes and pushed his chest. "What are you doing?"

"I'm kissing you." What he wouldn't give for another taste of those velvet lips. *Why'd she stop?*

"But we don't even like each other." She took a large step back.

"It must be that spell you placed on me a couple months ago."

Her confused look changed to a large frown. "What the heck are you talking about? I didn't place any spell on you."

He laughed. The silly woman thought he was naive. "Like hell you didn't." There was no other explanation.

"What kind of spell?" She splayed her arms out by her side, palms up.

"Don't try to tell me you didn't place some kind of attraction spell on me the night you and Abby exploded the pot and the wild possums stampeded."

She shook her head like she had no idea what he was talking about. He had to hand it to her, the woman was a great actress. He'd bet she'd be great in bed.

"I didn't place any kind of spell on you." She paced to her four-wheeler and hopped on. Over her shoulder she said, "You're just a horny bastard who got all excited when you saw us naked." And the temptress grew sexier when she angered.

~ ~ ~

Pepper needed to put as much distance between her and Ottar as possible. That kiss. *Oh my gosh.* He was a master. The possessive, wild kiss made her want to strip his clothes and take his exquisite body next to the stream. What the heck had gotten into her?

Did he really believe that crap about a spell? *Nonsense talking Aussie.* There was no way she spelled him while she and Abby were trying to banish the evil jinn. Ottar must be one of those crazy conspiracy theory people, though, she'd never pegged him as paranoid.

She gunned the gas and took off down the overgrown path into the forest.

A gunshot sounded. Pain exploded in her upper arm. Glancing down at the blood on her sleeve, she looked up too late. A low branch smacked her across the chest. She flew off the four-wheeler and crashed onto the ground.

Her body throbbed. The coolness from the dirt chilled her spine. *Breathe.*

Ottar ran toward her, screaming, with his gun drawn.

The bastard shot her? First her dinosaur and now her. *What next?* He'd lost his sanity. She'd always suspected something wasn't right with him. Now she had proof.

Her arm ached, and blood seeped through her sleeve. The pounding of her heart accelerated, each beat almost blending into the next.

Ottar closed in, but she wasn't going to let him finish the job. Was the kiss so upsetting that he wanted to kill her?

Heart pounding, Pepper jumped back onto the four-wheeler and hit the gas. River's office was only a mile out. She revved the throttle through the trees, so Ottar couldn't get off another shot.

It only took five minutes before she arrived at the police department. Pulling into the blacktop parking lot, she hopped off the four-wheeler and raced inside.

"River," she called out frantically.

The blond sheriff sat at his desk and raised his head. "What's up?" River's eyes zeroed in on her arm. He raced to her side. "You're bleeding. Did you fall off the ATV?"

"No. That dumb Aussie bastard shot me." She pulled on the long sleeve of her shirt.

"Let me see."

A quarter-inch deep inch-long gash ran horizontal right above her elbow. The wound dripped blood on the floor.

River snatched the first aid kit off the wall. He cleaned the wound and wrapped some gauze around her arm. "It's only a graze but you'll need to get it checked out."

"I can't believe he shot me for no good reason. The man needs to be locked up and his head examined." Her breathing picked up and needed to slow down before she hyperventilated.

River frowned. "Are you sure *he* shot you?"

"I heard the shot, my arm started bleeding, and he ran at me screaming with a gun in his hand. What more do you need?" She had a feeling he'd hurt or kill someone soon. Too bad it was her.

River shook his head. "There has to be some kind of explanation. I'm sure this is all a misunderstanding."

"Yeah, like my dinosaur? Really, he needs to be arrested. He's out of control."

The door swung open. Ottar sprinted inside, his face deep red, and his crazy eyes, wild.

She latched on to River's shirt and jerked him in front of her. "Don't let him shoot me again."

"Ottar, what the hell are you doing?" River shouted.

"Is she okay? I never saw who shot her." He lunged around River, so she bolted to the other side.

She refused to let him get near her. "Arrest him. He's a danger to society."

"Settle down. Let's hear what he has to say," River said.

Ottar flinched. "She thinks I shot her?"

"Yes. I do."

River straightened his shoulders. "Give me your gun."

"I'm not handing over my weapon. I've done nothing wrong." He crossed his arms over his broad chest.

River held out his hand and narrowed his eyes. He waited in silence with his fingers curling toward his palm.

Ottar threw up his hands. "I don't believe this." He handed River his weapon, handle out.

"Thank you. Now tell me the whole story," River said while inspecting Ottar's gun.

Pepper stepped back putting another foot between them. Who knew what he'd do next. What if *he* had rabies? Oh my gosh, could she catch rabies by kissing?

"She hopped onto the ATV and took off. Next thing, I heard a shot. I looked around but didn't see anyone. Then she fell off the vehicle. Yeah, I drew my gun. I ran to see if she was hurt."

Could that be what had happened? "Who would want to kill me? Besides you."

He scratched his head and a twig fell from his hair. "I don't know? Maybe the person who sent you that threatening letter?"

"How do I know it wasn't him?" She pointed to Ottar. His hair was a tangled mess. branches stuck out every which way. "First, he kisses me and shoves his tongue down my throat, then he accuses me of placing a spell on him, and then he shoots me."

River's eye brows shot up. "You kissed her?"

It figured he'd focus on the kiss. *Men.*

Ottar shrugged off the question. "I didn't shoot her. Instead of standing here wasting time, we should be out there looking for whoever *is* trying to kill her. Although right now I have mixed feelings. I need my weapon back."

River handed the gun to him.

"Why are you giving it back to him?" That was just great. Would he try to shoot her again? "You should lock him up or taze him. Better yet, let me taze him."

River shook his head. "Ottar didn't shoot you. His weapon hasn't been fired. You should see a doctor about your arm."

"I'm going to search the woods." Ottar slammed the door behind him.

Pepper's head started to spin, along with the floor. "I think I need to sit down." She reached for a chair with shaky hands.

If Ottar hadn't shot her, then who pulled the trigger?

Chapter 12

It took forever at the Urgent Care facility. The bullet had barely grazed Pepper's arm, but she needed a couple stitches and a Tetanus shot.

River received a call to attend to a disturbance in the park, so he asked Abby to pick her up from the facility.

Pepper sat inside Abby's small car. "Thanks so much for driving me home."

"Oh my gosh. I totally freaked out when River called. Who do you think shot at you?"

"At first I thought it was Ottar. Now I'm not so sure." It didn't make any sense. Why would he kiss her with so much passion, and then try to kill her? And what a freaking awesome kiss it was, too.

"You lost me."

"Ottar showed up while I was looking for the hounds. He kissed me, and then accused me of casting an attraction spell on him. Really, the man is a looney bird. Anyways, I took off on the four-wheeler and boom, someone shot me. I looked back and he's running after me with a gun. What was I supposed to think?" She still had her doubts about his innocence.

"Did you kiss him back?"

Geez, why did everyone zero in on the kiss? "What does that matter?"

"Enquiring minds need to know." Abby looked way too darn happy. The truth was, the kiss upset her more than anything else.

She rolled her eyes. "Yes. I did kiss him back."

Abby pulled down Pepper's driveway and stopped in front of the barn. "And . . . ?" She motioned to continue.

"And, he's a good kisser. But that doesn't matter. He's insane, even if he didn't shoot me." Good was underselling his kiss. It was almost magic.

"I knew it. You two are perfect for each other. He's untamed and you're so good with wild animals. You can whip his feral butt into shape. I remember how undomesticated Fred was when you adopted him. Now he's one of the sweetest horses alive."

Tame Ottar? Never. "Oh, boy. Stop your goofy ideas right now. We don't even like each other."

Abby shrugged and drove down the rest of the driveway. She parked next to Pepper's pick up. That's when Pepper noticed it.

Bob, her blowup doll, looked like he'd lost some weight. His usual rounded face was flattened against the back of the passenger seat, an arrow stuck between his eyes.

"Oh my gosh, they shot Bob." She jumped out of the car, racing to her beloved inflatable friend.

Abby pulled out her phone and called River.

Pepper circled around the vehicle. Someone had left the window open, and Bob's deflated head hung off the arrow.

"River and Ottar are on their way over. They said to get inside of the house, now."

Glancing over to her barn, her heart squeezed in her chest, making it almost impossible to breathe. "I have to check my horses to make sure they're all right." She raced to the paddock where Fred and Wilma were huddled into the far end. Her pulse pounded. "Hey guys, are you all right." They took their time clomping over to her. She climbed in between the timbers of the fence and ran to them. Running her hands over their furry bodies, she'd realized they were all right. Her body felt a little lighter after she exhaled.

Abby hung her arms over the fence. "Are they okay?"

Pepper nodded. "How am I going to keep all my critters safe?" If anything happened to them she'd be crushed. They were her babies. She'd saved them, gave them a home, and protected them from animal abusers. Putting them at risk again was not an option.

"The guys will find who did this. We'll figure out something." Abby hugged her tight. "Here comes Ottar now."

The black SUV pulled up next to Abby's car. Ottar jumped out. "Who's Bob?"

"Bob is my car pal. He rides with me so I never get carjacked." She pointed to the pickup truck where poor Bob laid at rest.

"Did you call an ambulance?" He rushed to the truck and stuck his arm through the window. "What the?" He tossed Bob's flattened body out of the truck, turning to stare at her with an incredulous expression. "He's nothing but a blowup doll."

She fisted her hands, unease skittering through her. "It's still disturbing, and I'm worried about my animals. How am I going to protect my horses? My dogs?" She chewed on her bottom lip.

At her obvious distress, Ottar's expression softened.

"Where's River?" she asked, ignoring how handsome he was when not glaring at her.

His mouth tightened, as if he'd just remembered what a pain in the ass she was.

"River's still at the park." His eyes narrowed. "Something about the fountain exploding and large paw prints. You wouldn't happen to know anything about that, would you?"

She shook her head.

Ottar scanned the property, his hand shading his eyes. "We can talk inside where it's safe."

They climbed the wooden porch stairs and walked into the front room. She did feel safe here. The warm yellow wall paint comforted her. The whole house soothed her like a cozy blanket.

She'd never felt safe when she'd lived with her mother. The rundown apartments were cold and dirty. Her mother never hugged her or told her she'd loved her. Nope, instead the woman yelled and screamed, always looking for her next fix. And the men she brought home bothered Pepper. There was a revolving door into her home.

Once she moved in with her aunt, she learned what love meant. Her aunt helped with her homework, taught her how to cook and garden, and most of all hugged her every chance she got. At night her aunt tucked her into bed and told Pepper how happy she made her. Love made a house a home.

"I'm going to make some hot tea. I'll be back in a few." Abby headed to the kitchen.

Then it hit her. The Hellhounds were probably at the park. Holy cow. More than anything Pepper wanted to run over there and see if they were still around.

"River wants a list of all your boyfriends from the past six months," Ottar said, crossing his arms, glaring at her.

No way. Ottar didn't need to know that kind of information. He'd think she was a floozy. Sure, she dated a lot, but she didn't go to bed with all of them. In fact, she hadn't slept with anyone since Thomas. After he'd kidnapped her and Abby, she'd sworn off going all the way on dates. "Six months?"

He nodded. "He also needs the list of people you turned down for pet adoptions."

"I'll put it together for him." She'd need her files from the store.

"River has his hands full with everything going on, so I'm your new shadow." He grinned.

Abby strolled into the living room, her expression confused. "I thought you were handling the Cryptid thing and River was going to take care of Pepper."

Ottar tugged at his T-shirt collar. "River has been contracted by L.A.M.P.S. to hunt down the present Cryptid threat. I'm helping him but still have some loose ends to tie up from the last case. So, I'm your man." He clasped his hands in front of him and cracked his knuckles. "Looks like we're going to be spending a lot of time together."

~ ~ ~

Ottar couldn't tell the women he was in fact on a Cryptid case—Pepper's mysterious Cryptids. Sticking close to her was the best chance he'd have of cracking it.

He thought about the note and the attempt on her life. How dare someone try to kill Pepper on his watch. If he hadn't seen it with his own two eyes he might have thought she cooked the whole ordeal up. He wouldn't put it past these two.

"Pepper, stay away from the windows." He pulled her to the other side of the room.

The silly woman tugged free from his grip. "I'm still worried about my horses."

"I'll sleep in the barn with them." He preferred to be outside anyways.

River stepped into the house. "Is everyone okay?" He hugged Abby and then Pepper.

"I'm going to put some cameras around the house. If someone comes near, we'll catch them," Ottar said.

He couldn't very well tell Pepper that he'd already installed them. In fact, he needed to check the footage when she wasn't looking.

"I think I should stay with Pepper," Abby said.

"No," said River and Pepper at the same time.

"Why not?" She puffed out her bottom lip.

"Because it's too dangerous," River said. "Ottar will keep an eye on her. Won't you Ottar?"

He gave River a nod. Oh yeah, he'd watch her like a hawk tracking a mouse. He pointed to his eyes with two fingers and then pointed them at Pepper.

She shifted from foot-to-foot with her arms around her waist, her eyes large circles of terror.

"She's scared to death," Abby said. "I think I should stay with her for moral support."

Pepper's features softened. "Abby, if you could run the pet store I would forever be grateful."

"I can do that."

"Ottar, maybe we should bring Pepper with us," River said. "I'd like your take on this situation over at the park."

"It was probably kids playing a prank." Most likely this was a waste of his time.

"Nope. We have surveillance footage from a street cam. We installed it when kids kept putting bubbles in the fountain. You need to watch it."

Chapter 13

River informed Ottar that he needed his expertise. Pepper perked up. It could only mean one thing—a Cryptid was involved. Was it her Hellhounds, or whatever killed the taxidermist? Either way, she'd check it out. Jumping into the back seat of River's SUV, they drove to the fountain in the middle of the park. She kept her mouth shut.

When they arrived at the park, they exited the vehicle.

Ottar strolled over to River with his hands in his pockets. "Bloody hell, who blew up the fountain?"

Pepper stared at the enormous stone fountain that used to stand a couple stories high. Water had cascaded from the top, spilled over four tiers, then fell into a round wading pool about two-feet deep. In the summer she'd loved to sit on the bench and watch the birds splash around in the water. Now the center was broken off, several of the tiers had chunks chiseled from the bowls, and the wading pool looked like a herd of elephants had stampeded through the middle. Water drained from the pool onto the surrounding cobblestones.

River pulled out his phone. "They sent the footage to me." He pressed the screen several times and sidestepped over to Ottar.

Ottar's bushy eyebrows shot up. "There's a lot of static, but from what I could tell, they're invisible, mate."

Pepper's stomach flipped and knotted. It sure sounded like her Hellhounds were the culprits. Those little troublemakers. Once she got her hands on that whistle, she'd take away their cookies for a week, maybe longer.

River tapped his phone replaying the footage again. "We should contact Houston. The Paranormal Division needs to be involved. What if it's a phantom or demon?"

Pepper swallowed hard. Who knew L.A.M.P.S. had a Paranormal group? Did they run around with packs on their backs and have traps like in the popular movie with the marshmallow man? Could they catch her Hellhounds?

Ottar stared at Pepper, long and hard. Surely, he didn't think she was involved. Did he? Had he put together the stray dog story and the fountain?

She thought fast and asked, "What if it was some kind of explosive?"

"Na, River show her the footage."

She stepped to River's other side. He played the recording.

White static lines cut through the video. The sides of the fountain crumbled inward before the center toppled. Large paw prints appeared on the patio surrounding it. Sure enough, her playful hounds tromped around destroying the fountain, having a puppy play day in the water while they remained invisible. Splashes and water droplets flew everywhere as if they shook their wet coats. She bit her bottom lip. What were the men going to do next?

After the video played, River dialed a number and walked out of hearing distance.

"Wow, freaky," she said to Ottar.

Ottar studied her face for a moment which felt like hours. He broke his gaze and reached for his phone. "Wait right here."

Pepper wandered over to the bushes on the other side of the fountain, not caring about the Aussie's orders. If L.A.M.P.S. sent another team, all hell could break out. Also, Abby had invited a heck of a lot of agents to the wedding. The poor little hounds were in grave danger. Her throat tightened when she tried to swallow.

Her phone chirped indicating a text.

Hey bitch. Who let the dogs out?

Finders Keepers.

A huge sour pit punched inside her stomach. No one knew about her hounds. She looked at the phone. The number said private.

Someone tapped on her shoulder and she jumped. "Ottar! You scared the bejesus out of me."

He shrugged. "Be more alert. Someone is trying to kill you. What are you looking at?" He snatched her phone from her fingers and narrowed his eyes when he read the message. "What does this mean?"

She breathed in deeply and tried to smile, but her lips didn't cooperate. "I don't know. Maybe it has to do with the strays I heard the other night?" She knew damn well this text was about the Hellhounds but couldn't tell him. Darn, she wanted to trust Ottar so bad. It would make her life so much easier, but still, she kept her mouth shut.

"Do you know who sent this?" He pressed his lips together.

"No." Her world spun around her. She was blowing this, bigtime.

"Is it the person who's trying to kill you? Or another whacked out animal person trying to snatch your dog rescue claim on the strays?"

"Wow, you have no clue about rescuers." Some people didn't get it. "I rescue those that can't stand up for themselves or take care of themselves. Those who are abandoned and need love. Not because I'm a crazy dog lady or in some kind of competition."

"I don't know how you think. You're a sheila and a tree hugger. That makes you a whacko in my book."

Her fingers ached to grab him around the neck and squeeze hard. He knew how to irritate her to no end. "Yeah?

Well, you're a blood hungry animal killer. *In my book*, that puts you in line with potential serial killers."

He flinched like she had smacked him in the face. A deep dark haunt flickered in his eyes, but only for a moment. Was there more to him than some out of control Tarzan? What kind of secrets was *he* hiding?

River strolled up next to them. "I have to go. Mrs. Jagger called and said someone stole her car. She probably misplaced it again."

"She forgot her purse in my store the other day. I had to track her down and when I returned it, she accused me of stealing. Her family really needs to keep a better eye on her." Pepper liked the old woman. She was in her late nineties and had a lot of spunk.

River turned to Ottar. "Did you talk to Houston?"

"Yep. Before you go, look at the message Pepper received." He held out her phone.

River read it and glanced up at Ottar. "Well, it looks like you're going to be busy. Try to keep your lip-locking to a minimum."

~ ~ ~

Ottar rolled his eyes. This whole mission sucked scaly crocodile dicks. To top it off, Pepper, and whoever was out to kill her, were clearly linked to those stray dogs. He wasn't sure how much Houston had told River, but he had a feeling it wasn't much, due to his relationship with Abby. Nope, he couldn't bring River in on this mission.

Pepper stared at the fountain with a puzzled look. Her blond hair glistened like spun gold in the sunlight. Her lips—plump and pink—begged for another kiss. A sudden urge to bury his nose in the crook of her neck and take a big sniff of her scent. It was almost if he could sense fear on her, and he wanted nothing more than to make her feel safe.

He scratched his wrist. The damn tracking device itched to no end. The chip moved under his skin with each scrape of his nails.

"I want to go home," Pepper said quietly. She looked down at the ground while moving a rock with the toe of her gym shoe.

If only he could gather her in his arms and comfort her. She was clearly shaken. He reached for her hand and grasped her fingers. "Don't worry, I won't let anything happen to you."

She didn't pull her hand away. Instead, she leaned into him. "I'm not worried about me. I'm worried about my animals." Her hand trembled in his.

He placed his lips on her long slender fingers and kissed them gently. "I'll protect them. We need to get you home. When was the last time you slept?"

She removed her hand from his. "I got in a few hours last night. You don't understand, these animals are my babies. Even the stray dogs. I heard them on Halloween and knew they were in trouble. Strays are usually victims to demented sickos."

A little white furry dog ran up to her. He hopped on his back feet in excitement, trying to gain Pepper's attention. She crouched down and addressed the little fluffy rat dog. "Who's a big boy?" She rubbed his small body and scratched behind its ears. "Where's your mommy?" She picked it up and looked around the park.

"What are you, the pied-piper of dogs?" He needed to get her out of here before every dog in the neighborhood followed them home. She was easy to talk to and had a magnetic draw. Apparently, dogs felt the same way about her.

"Pretty much." She kissed the pup on the head. "I need to find its owner." Pulling out her cell phone with her free hand, she dialed the number on its tag.

Ottar watched as Pepper talked to the owner. The little white dog relaxed in her arms. Its long pink tongue licked her cheek. She possessed some freaky animal magnetism, all right. Never in all his years had he seen animals respond like that to a human.

"His owner said Hughy ran into the park and she couldn't follow him. Someone roped off the entrance. She was super worried about him." She kissed the mutt on his furry head.

For some stupid reason, he wished her lips were on his.

Chapter 14

Pepper bounded up her stairs, two at a time, and beelined into her room. Ottar escorted her home after the fountain investigation. It seemed like she'd never get away from him.

Ha!

Abby texted her the whole drive home, making plans. Big plans. Pepper shimmied out her window and jumped onto the nearby oak tree branch. She swung her legs over to another tree and climbed down. Jogging away from the house, she looked over her shoulder.

No Ottar. *Easy peasy.*

Abby waited in her car down the street. She wore a wide-brimmed ball cap slung low, and sunglasses. Her idea of incognito, but she hadn't realized her car would give her disguise away. "I thought you'd never get here," Abby said.

"Oh my God, you know Ottar. I've had enough of his protection." Pepper's heart beat faster than a drum in a disco. If the barbarian followed her, he would have blown this whole idea into oblivion. Happy he hadn't, she sucked in a large gulp of air, attempting to slow her breathing.

"You'll get used to it. These boys are very obsessive about their women." Abby put the vehicle in gear and headed down the two-lane road.

Their women? She was nobody's woman, especially not his—and she liked it that way. Rethinking their new adventure, she said, "I'm not sure this is a good idea." The last time they did something like this it blew up. Literally.

"If you want your hounds back, we'll have to use all our resources. What do we have to lose?"

True. Running around in the forest calling their names hadn't accomplished much. Except for that kiss Ottar laid on her. And wow, what a kiss. His strong lips latching onto hers was heaven. Just what was he up to?

Abby pulled the car into a parking spot outside a small building. Blazing Broomsticks flashed in script on a neon sign, along with a picture of a broom on fire. The cute spiritual shop sold candles, incense, and other witchy trinkets. A middle-aged woman named Tammy owned the place. She'd helped Abby with a spell to remove her Jersey Devil curse. Too bad it backfired. The spell should've worked but they botched it up. Big time.

"I can't wait to see Tammy," Abby said as they hurried to the shop.

They opened the door and a chime dinged. The smell of lavender, vanilla, and sandalwood filled her nose. A soothing new-age melody played overhead. The muscles in her neck relaxed.

Pepper strolled past the candle display and over to the crystals hanging in front of a window. The light reflected off the glass and caused a rainbow of prisms on the wall.

A woman with long straight black hair, wearing a black flowing skirt, strolled up to them. She appeared to be about their age and wore a hefty helping of black eyeliner. Her large brown almond-shaped eyes had a warmth to them. "Welcome to Blazing Broomsticks. How can I help you?"

Abby shook her hand. "Hello. We're looking for Tammy. Is she around?"

The woman smiled. "Tammy isn't here today. I'm Tabitha, her daughter."

"Do you know when she'll be back? We kind of need help with something," Abby said. She leaned toward Tabitha and in a quiet voice she added, "with a spell."

Tabitha's eyes lit up as if she was the next contestant on

a game show. "I can certainly help you. I studied at the Acme Witchcraft Academy and graduated with honors."

Somehow a college named Acme Witchcraft Academy didn't seem all that promising. "When will Tammy be back?" Pepper asked.

Tabitha's smile drooped a tad. "She's out of town for the week."

"Maybe you can help," Abby said. "My friend here"— she pointed at Pepper—"lost something very important, an heirloom, and needs help finding it."

"I can do a basic finding spell. That's no problem. If you like, I can meet you at your house and perform the spell tonight."

Wow. If Tabitha did the spell herself, there'd be no chance of the witchcraft backfiring. What did she have to lose? Joy tingled through her body.

Then it hit her. The stupid nosy Aussie was hanging around her home. She waved Abby over to the side for some privacy and then held up her pointer finger to Tabitha to hang on a minute. "What about Ottar?"

"Ottar Shmottar. Don't worry about him. We can come up with something to get him out of the house," Abby whispered back.

"Are you sure? He accused me of placing an attraction spell on him. I think he gets a little wigged out by witchcraft. His eyes get all whacky when he talks about it."

"That's because we were naked when we performed the spell. Besides, why do you care? I thought you said you didn't like him?" Abby raised a suspicious brow.

Why did she care? For some reason, she did. Which made no sense. After the wedding, and after he found whatever Cryptid he was hunting, Ottar would leave town. She'd probably never see him again. Another good reason not to ride him like a pony. Well, she'd imagined he was more like a Clydesdale. Not that she was thinking about having sex with him.

She stepped back by Tabitha. "We'll do it."

Tabitha clapped her hands in front of her. "Great. I'll gather all the supplies for the spell."

Pepper shook her hand. "My name is Pepper, and this is Abby."

"I can't wait. This is going to be epic," Abby said.

Pepper had a feeling the night would be more than epic. It might even elevate to atomic.

Chapter 15

Ottar slammed his fist into a nearby tree. Those damn women. A few hours ago, after Pepper went upstairs, he'd watched the footage from the cameras. Her truck was parked just outside the camera radius, so no info there on whoever shot an arrow through her blowup doll.

He'd paced around the guest room and listened for noises upstairs. Nothing. Silence. He'd run up the stairs to see if she was okay. No Pepper just an opened window. He'd placed a call to River, only to find out that Abby was also missing.

River met him in the woods behind Pepper's home.

"The last time the girls went missing someone kidnapped them," River said. The poor bloke rubbed the back of his neck. It was his signature move when he worried.

Ottar frowned. He didn't want to think about how Thomas and his mother had taken the women a few months ago. The kidnappers were in jail now, but whoever mailed Pepper the threatening letter was still on the loose, along with Lord knows how many ferocious Jackalopes.

He pulled his hair back and secured it into a ponytail with a leather strap. "There's no sign Abby and Pepper went to the woods today. Wherever they went, they went by car."

Even though Abby's car was missing, they decided to check the woods to be safe.

"I'm going to install another tracking device on Abby's car. She found the last one and removed it." Lines formed around River's eyes. He felt sorry for River, but he knew what he was getting into by proposing to the woman. Abby and Pepper never hid their knack for trouble. In fact, they flaunted it.

"Maybe they went home. It's been hours. We should head back," Ottar said.

River nodded.

Once they sat in the vehicle River asked, "So what's with you kissing Pepper? Are you two an item?"

Oh, hell no. "No."

"Pepper may be hot, but she's a handful," River said. "Somehow, I don't see you sticking around to play house. If you hurt her feelings, I'll kick your ass. She's a good friend to Abby. If it wasn't for her, Abby and I wouldn't have gotten together. Pepper is like a sister to me."

Stone the crows. No wonder Houston didn't want to bring River into the heat signature investigation. He was too close to the woman.

"I won't hurt her." At least he hoped not. Pepper seemed to be the love-them-and-leave-them type, from what he'd heard. What if they both agreed to shag and then part ways? If it was mutual, no problem, right? What the hell was he thinking? She drove him batshit nuts.

"I'll remember you said that," River replied, staring him down.

Abby's car pulled into Pepper's driveway. The women exited Abby's car loaded with shopping bags.

Abby ran up to River and gave him a huge hug.

Ottar looked to Pepper. "What the hell were you two doing? You two took off without telling us. Do you have a death wish?"

~ ~ ~

"Abby and I decided we needed a little girl time. Which couldn't be accomplished with you lurking behind us." Pepper pointed at Ottar. He flashed her that angry bear face he liked to wear. Maybe she'd poke at the beast just for a little fun. "Look, we're fine. I think whoever is trying to kill me is taking a break. Besides, on television, they always wait a day or two in between attempts to kill their target."

This life threating stuff was inconvenient and exhausting.

The weather was still outside, but a blur of brown caught her eye in the garden. She strolled over to investigate which of her furry friends feasted on the vegetables she planted for them.

A little brown bunny with small antlers peered up at her. A giant lettuce leaf stuck out of his cute mouth. "Hello, little fella. Help yourself to my garden. I planted it for you and all your furry friends." She crouched down to get a closer look at the new rabbit.

Ottar lunged behind her. His warmth seeped into her chilled skin. "Stay back," she ordered. His hulkiness intimidated everyone. She didn't want him to scare away her new friend.

"River, she's got a bloody Jackalope here," Ottar yelled. "Get your net out of the car, now."

"You guys are idiots. It's not a Jackalope. It's a rabbit with the Shope Papilloma virus. The virus causes horns to grow on their heads." She refused to let them capture her new bunny friend and do experiments on him. Stepping in front of the rabbit, she protected him from the men, who clearly took their job too seriously.

"Come here, Pepper. Move slowly," River said, stretching the metal net between his hands.

She spread her arms wide. "No way. You guys need to leave my wildlife alone. Go hunt something else. My land is an animal sanctuary. No hunting is allowed here. You hear me?" She wagged her finger at them.

Ottar's lips drew back into a snarl. "Bloody hell woman, that Cryptid will kill you. Jackalopes killed the taxidermists." He inched closer.

"I find that hard to believe. It's just a bunny rabbit." She knelt by the small fence surrounding her garden. The rabbit's little pink nose wiggled. He looked scared with his huge brown eyes, and twitching whiskers. The bunny let out a low growl.

Then Bam! Out of nowhere, the rabbit sprung five and a half feet into the air and latched onto Ottar's T-shirt collar with its sharp teeth. He swiped the small furry animal off him. The rabbit landed on the ground, scampered through the garden, and disappeared into the forest.

Ottar and River chased the bunny into the woods.

With her heart pounding faster than her feet, Pepper took off after them. "Don't hurt the little guy. He's scared."

"It's a murdering monster. Stay back at the house," Ottar yelled over his shoulder.

The big oaf had a lot of nerve ordering her around. These guys were nutso. It was a scared little bunny who happened to have a virus that made him look different from the rest.

Abby ran up next to her. "Maybe we should listen to them. I've never seen a rabbit growl or attack someone like that."

Pepper slowed to a jog. "I've heard rabbits growl before. It's quite common. They also jump straight up in the air when they're startled. Ottar scared the bunny and the little guy freaked."

The men slowed ahead of them before stopping. They walked around in a circle and searched under bushes.

A wave of ease released in Pepper's tightened stomach. It seemed the little guy escaped. If it was indeed a Jackalope she didn't blame the bunny one bit for attacking Ottar. She herself, wouldn't want to be captured by the big scary caveman. "Haven't you heard of the Shope Papilloma virus?"

River shot Ottar a look and then shrugged as if it was up to him to tell her something.

The Aussie cleared his throat. "L.A.M.P.S. made up the virus for a cover story. The rabbit is a Jackalope and they're deadly. Usually, they hunt in packs. I don't know why this cheeky fella strayed out by himself." Ottar shook his head as if he was confused.

Why did this news surprise her? Sure, she knew some legendary monsters were real. She took care of the Hellhounds, her bestie had turned into the Jersey Devil a few months ago, and there was that pesky gnome that sucked people's brains, but little horned bunnies killing people? Yeah, for some reason that one was harder to imagine.

She pressed for more facts. "How could little bunnies be dangerous? He can't weigh more than five pounds."

"They choreograph attacks. One goes for the cardioid artery while the rest slash the Achilles tendon. Their prey goes down, and they drink him dry," Ottar said almost as if it was common knowledge.

She swallowed. "What do you mean, drink him dry?" They really were dangerous. Oh no, she'd bent next to it, just inches away from him. Did they attack other animals? She'd protect her horses and dogs.

Ottar stepped so close to her his minty breath whooshed across her face. He gritted through his teeth, "They're bloody pint-sized vampires."

Chapter 16

Ottar watched as Pepper's face went from a nice shade of peach to almost paper white. He'd snared her attention with his last comment. Apparently, the only way to get through to Pepper and Abby, was to scare the bloody piss out of them. Now, he needed to get them out of his way and to safety.

"The Jackalopes are deadly. River, can you walk them back to the house? I'm going to see if I can find some tracks." This was the closest he'd gotten to the savage little beasts. He wouldn't blow it now.

"Oh, honey, you don't have to watch over us," Abby said to her fiancé. "We'll go straight home. If they're as dangerous as you say, then you should stay and help Ottar."

Pepper's eyes squinted in protest. "I don't need anyone to watch over me."

"I'll take the girls back and make sure they're safe inside. Then I'll return," River said to him.

He nodded. At least he wouldn't have to worry about them for now. No telling how long it would last. "Promise you'll stay inside? No more excursions."

"We have a friend coming over later tonight. We planned on playing board games," Abby said.

"What friend?" Ottar asked.

"Tabitha."

A new piece to the puzzle?

"Who the hell is Tabitha? I've never heard you talk about her before," River said.

"Don't worry. We're going to drink wine and play some

games. You guys can do your hunter stuff outside. You don't need to bother with us," Abby said.

Bloody oath. These two were scheming again. He prepared himself for another challenge. When would these two learn?

River rubbed the back of his neck. "How do we know Tabitha isn't the one trying to kill Pepper?"

~ ~ ~

A light knock sounded on Pepper's front door. She greeted her visitor and motioned for Tabitha to come in. The witch carried in a shopping bag overflowing with candles and baubles.

"Thank you so much for coming," Pepper said. Excitement percolated inside her chest. Finally, some good luck for a change.

"This is going to be so much fun." Abby bounced on the balls of her feet.

Tabitha set her bag on the floor. Taking in the soft lemon-yellow walls and living room décor, she smiled a sweet genuine smile. "I love your house."

A warm tingling feeling swept through Pepper's heart. She loved her home, too. "Thank you. We're going to have to do this spell up in my bedroom. Will it be a problem?" They shouldn't be interrupted by the pesky big oaf upstairs.

Tabitha shook her head. "We can do it anywhere. But we can't be disturbed."

Dino the Sheltie bounded up to the young witch and spun. He rubbed his brown and white furry head on her leg. She patted him. He gave her a hand a sloppy kiss with his pink tongue.

"He's such a cutie. He looks like a mini Lassie dog. What's his name?"

Pepper liked Tabitha even more now. "His name is Dino.

And that's Barney, Betty, and Bam Bam." She pointed to her other dogs.

"Cool. I love your dinosaur outside. I'm a huge fan of the Flintstones, too." Tabitha waved the other dogs to come. She rubbed their wiggly bodies and let them slurp kisses on her cheeks. "They're so sweet."

Pepper trusted her dogs' judge of character. If they liked someone, then she did too. It seemed her gang loved Tabitha. "You passed the dog test. Looks like we're going to be good friends."

Tabitha's smile beamed. "I'd like that."

"Let's go upstairs," Pepper said.

Abby followed after Tabitha. "How's your mom?"

"She's great. Wait, are you the two that had trouble with the opossums?"

"Yes," Abby said with a little too much excitement.

A wary look crossed Tabitha's face. "It's a good thing we're doing this spell together. Mom was so worried about you. I can't wait to tell her about tonight."

"We were in over our heads before. Thanks so much for helping us," Pepper said.

"Mom should've never encouraged you to try the advanced banishing spell on your own. I'll be happy to help you out any time you need it." She spread out a blue, green, and yellow tie-dyed tapestry on the bedroom floor, then placed candles in a circle on top of it. "Come on and sit down." She patted the blanket. "We can do the spell right here. What are we going to search for?"

Pepper sat on Tabitha's right. "My aunt left me a necklace. It's a golden whistle. It's very special to me. I lost it on Halloween."

Tabitha tilted her head to the side. "Is it magical?"

Pepper sat quietly debating on if she should answer her. Would it make a difference?

Abby plopped down on the other side of Tabitha, so they were sitting in a circle. "It is."

Her friend had a big mouth.

"Does that matter?" Pepper asked hoping Tabitha wouldn't bail. The spell was the best chance she had of finding the whistle to call the hounds home. *What if they couldn't locate the whistle through the spell?*

The witch stopped still. "It does matter. Magic has a way of messing with spells sometimes. Is it good magic?"

And there you have the million-dollar question. Would calling the Hellhounds be considered positive? "I think it is."

"Okay. Is it what you seek most right now."

She didn't have to think about that one. Not one bitty bit. "Yes."

"That makes it easy. Just to be safe." She pulled out a small whisk broom and held it up.

"What's that?" Abby asked.

"It's a cinnamon broom. It's to sweep away any negativity in the room."

The spicy aroma of cinnamon filled the room. It reminded Pepper of the steaming apple cider her Aunt used to make for her every autumn. The memory sent gooey warmness into her stomach.

Tabitha lit the small tea light candles with a long fireplace match. "This works better with the waxing of a full moon, but we'll make do. Now concentrate on the candle in the center of the circle. See the whistle in your mind and wish as hard as you can."

Pepper's eyes snapped to the flame dancing on the small tea light. She saw the glistening of the gold whistle with sparkling rubies in her mind. Saw her aunt lovingly place the chain around her neck the first night she took over as caretaker of the family's ritual.

In the background, Tabitha made a sweeping motion with the broom. "Goddess, hear us tonight. Help us locate what

Pepper needs the most. Bring her the item she desperately seeks. Without this heirloom her mind weaks. As I will it, so mote it be."

For the next few minutes, Tabitha swept the broom again and chanted her spell several more times. The candles flickered, and the room lit up with a crack of lightning. A thunderous boom sounded, rattling the window glass.

Pepper's gaze snapped to the window. Funny, she hadn't remembered any rain in the forecast.

~ ~ ~

Ottar was searching outside of Pepper's house when a flash of light blinded him. A loud clap of thunder boomed in his ears. The ground bounced and he landed flat on his back.

"Are you okay?" River bent down next to him.

His body felt like a large truck hit him and then backed over him a few times to finish the job. His wrist burned and he lifted his arm. Smoke twisted from his fingernails. *Freaky.*

He stared at the tendrils of smoke in silence. *What the devil happened?*

"You were hit by lightning. Maybe you should stay down for a little bit," River said, an expression of concern knitting his brows.

Ottar struggled to sit up. His body felt like it weighed eight-hundred pounds. It was all he could do to suck in a breath.

River pointed to his head. "Your hair is smoking."

Ottar's thigh burned as if his leg was on fire. He reached into his cargo pants side pocket and pulled out his cellphone. The lightning had fried and blackened his device. Tossing it to the side, he glanced at a large blister forming on his wrist. The damn lightning scorched his microchip.

He smiled. *That couldn't be all bad, right?*

"Help me up." His voice was scratchy, and he barely

croaked out the words. His raw throat needed moisture. "I need something to drink."

River pulled Ottar's arm over his shoulder and he helped him walk into Pepper's house. Four dogs barked and twirled when they entered.

River leaned him against the wall for balance and hurried into the kitchen. His friend popped back with a glass of water in his hand.

Ottar drank it down in one gulp. Swaying on his feet, he placed his hand on the wall to steady himself. "Where are the women?"

River looked around the living room. "They must be upstairs. Maybe you should wait a while before you go up there. You look scary, dude."

Wait? No chance. He needed to find out what they were up to. Ottar pulled on the handrail while climbing the stairs. Each one felt as if they were a mountain. Step by step he pushed himself upward. When he reached the top, he swung open Pepper's bedroom door with a bang.

Pepper, Abby, and another woman sat in a circle with burning candles. Pepper jumped and sucked in a huge breath.

"Crikey!" Witchcraft! The damn women were messing with witchcraft again. He had a feeling Pepper wasn't innocent. He hated spells and magic. Nothing good came of it. "Pepper," he called out. "What have you done?"

The candles flickered out and the room darkened. A good-looking black-haired woman holding a small broom flicked a lighter and lit the candles again.

"You ruined everything," Abby said.

River rushed in behind him. "Abby, what did I tell you about messing with magic." He turned on the light switch.

The women squinted and shielded their eyes.

Pepper still seated, slammed her hands on her hips. "I didn't invite you in here. Please leave."

Wrong answer. "You invited me to stay at your house. Therefore I'm not budging until you tell me what's going on."

"Are these friends or foe?" the dark-haired woman asked.

Pepper's frown deepened. "Right now? I really don't know."

~ ~ ~

"What the H-E-double-hockey-sticks happened to you?" Pepper asked as she looked at the shaken Aussie. Was he okay? Did they get attacked by the Jackalopes?

"You." He pointed his finger at them and then waved it at the candles. His body vibrated as if he would combust.

"You're nuts. Do you know your hair is smoking?"

"Your Witchcraft did this to me." His gaze zeroed in on her. A shiver ran across her spine, skittering up the back of her neck.

What on Earth was he talking about? "We didn't do that to you."

"I was struck by lightning."

Her gaze traveled to the window. "It's not raining outside."

"Exactly."

She glanced over at Tabitha. "Tell him that it wasn't us." This couldn't be happening. Why did he think his bad luck was her fault?

Tabitha raised her chin. "I performed the spell correctly. We did a simple finding spell for Pepper's heirloom—for what she wanted most. There is no way it would have affected you or anyone one else."

"What kind of heirloom was Pepper searching for?" He pulled on the collar of his T-shirt. More smoke puffed out.

"A necklace. See, it had nothing to do with you," Pepper said. It figured he'd think this was about him. The barbarian thought the world revolved around him and his stupid hunting job.

"Um, Pepper. Come here." Tabitha signaled her to come over by her.

Pepper crawled across the tapestry to the young witch and leaned toward her. "What happened?"

Tabitha cupped her hand over her mouth so Ottar wouldn't hear her. "Were you thinking about the whistle the whole time you were looking at the candle?"

She thought for a moment. Yes, she was, well almost. She gasped. At one point her thoughts drifted to Ottar and that darn kiss.

Holy blazing cow pies.

Chapter 17

Ottar punched his pillow and pulled his sleeping bag around him. Witchcraft. He should've known Pepper was up to no good. The lightning fried his energy and he needed a good night sleep. Before he knew it, his eyes grew heavy and he dozed off in the woods behind Pepper's barn.

Ottar hid behind a rock beneath the trees. Birds screeched and cawed their warnings from above. Spikey Yakka plants intermingled with softer mint bushes. The heavy scent from eucalyptus leaves lingered in the heated air. He was no longer in Haber Cove New Jersey—this was Australia's bush.

A thump sounded to his right. A headless Goanna laid shredded on the ground. It looked like something had eaten the large lizard's head. What the hell? His gaze snapped to the branches above him. A bloody Drop Bear, a koala-looking beast about five times the size of a normal koala bear, locked gazes with him. Its sharp fangs dripped saliva and blood. The monster's red eyes blazed in the night. A twig snapped above him. Oh crikey, another Drop Bear. As he searched through the trees, he found three more.

They roared in unison. Vicious carnivores, they attacked their prey by dropping on them from the trees. The Cryptids hunted in packs which made them extremely dangerous to people. An unsuspecting tourist would have no chance should they wander into the bush alone.

He glanced to his right. A village of Aborigines lay in the path of the beasts. His heart thudded in his chest. This tribe helped raise him when he was a boy. He grew up with these people. They took him and his grandfather in after his parents died, making them part of the tribe. Pulling out his gun, he shot at one of the beasts. They scattered in the trees.

Ottar sat up, sweat drenching his back. It was a bloody dream. Just a dream. He swiped the perspiration from his brow. He was still in the forest behind Pepper's barn. Checking around, he realized with relief, his food and gear were untouched.

He paced back and forth on the damp earth. *Freaking odd dream.* Or was it a memory? Houston had said he was hunting Drop Bears in his homeland when he was arrested, but he could never recall the events. Why was he dreaming about this now?

Bloody hell, that lightning must have zapped my brain.

He sniffed the air. The sulfur scent was much stronger now. The overwhelming odor of canine sabotaged his nose. He strolled over to a tree with a pungent scent of dog urine and relieved himself.

Light peeked over the horizon. The outdoors soothed his tormented soul. Soft dove coos whispered through the trees. Off in the distance Pepper's horses whinnied. An uneasy feeling crawled into his gut.

After packing up his camp, he headed to Pepper's house. Stopping to check on her horses, he found Fred and Wilma huddled together inside their stall. Something must have spooked them. He searched the barn for threats but didn't see anything, so he carried on to the house.

Pepper chopped greenies in her kitchen and stuffed them into a blender. "Good morning." She had a cheerful smile plastered onto her face.

"What's that?" He pointed to her concoction.

"I'm making a green smoothie. Want one?"

"Pass." Crazy woman drank salad for breakfast. He could really go for some steak and eggs. He'd have to stop by River's house or hit a diner to find some Man-Food.

"It's really good for you and boosts your energy." She stuffed a banana into the blender container.

He'd rather watch her eat that banana whole. Just thinking of her wrapping her lips around the slender fruit stirred his old fella in his pants.

"How come you don't eat meat?" He couldn't imagine life without a steak or burger.

"Because of the way the industry treats the animals. They raise and kill them inhumanly. The poor babies are so scared when they go into the slaughterhouses. They know what's going on. It's horrible. I get all the protein I need from my vegetables. Besides, meat isn't all that good for you. I feel better when I don't eat it. I think it has to do with my blood. They say sometimes your blood type can make a difference."

She turned on the blender and stuffed a baton down inside to make sure the greenies chopped and liquified.

Two dogs perked up from their sleeping positions and ran to him. One spun around in excitement, while the other sniffed his leg. He patted their heads to make nice.

When she finished with all the racket of the blender, she poured the thick green shake into a glass. She took a long drink.

Eww.

She licked her lips and set the half-filled glass on the counter. "How are you feeling this morning?"

"Pretty good considering you struck me with lightning last night." He did feel good. Actually, he felt better than good. He felt great despite the realistic dream about the Drop Bears and the Aborigines.

"I'm sorry you got hit by lightning, but we didn't have anything to do with it." She drew her eyebrows together and bit her pink lip.

Yeah, right. "Lightning struck the same time you were doing your voodoo."

"Coincidence?" She nibbled some more on her bottom lip. Her mouth tempted him for another taste. He adverted his gaze to her eyes.

"There's no such thing as coincidence." He wasn't buying it. This woman was dangerous. Beautiful, but a magnet for weird things. If he had any damn sense in his head, he'd hightail it out of here and leave her be to her own demise.

Pepper answered her cell phone. "It's for you." She handed the phone to him.

River's number displayed on the screen.

"What's up?"

"We have another situation down here," River said.

"What's going on, mate?"

We have dumpsters overturned, and a shoe store was hit last night. I swear, whatever we're dealing with is huge. Do you know how hard it is to tip a dumpster?"

Yes, he did. Almost like tipping cars.

"There's also another dead body. Get down here fast. I'm going to need your help."

Chapter 18

Pepper finished feeding the dogs and walking them. Eager to get back to her normal routine, she climbed into her yellow pickup truck. She glanced over at her empty passenger seat. She missed Bob, her carpool buddy, and would have to replace him soon. Pulling onto the road, she drove downtown to Pepper's Perky Pets, her shop. Ottar followed right behind her in his SUV.

Man, she couldn't shake the Aussie off her tail. She liked her freedom and he was seriously cramping her style.

The aroma of cedar chips and bird seed filled the medium sized pet shop. A happy peaceful calm filled her chest. She'd worked so hard to make her dream come true, and she felt fiercely proud of her little store. This was where she united pets with their forever families.

She only had a couple of puppies left that she'd rescued from the pound. Funny, people thought puppies were immune from abandonment at shelters. That wasn't always the case. If only everyone would spay and neuter their pets, the country wouldn't have such a mass over-abundance of strays. At least she did her part to help the situation.

She picked up a brown and white pup and snuggled his soft little head. His pink tongue shot out and slurped her cheek. She squished her nose at his stinky puppy breath. Hooking up a leash on his collar, she walked him outside the back door, breathing in the fresh air.

The narrow alley had a thin strip of grass, perfect for the puppy to sniff around. Flashing blue police car lights caught her eye. Down a few stores, River and Ottar paced around a body next to an overturned dumpster.

Her stomach clenched. Haber Cove's crime rate had escalated.

She picked up the pup and walked over.

A man's body was on the ground inside a chalk outline. The muscles in her neck tightened, making it hard for her to catch her breath. No wonder Ottar rushed over here.

"What's going on?" she asked.

"Bloody hell. What are you doing out here, woman?" Ottar tugged at her arm. "Get inside. Need I remind you that you have a target on your head."

She looked both ways down the alley. Crime tape roped off the entrances. "Isn't it safer to have two big bad monster hunters surrounding me?"

"She's got a point." River chuckled, busy inspecting something goopy next to the dead man's leg.

"I don't give a platypus's watertight ass about her point. There's a chance the Jackalopes might show back up."

"Did the Jackalopes tip the dumpster?" she asked.

River walked over to her. "No. Whatever did this is too big to be a Jackalope."

"So, did the creature who tipped the dumpster kill the man?" Her gut constricted, and the sensation of big hairy bumblebees ricocheted off her stomach lining. Her Hellhounds were large enough to do this. Surely they wouldn't kill someone. They weren't supposed to harm people.

"Negative. The Jackalopes killed the nightclub manager," Ottar said.

"Oh my gosh. Why would they do that?" She asked.

"Because the idiot mounted a Jackalope head over the bar," Ottar added. "Now we'll have to track down all the blokes who purchased a Jackalope trophy." He scratched his head. "It seems these critters are looking for payback."

He searched inside the dumpster, poking around with a stick. "Nothing but refried beans and Jalapeno peppers in here. Whatever ate out of this wheelie bin is going to have massive gas."

She cringed. If her poor Hellhounds were responsible, they'd have a tummy ache.

River's phone rang. He frowned and walked away from them.

"You need to get inside. I don't like you being out in the open," Ottar said.

Wow. The wild caveman cared for her? Or at least he acted like it.

"The alley isn't out in the open." It looked secure to her. They were the only ones around.

"Why do you sheilas have to argue all the time? Get inside woman." Ottar pulled on her arm.

She clutched the puppy tighter. "Fine. I have to open my store anyways." *Stupid bossy Aussie.*

River walked up to them, his face etched in worry lines. "I've been called to another site. Looks like we have a dogfighting ring in the area."

"No. That can't be." She covered her mouth with her hand and her heart throbbed. Dogfighting rings represented the worst of humanity as far as she was concerned. The people who ran these operations were most evil. They picked dog breeds that were powerful, and devoted to their masters. Those money-hungry assholes put their dogs through awful abuse. Not only that, they dognapped family pets, usually from backyards, and used them as bait dogs. Her worst nightmare.

"Please stop them," she said in a soft tone. Thank goodness she kept her dogs inside. "This town has gone to hell. If you two don't get busy and catch them, I will."

~ ~ ~

Ottar wanted to wrap his arm around Pepper and hold her. He could almost feel her pain and anger. Which was weird. Never the less, it bothered him, and he wanted to make her sorrow go away.

She hunched her shoulders and clung to the pint-sized pup nuzzled in her arms when she walked back inside her store.

"You shouldn't have said anything about the dogfighting ring while Pepper was here. You know how she is," he said to River. Sensitive. She was sensitive to all animal's rights. And he furrowed his brows as the puzzle that was Pepper fell into place.

"I know. Abby's going to give me an ass peeling. It just came out. I swear, I'm getting married in a few days and this whole town is going berserk. My deputy is sixty-five years old and he's retiring. Not to mention I can't tell him half of what's happening here. I need to hire another."

"Don't chuck a wobbly. Maybe you should come back to L.A.M.P.S.? Forget all this small-town sheriff stuff." He could at least tell Roman he tried to get River back.

River shook his head in disagreement. "No, I'd have to leave Abby for days, or weeks at a time, and I can't do that. I'd miss her too much."

Ottar grimaced. The poor wanker was whipped. "And besides, she'd get in trouble with Pepper."

They walked to his squad car at the end of the alley. "Can you handle the cleaner? I need to investigate this lead."

Ottar nodded. "Vulture is bringing Holly to clean up the site. She's got a thing for dumpsters."

"Good. They're coming to the wedding, too. I imagine they'll stay in the area then."

The lines around River's eyes were more defined and deeper since the first Jackalope episode. It would be rough to balance the Sheriff's gig, hunter freelancing, and a wedding to one of the most stickybeak-busybody women in the world.

He did feel a little sorry for the poor bloke. But he could say one thing about River, he was fair dinkum, and Ottar was happy to call him his friend.

"Don't worry, mate. I'll take care of the mess here, then I'll head to the clod hopper store to check things out."

"Oh God, I forgot about the shoe store." River shook his head. "You can be my temporary deputy assistant. There's a badge in my desk drawer if you need it." He turned and jumped in his car. "What about protecting Pepper?"

"I can put Vulture on Pepper detail after he arrives."

Chapter 19

Pepper studied the huge, nicely built, olive-skinned man who Ottar had posted as guard detail in her pet store. He looked a little like Dwayne Johnson, the actor. The back of his bald head sported an interesting vulture tattoo. Standing beside her, he crossed his muscular arms over his chest and studied her. She pulled her sweater closed and flipped up the collar. Was Ottar tired of guarding her?

She circled Vulture, taking in his gorgeous massive body. "You really don't have to watch over me."

He pursed his lips but kept quiet. The man was good looking but intense. He reminded her of one of the Queen's guards in England. Not that she'd visited England, but she'd seen pictures and movies.

"I'm so glad we can have a civil conversation," she said sarcastically. "You know, it's not every day that you run into a man that can't shut up. I hardly can get a word in with you around. Bob, my carpool buddy, may he rest in peace, had the same characteristic."

His dark eyes followed her around the shop. She was going to tear Ottar a new one the next time she saw him. Vulture didn't look amused with her or his new assignment.

The tattoo stretched across the back of his bald head with blue-black iridescent feathers. The skeletal head of the vulture appeared three dimensional, and in its talons, the bird carried a scythe. She shivered at how real the tattoo appeared. "Hey what's the name of the vulture on the back of your head?"

He thinned his lips while he glanced down at her. "Vulture."

He talks? "Oh, I have Vulture with a vulture tattoo named Vulture watching me. Interesting."

He shrugged.

She went on about her business to open the store. Her heart ached when she thought about the dogfighting ring in the area. River better get the case solved, and fast, or she would do some investigating on her own. No matter how dangerous it might be she wasn't going to live in a town where criminals maimed dogs for sport.

The bell dinged, and Abby swooped into the shop. "Hey, Pepper. Sorry, I'm late."

Relieved that her friend had arrived, Pepper let out a long breath she didn't know she'd been holding. "No problem. I'm so glad you're here."

Her friend turned to her new bodyguard. "Hey there, Vulture."

He cracked a small smile and nodded to her.

"What's Vulture doing in your pet store?" Abby asked.

"Ottar put him on guard duty. It seems a lot of stuff is going down in Haber Cove. I don't envy your husband right now."

Abby's forehead wrinkled. "Oh gosh, he's already at DEFCON TWO with everything going on around here. What happened now?"

Pepper filled her in on all the events.

Abby let out a sigh. "I hope he doesn't overdo it. I have big plans for him after the wedding." Her mouth formed an O. "He'd better kick it in gear and wrap up these cases. I'm not postponing my honeymoon."

Vulture let out a small chuckle.

Really? Now the guy decides to come to life?

She wrapped her arms around Abby. Her friend didn't deserve this during her wedding week. "Don't worry, the boys will pull through for you. Holly is here, and Leif will be here in a couple days to help."

"We need to find your heirlooms too," she whispered into Pepper's ear.

Pepper couldn't hold back her smile. Abby was the best friend ever. "Don't worry, I'll figure something out. Oh hey, we need to plan your bachelorette party."

Chapter 20

Before Ottar stepped into the shoe store, a strong sulfur scent ambushed his nose. He also picked up four, maybe five different dog smells. They were the same breed, whatever that may be, and the scent was fresh. Like they'd been here within the past couple hours.

He walked into the store. *Crikey!* The buggers must have rolled around in the shoes for hours. Shoes were everywhere except on shelves. Tossed and chewed toes and heels. The leather boots were the hardest hit.

"Anyone here?" Ottar called out.

An older man walked in from the back room. He wore wire-rimmed round glasses and a plaid vest. "Who are you?"

"I'm the new deputy. Sherriff River sent me. My name is Ottar." He shook the old man's hand.

"I'm Frankie. Where's River?"

"The Sherriff has another call. He'll stop by later. I assure you, I'm qualified to do this investigation." He couldn't reveal that he, in fact, was River's boss at one time. "Do you have any idea what happened here?"

The older man dabbed the perspiration on his forehead with a white hanky. "The window glass is broken." He pointed to one of the shattered panes. Glass shards covered the carpet. "I guess that's how the kids broke in."

Good, the old man thought vandals were responsible. Never mind all the saliva and bite marks on the shoes. Ottar pulled out a pad of paper and jotted down some notes, like a good detective.

"I came in about eight-thirty this morning. It looks like something chewed on these shoes. Do you think it's kids taking those psychedelic bath salts?"

Ottar looked up from his paper. Nice. He didn't have to make up any weird stories for cover. The man was doing all his work for him. "It's a good possibility that the culprits were kids doing drugs."

"I heard bath salts turn them into zombies." The shoe store owner scratched his head. "I'll have to warn the misses."

"I don't think you need to alarm her. Have you noticed anything missing?"

The old man went to his cash register and counted the contents. "They *had* to be on drugs. No money is missing." He closed the drawer and went into the back room.

Ottar took pictures, measured bite marks, and gathered samples for L.A.M.P.S. It took a couple of hours before finishing. For some reason, he didn't want Pepper to be alone with Vulture very long. It wasn't that he didn't trust Vulture to watch over her, he just didn't want his coworker to become a victim of Pepper's alluring qualities. The woman was quite the schemer.

Hell, she was the perfect vixen. Her never-ending long legs could wrap around a man like a pretzel. His cock pressed against the zipper in his pants. The woman reminded him of a siren. Hmm, he'd research sirens to see if indeed she was one. *Na, it had to be the spell.*

His ears twitched, which was weird, but he'd heard every sound the old man made in the back room, even his breathing. Hell, that lightning zap had enhanced his senses. He grinned to himself. They'd come in handy hunting down the beasties.

After gathering his gear and samples, he set off to the pet store.

Pepper and Abby sat at the counter, planning something. He grabbed a ghost-shaped biscuit and popped it into his mouth. It was a little dry and had an oatmeal, peanutty flavor. Best bikkies he'd tasted in a while. "Mmm. These are good. Did you make these?"

Pepper and Abby busted out, giggling their chicken cackles. Even Vulture laughed.

"What?" he asked.

"Those are dog cookies," Abby said.

"Really?" They didn't taste like dog biscuits. Though he'd never eaten dog treats before.

"Humans can eat them too. I use regular ingredients. I've tried them to make sure they tasted all right for the dogs." Pepper gave him a small smile with a nod.

He popped another biscuit in his mouth and chewed despite their glee. *These things are addicting.*

Holly came up to the counter, and her red curls bounced around her head. "Hey, Ottar. Are you going to start barking now? Want me to rub your tummy?"

Smart ass. He swallowed the rest of the treat. "Holly, don't you have something to blow up, or start on fire?"

"Nope, I wrapped up the sight. It's clean as a whistle." She clapped her hands and rubbed them together. "I'm helping Pepper with Abby's bachelorette party. We need a stripper. Do you want to volunteer?"

He shook his head. "No."

"I'll volunteer," Vulture piped in.

All the women turned to look at Vulture. They studied him up and down, taking in his physical body.

Ottar had spoken too soon. He didn't want Pepper watching his transporter strip. "I changed my mind. I'll be the stripper." That way he could keep a close eye on her. How hard could it be?

"Nope, you already turned it down," Holly said. "Vulture is going to be our man-candy for the night."

The girls laughed.

Pepper caught his gaze but quickly looked to Vulture. "You'll have to practice."

"I already have my routine," Vulture said.

"You do?" Abby asked.

"Yes, I worked my way through college as an exotic dancer." Vulture grinned. Funny, he hadn't put that on his application for L.A.M.P.S. Well, he might have. Ottar had never really read past all the mercenary jobs. Hell, he never knew Vulture went to college. Would Pepper find Vulture more attractive? A squiggle hit his stomach and the back of his neck burned. Since when had he worried about competition when it came to a sheila anyway?

Chapter 21

Pepper leaned back on her sofa. Barney and Betty sat on the cushions next to her. Dino, the Sheltie, and Bam Bam, the Golden Retriever, played tug-of-war with a rope near her feet. The long day wore on her and her pups needed their pets. Before she came inside, she checked Fred and Wilma. Both horses galloped around the paddock, happy to exercise.

Bam Bam gnawed on something. The dog constantly picked up things that didn't belong to him. "Hey, buddy, come here."

The golden retriever trotted over to her but before she could grab his collar, he darted away. *The little brat.*

"Get over here right now."

He laid down and dropped the gray fabric between his paws. He nibbled some more.

"Stay," she commanded.

He looked up at her and wagged his tail, his treasure in front of him.

Reaching down, she snagged a drool-soaked sock from his paws. It was a man sock. *An Ottar sock.*

She let out a long breath. Heck, she'd told him not to leave his socks laying around. Bam Bam loved to steal them. He also loved to chew and swallow things. He was super sick when she'd rescued him from the shelter. She'd rushed him to the vet and he had to have emergency surgery. They found three socks and a knit hat blocking his intestines.

Some people were so irresponsible when it came to their pets.

Her teeth clenched until her jaw hurt. If Ottar left something out that hurt her dogs she'd wring his Aussie neck. It looked like she'd have to have another talk with him.

This whole "victim stuff" was getting old. She hated that the men had to watch over her. Ottar and River were on another investigation. This time it was something about the toilet paper factory. From what she'd gathered from their conversation, toilet paper rolls were torn apart and the whole warehouse had been TP'd. The niggling in her tummy indicated her hounds were involved.

She stretched her arms over her head. Ottar had looked good today, even though he was grumpy. His cargo pants hugged his butt and it was all she could do not to pinch his tight rounded bottom. His tight T-shirt had clung to his hard cobblestone abs, and his biceps burst from the short sleeves. If only he would act normal. Holy cow, honest to god, what was she doing? She shouldn't think about the barbarian. What would he kill next?

Gathering up a water bottle and her phone, she decided it was time to go look for her Hellhounds again. She set out into the woods. The birds chirped and cicadas sang their mating calls. A breath of forest clean air filled her chest. Her love of the woods and nature stemmed from when she was a little girl. The forest was her escape from all the drama in her life.

The leaves were turning pretty shades of orange and red. Pinecones dropped from the evergreens. A sense of peace filled her with the November chill in the air.

"Jeb, Granny." They didn't answer. She didn't blame the stubborn pups. Who would want to live in hell? They were causing so much trouble in Haber Cove, though. She simply had to round them up and get them back where they belonged. A cool breeze whispered against her neck.

Ottar popped out from behind a tall pine tree. Startled, she jumped back.

She smacked his hard arm. "Don't scare me like that."

"Oi, if I was the one threatening your life, you'd be dead. Abby would kick my arse for not protecting you."

"Still, that's not nice. You need to take a course on how to be civil." Her gaze traveled to his broad shoulders and strong arms.

Wrinkles of tension forked from his eyes, his forehead creased. "You shouldn't be out here alone." Not many people really worried about her safety and it seemed that Ottar really cared about her. She should be flattered not irritated.

Play nice with Tarzan.

"I'm fine. No one has tried to kill me for a while. Maybe they gave up?"

He moved closer, warmth radiated from his body. The man gave off a ton of heat. She nibbled on her bottom lip. He emitted an untamed energy that called to her.

"You." She poked him in the chest with her pointer finger. "You left out a sock and Bam Bam stole it. I told you he's a sock thief. What if he swallowed it? It's dangerous for dogs to eat foreign objects."

His eyes caught hers and his intense focus zapped the breath from her lungs. Big brown beautiful eyes, almost like puppy dog eyes with a dash of gold in them. His long thick lashes fanned across his cheekbones. Men shouldn't be allowed to have such thick lashes. For such a barbarian, Ottar was truly gorgeous.

Her stomach clenched with want. His face softened as his gaze slowly scanned her, pausing on her breasts. Her skin chilled. Her heart beat wildly, and her core heated. Darn, she could get lost in those big brown eyes.

He stepped even closer and pressed her back against the rough tree behind her. Placing his palm against the bark over her head, he leaned in. "I've been thinking about that kiss from the other day," he said in a quiet, gentle voice.

Her eyes widened. Oh, yes. The wonderful, wet, moist kiss. The kiss that almost brought her girly parts to a quiver. *Don't think about it again.*

"What about it?" she asked, trying to play it off as if it was no big deal.

"I think I need another one." He studied her lips.

"So do I," she blurted out. Then, so he didn't think she craved him, she added, "You know, so I could see if it was a fluke."

His smile grew.

Darn, she was toast.

"You enjoyed it." His dimples deepened.

Yes. Yes, she did. Very much so.

He touched her lips with his. Then he went in for the kill. And heck, he nailed the kiss of all kisses. It was hot, strong, and took no prisoners. A savage passion burst from his mouth into hers. Their tongues collided and danced a ferocious fevered mambo. Suddenly she didn't care what a pain in the ass he was.

He wrapped his arm around her waist and pulled her even closer. Her body melted into his, chest to chest, thigh against thigh, and well, all the rest of the parts in between molded together, too. His tongue ravaged hers in long seductive strokes. Tingles waved through her limbs from her fingers and toes. She kissed him back letting out all her bottled fear, love, and strength.

"Whoa, what the hell are you doing to me?" His mouth covered hers again before she could answer.

The bone hard bulge in his pants rubbed against her and she loved the feel of his massive body close to hers.

Ottar pulled her shirt up revealing her lace covered bra. With one snap, he loosened the elastic, and cool woodsy air hit her nipples. He grasped her breast in his warm hand.

"We shouldn't be doing this." Her voice came out breathy and needy, the way her body felt. He hadn't only kissed her, and touched her, he claimed her like she was the only woman meant for him.

He placed his mouth on her breast. His sizzling tongue swirled around her nipple. Her breathing picked up to the point of almost panting. If he brought her this much pleasure at second base, how would she feel when he hit a home run? An undeniable urge plunged through her to find out. "Never mind," she moaned.

She glided her hand down his tight, ridged stomach and over his hip. His hard muscles contracted under her touch. She traced her fingertips down his little track of hair running from his navel down the treasure path. Surely, the bounty would be worth it.

"Oh woman, you better not be toying with me. I don't think I can stop," Ottar murmured.

Eagerness spiked with adrenaline ambushed her. She plunged her hands down the front of his cargo pants and smoothed her fingers around his hardness.

His wild hair fell across his chiseled face. "I won't hold back. I've been waiting too long for this."

"No one is asking you to hold back. I need this too. Don't disappoint me," she warned. Then she unzipped his pants and yanked them to his ankles. His shaft bounced free.

He stepped out of his cargos, kicking them to the side.

She gasped and bit her bottom lip. Ottar was huge.

He lifted her shirt the rest of the way over her head and wrapped his hands around her waist. Picking her up, she grasped the branch above her.

In one motion, he pulled her jeans off. She swung naked, hanging from the sturdy branch above her head. Her toes were an inch from touching the ground. He stepped back and flashed his famous Ottar smirk. "Now that's an exquisite sight. I never tire of seeing you naked."

Oh damn, she was in big trouble. Hopefully, she wouldn't scream too loud. The anticipation was killing her.

He knelt, starting at her feet. With skillful fingers, he paid attention to each toe. Patiently massaging them with his large hands.

This whole experiment was worth it for the foot massage alone. *Heaven.*

He placed his tongue on her shin, making small circles on the skin. Then behind her knee. Between her legs pulsed with desire.

Taking his sweet time, he moved up her inner thighs.

A small whimper escaped her. She readjusted her grip on the branch. She arched, aching for more.

Only a couple inches from that special spot, he pulled back. He cleared his throat. "Um, Pepper, do you want me to continue?"

"Hell yes! Get on with it, Aussie." The man drove her crazy. Crazy with desire. She might hit that big "O" before they got down to the serious business. *A girl could dream, right?*

He didn't hesitate and dove in.

Wave after wave of shudders pulsated through her as soon as his tongue hit her bundle of nerves. She let out a scream. Oh, the euphoria. He placed his large shaft against her folds.

Still riding the quakes from her pleasure, she wrapped her long legs around his waist.

~ ~ ~

Ottar figured he'd have his one-time bang with Pepper and get the damned woman out of his system. Now he wasn't so sure. She was like an addictive drug. Once he had a taste, he wanted more. He figured another kiss was all it would take. *Wrong.*

She kissed him back with eagerness and need, and he didn't want to disappoint her. Plus, he had to see where this would lead. If it wasn't for that stupid attraction spell, he would have run the other way. At least that's what he kept telling himself. He nuzzled her long silky neck. She smelled so alluring. It was like she was created only for him.

And she'd said *Get on with it.*

He'd had never wanted to take a woman like he wanted to take Pepper. His cock hardened to the point that it ached for her. He rubbed it between her legs. Her core was primed and ready for him to enter.

Unable to wait another moment, he slid into her. He clenched his teeth, wanting to prolong the pleasure. Her long never-ending legs tightened around him, and she pulled him in deeper. If he wasn't careful this would be over in about two seconds. Disappointing her was not an option.

He pushed her back against the tree, and her arms tightened, as she switched her grip on the branch above her. Damn, she turned him on. Every part of her body, from her toes to her eyes, were sexy.

She let out a sultry moan into his ear. Her hot shortened breaths grazed against the side of his face.

He pumped harder, wanting to bury himself deeper into her.

She moaned again and bucked her hips, giving back all the pure, raw, edgy passion a bloke could only hope for.

He sped up. Clenching his teeth, he took her savagely.

Pressure from the swimmers threatened to explode from him. Not able to control himself any longer, he pumped three more times.

He roared on his last thrust. Shudders slammed into him and pulsed through his erection. The tadpoles were free.

Pepper let out a loud scream and began quaking again. She let go of the branch. Still locked together, he cradled her soft round bottom in his hands as the waves of passion stormed her beautiful body.

He plastered his mouth against hers and sent in his tongue.

She returned the kiss. Unwrapping her legs, she slid off him. Her eyes widened. "What did we do?" She covered her mouth.

"We bumped like a couple of horney lizards."

She gathered her underwear. Her hands trembled when she tried to hook her bra behind her back, so he helped her with it. She leveled her gaze on his. "We can't tell anyone this happened."

Mine.

Chapter 22

Pepper paced around in her kitchen while Ottar lounged on her couch in the other room. She placed a teapot on the stove and turned on the burner. One thing was for sure, she needed a cup of herbal tea to settle her nerves. Thinking back to the hot passionate sex with Ottar, caused her to shiver. It had to be a one-time ordeal because she didn't want things to get all weird between them. *No more Ottar sex.* The barbarian was so wrong for her in so many ways. Still, she loved his humor and didn't mind his hotness, at all. He seemed like the obsessive type with his intense personality. But a relationship? Nope, she doubted it could be done. She'd have to end this before it went any further.

She popped her head around the corner. "Do you want some tea?"

Ottar sprawled out on the couch, his legs spread wide, with a very satisfied look plastered on his face. "Grab me a stubby, would you, Lovey?"

Lovey?

She felt herself falling for him, and he would leave her for his next mission. This had to stop before she risked caring for him, anymore. She grabbed a beer from the fridge and threw the can to him. "Listen here, bud. I'm not your *Lovey*. We are not a couple. And we are not going to have a replay of this afternoon."

He let loose a teeth-baring grin. "As you wish."

"Don't mock me."

"How the bloody hell am I mocking you? If you don't want to bump the uglies anymore, no worries." He shrugged.

"Good." But somehow his agreement didn't sit well in her tummy. She still wanted his touch and craved his body. Did their time together mean so little to him?

He raised the channel changer and pointed the device at the television. He flipped from channel to channel, ignoring her.

Suddenly her house seemed too small for both of them. "I'm going to check on my horses." Grabbing a bag of carrots off the counter, she turned and traipsed out the back door.

She passed her *still* unfinished dinosaur on her way to the barn. Once inside, Fred and Wilma clip clopped over to greet her.

"Hello, guys. Do you want a treat tonight?"

Fred, the big gray Arabian horse nibbled the carrot while she held it. Wilma, the timid, waited for her turn. Fred was more outgoing and loved affection. She snuggled his neck and stroked his mane.

Out of the corner of her eye, she saw a hay bale move. "Who's there?"

No answer.

The saddle perched on a stand fell to the ground.

Her heart pulsed.

A small black Pomeranian materialized and ran up to her. He twirled and hopped on his hind legs. His long purple tongue hung out the side of his mouth.

"Jethro." She knelt next to him. "I hear you guys are causing all kinds of trouble."

He slurped her face.

"How are you doing?"

His plumed tail swished so fast it was a blur.

She looked around the barn but didn't see the others. "Where are your friends?"

He bounced around from one hay bale to another. A piece of toilet paper trailed from his back end. She picked it off him. "Oh boy, you *were* involved in the toilet paper factory fiasco. You need to behave. Where's my whistle?"

He hunkered down on his belly and covered his nose with his paws. Apparently, he knew but wasn't going to help her.

The door creaked open, and Jethro disappeared into the air as if he'd never been there.

Ottar strolled in sniffing the air. "What's going on in here?"

~ ~ ~

The first thing Ottar noticed when he entered the barn was the thick stench of sulfur. Pepper's worried eyes swept to him.

She fidgeted with the hem of her T-shirt. "I'm checking on my horses, why?"

Ottar slammed his lips together. *Lie.* He'd have to tread softly so she didn't spook. He'd get her to slip up somehow. "Don't you smell that smell?"

"What smell? I cleaned the stables earlier today?" She even mustered up a confused look on her face, as if to trick him. Silly sheila.

He was no fool. She gave safe harbor to the beastie he hunted. Didn't women have an obligation to speak the truth to someone they made love to? Crikey! He meant had sex with.

Pepper was making him lose his marbles.

She swept her fingers through her golden long hair. The memory of those silky strands brushing his face as he took her spun through his mind. The fresh sent of petals from wildflowers filled his senses. He shook his head to dislodge the memory.

"You shouldn't be out here. What if the person who's trying to kill you was hiding in the barn? Or what if I was the killer?"

"Exactly. I'm still not convinced that you weren't the one who shot me." She let out an exhausted breath.

"I have no motive, although you're sure trying to give me one." He raked his hand through his hair.

"Speaking of shooting, when are you going to finish my dinosaur? I'm kind of tired of looking at that gaping hole in his head. You know I saved up for that statue for over a year?"

He'd never thought about where or how or why she'd acquired the hunk of resin. The woman sure didn't forgive easily, but she was sexy as hell when she got fiery. "I'll have it completed by the wedding."

"Good, because Abby and River are getting married here. I don't want my dinosaur looking like a ragamuffin."

Ottar almost didn't notice how she side-stepped on the piece of toilet paper sitting on the floor. *Ah ha!* She was involved in the toilet paper factory break-in. He knew it. Did she sell her soul to a demon? Maybe to make her pet store profitable? Na, she'd be the type to make a deal to save the life of a wounded animal. He'd have to do more research.

Or maybe she was covering for Abby again?

Pepper had covered for Abby big time when a genie popped out of a tampon box and turned her into the Jersey Devil. But they'd captured and secured the evil jinn.

Could the genie have had a partner? One that would take over if he got detained? Could Abby have another curse placed on her where she turned into a phantom or some other vile paranormal creature?

He'd have to grill River on Abby's whereabouts when all these current events had taken place. After all, Abby had been at Peppers house when the hot spot hit on Halloween night. He found it oddly suspicious that a second heat signature hadn't shown like in the past.

He stopped stroking his chin and sucked in a deep breath through his nose. Pepper's arousal wafted on the air. *Mine.*

How crazy was that? The scent was sweet and enticing, almost calling to his shaft, which responded immediately. He tugged on the front of his pants. Crikey, his cock had a mind of its own.

Pepper's gaze locked onto him. She studied his every move. Too smart for her own good. Too bad he was smarter.

He pushed the erotic thoughts of her rounded breasts and perky nipples out of his brain and pointed his index finger at her. "What do you know about the sulfur smell in here? Did another genie place a curse on Abby?"

She crunched her eyebrows together and took a step back from him. "What? No." She shook her head in disbelief.

Either she had excellent acting skills, or his genie theory was blown to hell. He'd have to go with his next idea. "Did you make a deal with a demon? Come on, Pepper, I can help you if you'll just let me in."

"Where are you coming up with this stuff? Geez, you have a great imagination. You should write a book. I bet you could come up with all kinds of freaky storylines." She brushed her hair from her face.

The brown horse made a whinny.

"I'm coming, Wilma." Pulling a carrot out of her pocket, she held it out to the mare. The horse snatched it from her fingers and chewed. Pepper stroked Wilma's long nose and placed a kiss under her eye. "There, there. I wouldn't forget you. Do you remember Ottar?"

The horse made a raspberry noise at him.

"She remembers you. I don't think she likes you much, though. Maybe you should give her a treat?" Pepper handed him a carrot.

He held it out to the horse. The beast snatched it from his hand and cracked the veggie between its teeth. She lifted her tail and blew a fart.

Pepper giggled, and her eyes sparkled like gemstones in the bottom of the Coral Sea. "You give her gas."

The smell of the horse butt overtook the sulfur odor and Pepper's alluring scent. "You could bottle that and use it as biological warfare."

"Unfortunately, things like this are an everyday occurrence when you're around animals. You'll get used to it."

He fanned the air in front of his nose. "I don't want to get used to it. I think the stench is frying my nostril hairs."

"I'm done giving them their treats, so we can go outside." She headed out the door.

He searched around the tidy barn, but nothing seemed out of place.

Just as he walked outside, a rifle blasted off in the distance. He tackled Pepper to the ground a split second before a bullet pelted the side of the barn.

"Um, Ottar?"

"Wow, that was close. Are you okay?"

"Yes," she said, her voice was shaky and hesitant.

"What's up, love?"

"How the heck did you move so fast?"

Chapter 23

Good question. Ottar hadn't realized how fast he'd moved until he thought about it. "Adrenalin can speed up your reflexes."

"Not like that." Pepper shook her head. Her face revealed she didn't believe him one bit. If he wasn't mistaken, he also saw a little fear.

"More important, someone shot at you. We can worry about my fantastic moves later." Another bullet exploded into the dirt next to them. "What the hell did you do to make someone want to kill you this bad?"

She squiggled underneath him, the movement like a snared rabbit. Instantly, a shot of excitement flooded his body.

"Stop moving." He studied the woods behind her house but saw nothing to give away the shooter's location. It was dark, but his vision wasn't impaired, and the woods looked clear as if it were daytime. *Freaky.* It must be another side effect from the lightning strike. Like the speed in his movements. Bloody hell, the zap gave him superpowers. A smile spread across his face.

"This isn't funny," Pepper said. "My life is in danger and you're laughing at me. Please get off me. I want to go inside." She shoved against his chest.

"You're not going anywhere. Give me your phone."

"No. First of all, I can't reach it with your huge gorilla body draped across me. And second, get your own phone."

"If it wasn't for you frying my phone with your damn spell, I'd still have it." He felt down Pepper's ribs, her flat stomach, and to her firm ass.

"Stop copping a feel. Now is not the time. I swear you're a horny hound dog."

"Bloody hell, woman. I'm looking for your phone." He grasped the device and pushed the button. The screen was locked.

Ping! Another bullet bounced off the shovel leaning against the barn, about three feet away from them.

"Unlock your phone. We need to call River." He handed the phone to her. He wished he'd had his weapon on him.

Pepper wriggled around until her arm came free. She placed her thumb over the small round circle on the bottom. "It's under favorites." After hitting the screen a few times, she handed the phone back to him.

"Hello, River? Get your arse over here. We're under fire." A crackling sounded off on the phone.

"I'm not that far away. Find some cover," River replied.

"We need to get into the barn," he said to Pepper.

"No way. I'm not going anywhere near my horses. They'll get shot." The woman was always thinking about her pets. Even when her life was in danger.

"If it comes down to you or them getting hurt, I'm picking them. Come on, let's go when I count to three." He wrapped his fingers around her wrist.

She jerked her arm. He tightened his grip. "I don't want to go. They're innocent."

"And you're not? What are you not telling me?" He sensed she knew exactly what was going on. A low rattle escaped from his chest.

Her eyes popped wider than an owl's. "Did you just growl?"

~ ~ ~

Oh my god, Ottar had growled like a wild animal. Pepper had enough of the Australian Tarzan sprawled across her body, rumbling in her ear. He was willing to put her precious animals at risk. Not happening.

She'd lure the gunfire away from them. Wilma and Fred lived through enough abuse in their past lives. Whoever was trying to kill her had mentioned the Hellhounds in the text. Weird thing was, no one knew about the hellish pups except Abby. And Abby wouldn't tell a soul, including her husband-to-be.

She swallowed hard. "I'll run but you need to get off me. I don't want you to get shot either." She'd feel super horrible if Ottar ended up wounded. But with his speed, he could probably outrun a bullet. How freaky was that? He'd morphed into a bizarre outback superhero. And what was up with the growl? Egads, what if he was dangerous?

"We'll run to the barn on three," he said in her ear.

She nodded.

"One, two, three." He wiggled off her and bolted toward the barn.

She took off the other way and headed toward the dinosaur. Rounding its leg, she hid behind the statue.

"Pepper," Ottar called out, his voice fierce.

Uh, oh. Her stunt had pissed him off. Still, she didn't care about Ottar's fury because Fred and Wilma were now safe. Her heart smashed into her chest with each beat.

A blur zigzagged through the dark yard and plopped down next to her. She couldn't get over how fast he moved. Like he had superhuman speed. A picture formed in her mind of Ottar wearing tights and a cape. She let out a little laugh.

"You. Did. Not. Listen. To. Me."

"Nope. Dude, you're freaking me out with your mega-speed. It isn't normal."

He shook his head. "What's wrong with you? Do you have a death wish?"

"Certainly not. Who would take care of my animals and my store?" She had drawn up a Will and had named Abby-poo guardian of her pets, but she doubted Abs could take care of all of them. Sometimes they could be a handful. Like the Hellhounds right now, for example.

A crash sounded next to her. The gunman shot a big hole in her dinosaur's leg.

"I'm not fixing that," Ottar said pointing to the new damage.

"Urgh." She took off and slid behind a tree. Another round hit the bark causing it to splinter. *Crap.* Now she had to worry about the tree. She searched for a hiding place that wouldn't further damage her property.

Ottar landed next to her. "You're one of the most stubborn women I've ever met."

Right now she didn't care what he thought.

Flashing lights turned into her driveway. To her relief, River arrived. Now maybe the gunfire would stop.

"Pepper. Ottar?" River called out.

"We're behind the tree, two-o-clock," Ottar called back.

"Stay put. Where's the shooter?" River ducked behind the open car door.

"Probably gone now. Great entrance, mate." Ottar peeked around the tree. "He was about fifty yards to the right of the barn." He moved behind her, placing his hands on each side of her head on the tree. He caged her in, the moron.

Still, his woodsy scent sent shivers up her legs to her core. It reminded her of the afternoon's events. She'd never look at a tree the same again.

He leaned on her and spoke into her ear. "Woman, now is not the time to be aroused."

How the heck did he know she was feeling frisky? "I'm not," she answered him.

"Stop telling porkies. I can smell you, and it's driving me crazy."

"Now wait a doggone minute there, mister." She ducked

under his arm and stepped from behind the tree. Pointing her finger at him, she said, "I do not smell."

"We'll take care of those desires after this is over." He licked his lips and eyed her like she was a steak dinner.

Oh, no, he wasn't. She wagged her finger in his face. "Keep your man parts in your pants. We are not having a replay."

Ottar grinned wide. "Oh, lovey, you're wrong this time."

Chapter 24

Ottar scoured the forest surrounding Pepper's house. He caught a human scent in the area where the gunfire originated. The acrid gunpowder scent over-powered the unfamiliar human culprit. He'd have to work on his new superpowers. The thought of these enhanced senses brought a smile to his face. The Cryptid wankers wouldn't stand a chance after he perfected these gifts.

River walked over to him. "Do you think all this is related to the herd of Jackalopes?"

"I doubt it. But when Pepper is involved, anything is possible." He wished he could wrap up this investigation. He'd like another go-around with the sexy woman.

They searched deeper into the forest checking for clues to the shooter. So far there wasn't much to go on.

"Abby's mom is coming in a couple days. I'm afraid I'll be busy trying to be the perfect son-in-law. Do you want to come to dinner and help a bro out?"

The thought of another woman like Abby made his stomach all squirrely. "I'll have to chew on that one for a while. Is Pepper going?"

Lines formed around River's eyes. "I have no idea. I'm not getting cold feet or anything, but with everything going on, I want to blow off the wedding and head straight to the honeymoon."

"I don't blame you, mate. But you've been drafted into Abby's world of whacky shit. I have a feeling, days like this will be common. Get used to it." River's life would never be mundane. In a way he wished it was him. These past few days excited him to no end. Pepper made him feel alive and he never knew what would happen next. The woman was unpredictable.

"I don't see any evidence leading us closer to Pepper's attacker." River shook his head. "Abby is stressed out by all this."

"I have a feeling Pepper knows more than she's telling us." Ottar breathed in a whisper of smoke. Flames rose in the distance. Ottar's chest grew heavy.

He never should have left Pepper home alone. Her farm was on fire.

~ ~ ~

Pepper did go inside her home like she'd promised, but when Ellie Mae jumped against her back door, she went back outside to check on her.

The little black Pomeranian pack played keep away from each other in her yard. Jeb had a stick in his mouth and Jethro snapped at it. Mr. Drysdale ran around them, barking nonstop.

"What's going on guys?" she asked the fluffy pups. In the dark, they were hard to see, except for their glowing red eyes.

Granny ran up to her and hopped on her hind feet. Pepper sat on the cool concrete steps. The old hound jumped into her lap and she stroked her soft thick fur.

"You guys are causing all kinds of trouble." She hugged Granny's wiggly, frail body.

Jethro yanked the stick from Jeb's mouth, the golden whistle shimmered around Jeb's neck. "Ah ha. Jeb, come on over here. I need that whistle."

Jeb's gaze locked onto hers. He shook his head and darted behind Mr. Drysdale. The cranky pup crashed into Jeb, rolling him over.

Jethro stood off to the side. He stilled and let out a loud belch. A small flame shot from his mouth at the same time. *Good heavens, the hounds burp fire.*

After realizing his new cool trick, Jethro chased Ellie Mae, launching flames at her. Granny jumped from her lap and barked at Jethro.

"Shoosh, Granny. Someone is trying to kill me and steal you."

The old girl kept barking.

The other Hellhounds surrounded Jethro. He spun inside the circle of pups. He paused and his eyes glowed brighter. He let out another belch and at the same time flames shot from both his mouth and rear end. Mr. Drysdale's fur caught fire. He rolled on the ground to douse the flames. He didn't seem fazed by it one bit. She'd bet those pups were used to the inferno living in hell and everything.

Soon all the dogs were burping and farting flames. Jeb pointed his butt at Jethro and he jumped out of the way. Granny wasn't so lucky. Jeb blasted her in the face. She chased him around and cornered him by a stack of hay bales. The tiny dog shot a monster flame from her backside. Jeb scampered away.

Pepper rose to her feet and inched toward Jeb. "Hey, little guy, want some pets." If she could get close enough to him, she'd grab the whistle and put this to an end. The Pomeranian pranced around. Every time she closed in, he'd take off running.

She shoved her hand into her pocket. Her fingers latched onto a piece of a vegan treat. She always kept dog treats handy for her regular dogs. Positive reinforcement worked a heck of lot better than negative. Holding out the treat in her fingers, she called his name. "Jeb. Hey, boy, want a treat?"

Jethro materialized in front of her and snatched the treat from her fingers. "Shame on you Jethro." She scowled at the little thief.

Flames rose from the hay bales. One of the little rascals must have started it on fire. Smoke twisted and rose into the sky. She ran inside. Checking under her sink, she found the fire extinguisher. She yanked it from the cupboard and ran back out the door.

The fire grew, snapping and popping. The hounds disappeared, the little devils.

Ottar ran toward her with his gun drawn. "What the bloody hell is going on? Get into the house. Don't you realize the fire was most likely set to draw you outside?"

She ignored him, aimed the fire extinguisher, and doused the flames. "Gosh, that was close. The barn almost caught fire." A wave of relief washed through her muscles.

Ottar latched his fingers around her wrist and dragged her toward the house. "You're going to stay inside."

She whipped her arm away from his, trying to free herself. "I'm fine. I couldn't let my barn burn down." Thank goodness, the Hellhounds had disappeared.

He called over his shoulder, "River, check around outside. I can't leave her alone for a minute."

"What, now I need a babysitter?" She had a crapton of stuff to do, and it didn't involve certain L.A.M.P.S. personnel sticking his nose in her business.

"If you can't follow orders, I'll have to have someone on you twenty-four-seven." Ottar opened the door and nudged her inside.

Wonderful.

Barney and Betty rushed to greet them. Whenever she saw the two large pups her heart melted. They sat at attention, one on each side of her.

"Look, you're scaring them," she said to Ottar.

He narrowed his eyes at her. "You're scaring *me*. You are impossible to guard." He rushed to her windows, peeked out, then closed the curtains. He turned back to her. "You had a close call today."

No kidding. "I truly appreciate you trying to keep me safe, but I can't curl up into a ball and hide inside the house. I'm a busy woman."

~ ~ ~

Ottar held Pepper's arms. His fingers touched her bones under her thin skin. She stood about five-foot-ten and sported some bodacious breasts, a flat stomach, and nicely rounded hips, although, in his opinion, she could use some meat on her bones. "When was the last time you ate?"

"I eat. I ate a black bean burger this afternoon."

"Why don't I have River grab us a couple steaks?" His mouth watered thinking about the juicy, almost rare chunk of meat.

"I could make a quinoa salad. Do you want one?" She wriggled free from his grasp and he missed feeling her next to him.

"Sure, whatever that is." He was so hungry, he could eat cardboard right now. He followed her into the kitchen.

River opened the back door. "The perimeter is secure. I'm going home to Abby."

"Thanks," Ottar responded.

"Tell Abby-doodle to take the rest of the week off work. I figure she has a gazillion things to do for the wedding," Pepper said.

"I appreciate that."

Ottar turned to Pepper. "You should stay home too."

She gave him a you're-kidding look. "I have a business to run."

"I'm leaving before you two shed blood. Have a good night." River ran out the door.

Pepper chopped up an avocado, carrots, onion, grape tomatoes, and some broccoli. She mixed it into a bowl with some kind of round rice bits and then placed it on the table.

He picked through the concoction with his fork. "What are these round things? They look like tiny rolled up condoms." It was true. The small opaque rice balls had a ring around them. If mice wore condoms, this is what they'd look like straight out of the package.

"That's quinoa. It's good for you. Shut up and eat it—or starve. I don't care." She salted and peppered her bowl. "It's loaded with protein."

He scooped up a forkful and placed it into his mouth. It wasn't too bad if you liked veggies. The rice stuff seemed to go well with the smooth taste of avocado. He scooped up another heaping and chewed. Before he knew it, his bowl was empty.

"See. I'll make a vegan out of you yet." She sat back in her chair and folded her arms.

"Fat chance. I was so hungry, I would have eaten bushes. This wasn't very far from that."

She let out an exhausted sigh, rinsed out his bowl, and placed it into the dishwasher. "I need to take the dogs outside before bed."

"No, you don't. You're not leaving the house." Did she forget that someone shot at her tonight, then started a fire?

She batted her big blue eyes. "Okay, then *you* need to take them out. Believe me, if a hundred and twenty-pound dog has an accident, it's a puddle the size of the Atlantic Ocean. I'll leash them up. They'll know what to do. You have to hang on to them so they don't get loose."

"No problem." He could do that.

She pulled out four leashes. The two large dogs stood still as she hooked up the leather straps to their collars. The one she called Dino looked like a little Lassie dog and spun out of control. Bam Bam was a golden retriever and licked the drool from Barney's jowls.

Pepper handed the leashes to him. The dogs beelined to the door, tails wagging.

"Hang on tight. If you let one leash go they'll go crazy."

In his opinion, they were already spastic. He'd never seen animals so excited to go outside.

He bounded down the steps, following the pack. Not far off the pathway they squatted and did their business. Bam Bam finished first and sniffed the ground, tugging on the leash. "Heel dog." Ottar pulled back on the leash, but the dog seemed to be on a mission.

Bam Bam wandered over by the burnt hay bales, sniffing the ground. He wagged his tail. Ottar strolled behind him with the others in tow. "Hey, dude, what's going on?"

Pepper opened the back door. "What's taking you so long. I don't trust that blood-thirsty shooter. Please bring them back inside."

As he herded the dogs back to the house, Ottar smelled the sulfur odor. He didn't notice it earlier because of the burning hay. Sniffing again, he homed in on five different yet similar canine scents, and they weren't Pepper's Flintstone pups. They smelled like the ones at the shoe store.

He yawned. After being up for days, he needed a restful night. His investigation would have to wait.

Pepper unleashed the dogs. "I'm going to bed. Do you need anything?"

Ottar needed something, all right. He needed her. "I'm right behind you." He followed her to the stairs.

"What do you think you're doing?" She slammed her hands on her hips.

"We're going to bed." He looked forward to spooning with her.

"You're sleeping in the guest room."

Ouch. "Sorry lovey, I'm sleeping with you."

She narrowed her eyes at him. "Over my dead body."

~ ~ ~

Ottar tossed and turned in the guest bedroom. Pepper insisted her dogs needed to sleep with her. After all four pups jumped onto her queen-sized bed, he clearly saw there was no room for him. Maybe he'd invest in a king-sized bed with extensions? Wait, what the hell was he thinking? After the missions were completed, he'd be in another state. Would he miss his blond vixen?

More than anything, he wanted to nuzzle his face in the crook of her neck and breathe in her sexy scent, touch her soft skin, and bang her like there was no tomorrow. Which may not be far from the truth with the gunman running around.

His eyes grew heavy as he dozed off into sleep.

A bright light blared over him. And what the bloody hell was that beeping noise? He struggled to sit up, but couldn't.

White walls surrounded him. A face half-covered with a surgical mask, peered over him. The man's thick round glasses magnified his ice blue eyes. "Mr. Jones, nice of you to wake up. We prefer to have you conscious when performing our little experiments." His latex glove covered hand gripped a scalpel that hovered over his chest.

"Get me out of here or I'll rip you apart." Ottar's voice was weak and scratchy. He moved his shoulders from side to side, but they only moved an inch at the most. He looked down at his chest where large leather bands held his body in place.

Blood pumped in his temple. He would rip the asshole's throat out, whoever he was.

"The more you fight this, the more it will hurt," the masked man said in a sing-song voice.

Ottar elbowed the strap holding him down. It gave a tad. A sharp jolt zinged through his chest. He let out an "Umph."

"Stay still. I want to watch this one more time." The surgeon's eyes widened. "I'll never get over how fast you heal."

Next thing he knew a gas mask was placed over his nose. The lights dimmed.

Ottar opened his eyes. He sat on a stainless-steel bench in a jail cell. The same gleaming material covered the walls.

Houston stood on the other side of the bars with his arms crossed. "Do we have a deal?" he asked.

Ottar bit into his lip. He could feel the turmoil roll around in his stomach. A betrayed feeling rose to his throat.

He nodded.

Chapter 25

Pepper wanted to kick Ottar in his tight butt. Last night was the first time she'd had glimpsed the magic whistle since its disappearance. If that overgrown barbarian hadn't barged in on her and the hounds, she was sure she would have been able to snag it from them.

When she woke up this morning, Ottar was gone. Vulture was waiting outside in a large black SUV. He waved to her when she took the dogs outside.

She performed the duties of opening her pet shop and took out the puppies so they could do their business. Vulture, her new seven-foot-tall shadow, trailed her wherever she went.

Tabitha strolled into the pet shop with a large black raven perched on her shoulder. "Hello, Pepper."

"Hey, girl. Who do you have there?"

Tabitha shot a glance at Vulture, then turned back to Pepper. "This is Gwendolyn the raven. Say hello, Gwendolyn. She's my familiar." The bird's feathers shone pure black and shiny.

"Hello, beautiful. Would you like some peanuts?" Pepper headed to the bird aisle and opened the package that sat on a shelf loaded with different bird seed. She loved handing out treats to the pets people brought into her shop. This would be the first time a raven had visited.

"Please," Gwendolyn said in a birdish voice.

Tabitha set her down on the counter. The bird walked around in a circle.

"She talks. How wonderful." Pepper held out the peanut. Gwendolyn picked a small dog treat out of the bowl sitting next to her and held it in her beak. "Does she want the dog treat instead?

"She likes to swap out prizes," Tabitha said.

The raven placed the treat in front of Pepper and flapped one time.

"Oh, thank you." She handed the bird the peanut. "What a lovely soul."

"You wouldn't say that if you got to know her," Tabitha joked. She placed a kiss on its black head.

"I'm making birdseed ornaments for Abby's wedding, want to help?" Pepper pulled out a twenty-pound bag of seed mix. "Are you going to be able to come? Abby said she invited you."

Tabitha's face lit up like a blazing jack-o-lantern. "I wouldn't miss it for the world. I have a feeling it's going to be the event of the decade."

Vulture moved his arm. Funny, Pepper forgot he was standing ten feet away from them. He cleared his throat. "I'm going to check outside."

"Okay. Thank you," she replied.

"Who is the hunk of brooding man?" Tabitha asked.

"Vulture. He's my new bodyguard." The whole guard on patrol thing still didn't sit well with her. She was sure he had better things to do than stand around and watch her carry on with her daily routine.

"Why do you need a bodyguard?"

Pepper exhaled. Having your life threatened was exhausting. "Someone is trying to kill me."

"You're kidding. Who?" Tabitha's eye's widened.

"I have no idea. That's why Vulture is protecting me."

Tabitha looked outside, eyeing his physique. "He's hot. Will he be at the wedding?"

"Yes, along with several others. Are you single?" Funny, she hadn't asked Tabitha many personal questions. After the whole spell nightmare, the men had shut down their ladies' night fun.

"Yes, and I'm not sure I want to change that." Her smile tightened, indicating she didn't want to talk about it.

"No problem. I'm a happy single here." She sure would like to snag some Ottar beef again. But it wasn't meant to be.

"What's the story with you and Seal?"

"Seal?"

"Yes, the cray-cray wild looking dude who was struck by lightning." She widened her eyes and bared her teeth as if to imitate Ottar's expression from the other night.

"Oh, you mean Ottar. Well, nothing really. We couldn't be more opposite." But his skills as a lover were unbelievable. Not that she'd tell him. Humble he was not.

"I picked up some untamed vibes off him. I'd be careful if I were you. He may bite." Tabitha straightened out her super cute flowing purple lace skirt.

"He'll be gone after the wedding, so I'm not too concerned," Pepper said.

The door dinged and Abby-licious strolled in. "Hi-ya, girlfriends." She placed a shopping bag full of white ribbons on the counter. "I can't wait to make these ornaments. They're going to be awesome hanging from the trees. I'm hoping birds flock from all over and fill the branches to add the final touch. Who is this fabulous crow?"

The large black bird squawked and flapped her wings.

"Gwendolyn is a *raven*. She doesn't like to be called a crow," Tabitha said.

"I'm so sorry." Abby snagged a peanut from the bag and offered it to the bird.

Pepper enjoyed her afternoon making the heart-shaped birdseed ornaments with her friends. She loved girl time and didn't want it to end.

After an hour, Abby had to run for her last dress fitting. Tabitha left not long after.

Vulture returned after her friends left the shop. "I thought you women would like a little alone time."

She tilted her head as she studied him. He stalked around the store checking all the nooks and crannies. "Thank you. That was very thoughtful."

He nodded. "How long have you known Tabitha?"

"Not long. We know her mother though. She's a sweetheart."

"She's a witch?"

"Yes, but she's a good witch." Uh, oh. What did these agents have against witches?

"If there is such a thing." He frowned before his attention snapped to the entrance.

The door dinged. In came Charlotte, the widow. Her peroxide platinum hair was wisped up in a cotton candy hairdo. The sickening stench of her cheap perfume followed right behind her. Pepper bit back a gag.

"Hello, Pepper." She tottered in on her stiletto heels. Who in their right mind wore shoes like that into a pet store? "Hello, Mr. Tall, Dark, and Handsome." The widow's gaze traveled from Vulture's toes to his face.

"Charlotte," Pepper greeted her. The hussy was looking for a new victim to sink her glittery pink talons into. Her husbands had a habit of dying in mysterious accidents. One died from a tree falling on him and another was electrocuted in the bathtub. Both deaths seemed extremely fishy.

"How can I help you today?" She didn't want to help the widow, she wanted her to leave. Like immediately.

Vulture crossed his arms in front of him and didn't say a word.

"I heard Ottar was in town. I was hoping to run into him." She pouted her ruby red silicone filled lips.

When Charlotte moved to town, they'd been in high school. Pepper, being her friendly outgoing self, befriended Charlotte. She invited her to hang out with her and Abby and join in on the fun. The next thing she knew, the wench stole her boyfriend. True girlfriends didn't steal other girlfriend's dates. When she'd confronted Charlotte with that rule, she'd said, "You must not have been taking care of him, since he strayed." And since then, Charlotte had tried to steal every single one of Pepper's dates. For some stupid reason, the betrayal still hurt. She would never ever stab a friend in the back like that. She let out a long breath, relaxing a tad bit. "I'll tell Ottar you were asking about him." *Not.*

"Please tell him to pay me a visit. We had such wonderful chemistry the last time he came over." She raised her eyebrows a few times.

Pepper wanted to pluck the woman's eyeballs from her skull and pop them under her shoe like a grape. Had Ottar and Charlotte had sex? Surely not. Her mind drifted to the branch swinging sex they had yesterday in the woods. Egads, she would need to get tested for STD's. "How's Keith?" Did the hussy dump him already?

"We decided we're better off as business partners. You overreacted with that childish tampon stunt the other night."

A smile grew on Pepper's face while she thought of his mushroomed yard. The blooms brought joy to her heart.

"I have to run," Charlotte said. She headed to the door without buying anything. The only reason she stopped by was to snoop.

"Okay." She hoped the woman would run far away, like out of town, into the next state, or even Canada. Ottar would never fall for her skanky ways. Would he?

Chapter 26

Ottar had kept his distance from Pepper today. It wasn't that he didn't want to be around her, in fact, it was quite the opposite—and that scared the bloody piss out of him.

After the disturbing dream, he couldn't sleep. While he waited for Vulture to take over watch on Pepper, he paced outside. No matter how hard he tried, he couldn't make sense out of the nightmare. It seemed like part memory, part make-believe.

Not wanting to waste any more time pondering, he set off into the woods surrounding Pepper's house. The morning dew air filled his lungs.

His first stop was the area where the shooter had been standing. He picked up a human scent. For some reason, he knew it was male, but he had no idea why. These new Spidey-superpowers came in handy. He'd also smelled the sulfur back by Pepper's house.

After a thorough search of the area, and not picking up any more clues, he headed to meet River at a diner.

River sat in the corner booth with a new cellphone box in front of him. "Vulture said you left before he could give this to you." He pushed the box closer to Ottar. "Why is Houston blowing up my phone with texts and voicemails? Anything I should know about before I call him back?"

River had strong intuitions, and he was such a good friend that his blood was worth bottling. "He's probably pissed he can't track me now that my chip is fried." Ottar pointed to the blister on his wrist.

"Listen, I know about the chip. Hell, I think the rumors have been circulating for years about Houston holding it over your head. I think there's more. He mentioned a heat signature. What the hell is that about?" River had lifted his baseball hat up and down, adjusting it.

Did he trouble his friend with the investigation, or not? He didn't want to be the one to cause a canceled marriage. On the other hand, his friend had a right to be informed that his wife-to-be was thigh high in trouble. "The satellites picked up a heat signature that shows up on Pepper's property every Halloween. I was called in to investigate it."

"It could be a bonfire or anything." River scratched his temple.

"Na, it's not just any heat signature, it's the mother of all mother's heat signatures. As in the flaming-bowels-of-hell, heat signature. Crikey, it lit up her whole property in silver. I'm thinking Pepper is involved in something huge, and my guess is it's paranormal." He watched River mess with his cap again.

"You think Abby is involved, too." River lowered his gaze.

"I don't know, mate. All I do know is there's a strong sulfur odor surrounding Pepper's house, and a lot of weird shit has been happening." Like him getting struck by lightning and someone trying to kill Pepper.

"I'll have a talk with Abby. I thought she would trust me after everything we've been through." His voice trailed off, almost defeated. The poor bloke.

"Abby may not be involved. That's why I haven't said anything to you."

"Last night the fire department was called to several small fires around town. Do you think they're related?" River asked.

"No idea. But I'll find out."

An older waitress placed an overflowing plate of steak, eggs, and bacon in front of each of them. He stuffed a forkful of creamy eggs and spicy sausage into his mouth. Before he knew it the plate was empty.

River picked up his ringing phone. "Sheriff Stone," he answered.

There were a lot of ah huhs, okays, and a thank you.

"What's up?" Ottar didn't like the look that took over River's face. His expression said something sinister had happened.

"We have another victim." River stood up and signaled the waitress to bring the bill.

Ottar handed his company credit card to the woman. "Who is it?"

"The Butcher."

~ ~ ~

Ottar and River pushed past a small crowd forming in front of the butcher shop.

River addressed the people. "Everyone needs to go home. This is an investigation. Move lively, please."

The men and women turned and whispered quietly to one another. Soon they began to disperse.

"Oi, you've got this town wrapped around your pointer finger. It'll come in handy if this investigation goes on any longer." Ottar opened the door and let River go into the shop first.

The odor of meat, blood, and wild game saturated the butcher shop. Ottar breathed in, enjoying the smell. The steak and eggs clearly didn't fill him. His metabolism was speeding up, probably from the stress of the cases.

Derek the Butcher was a large man, weighing in at over three-hundred pounds. His body was sprawled out on the floor, behind the glass cases showcasing different cuts of delicious meat, and his apron was splotched with fresh red blood. Not the usual Jackalope murder. At least fifty shish-kabob stakes riddled Derek's body. The wooden skewers stuck out from his torso, making him look like a large sea urchin.

"Crikey, do you think the horned dickheads were pissed?" This didn't make sense. Why would the Jackalopes target the butcher? He searched the walls but didn't see any trophy heads.

"Maybe this is the reason." River pointed to one of the signs in the meat display that read Jackalope Meat $15.95 a pound.

"What a stupid plunker." Ottar pulled on his latex gloves and squatted next to the body. The butcher's blood had been drained, like the other victims. The skewers were shoved an inch deep all over the body. Bite marks and saliva coated the skewers, indicating the Jackalopes were responsible. Creative buggers. Derek chopped up their family members for stew meat and it pissed them off.

He called the location in to Holly, his cleaner. She'd have the bloody scene wrapped up in an hour. As soon as he hung up, Houston called.

"What the hell is going on there?" Houston barked out, his voice demanding.

Ottar filled him in on the new murder.

"I'll get the media control unit to cover it up. You and River are making a mess out of this investigation. You're spread out too thin. You should have had this wrapped up three deaths ago." He let out a sigh.

"I'm on it."

"You better be. Another thing, how come your tracker isn't showing up anymore?"

Yep, he had a feeling Houston would get upset when he couldn't see him on the GPS. "I was zapped by lightning. You don't have to worry about me taking off. River can keep you posted on my whereabouts."

He endured a long silent pause from Houston. Why was he so concerned? It wasn't like he would disappear. River was there. So was Vulture, and Holly. Soon Leif and other L.A.M.P.S. personnel would join them for the wedding. "Damn it, Houston, I told you I wasn't going anywhere."

"Yes. Well. We have an agreement with the Authorities in Australia," Houston said.

"So you weren't going to remove the microchip when I wrapped up these cases?" Ah, he'd caught the bastard in his porky lie. He had a feeling they'd never remove the chip. After all these years he'd never given them any flack. They snapped, and he jumped at their beckoning. Why couldn't they give him a fair go? A warm fury stoked inside his chest. He breathed in deep, counted to ten, and let out the air. *Calm down.*

"Do you have anything new on the cases?" Houston changed the subject.

"Other than a dead butcher? Nope." Ottar hung up the phone. He had enough of the pompous windbag.

He pulled one of the skewers from the butcher and inspected it. *How the hell did the Jackalopes do this?*

~ ~ ~

Pepper thought about her Hellhounds and her stomach twisted. Her poor hellish babies had to resort to digging through garbage to survive. She didn't know what they ate in hell, she didn't know if they were watered, and doubted they had little doggy beds. Who took care of them while they were down there? She realized she didn't know much about their life when they weren't with her. In fact, she often wondered how they "marked" someone for hell. What if Abby was right? What if they did lift their leg on the people who were damned?

She shook her head to remove the thought only to find it replaced with Ottar's amazing performance in the forest.

Did she want a replay of the Earth-shattering, swinging from the branches, sexcapades? The Aussie was a sex king, a true pleasure prince. Not that she'd tell him. She'd bet he already knew.

Tabitha entered the shop. "Hey, Pepper."

"Hello. Where's Gwendolyn today?"

Tabitha shrugged and looked out the window. "She's flying around out there looking for treasures. She'll peck on the window when she's ready to come in."

"I've got more peanuts when she does." Pepper placed a few shelled peanuts on the counter.

"She loves peanuts." Tabitha reached into her pocket and placed three whistles on the counter. Two were plastic and one was silver. "I told her you were searching for your heirloom and she brought me these this morning. She scoured the whole area. I think she took a liking to you."

Pepper's heart warmed. Gwendolyn wanted to help her. "Aww. And for that, I'll have to give her a special treat."

True to Tabitha's word, the raven perched on the door handle and pecked at the glass. She opened the door and the raven flew in. "Hello, Gwendolyn. Thank you for looking for my whistle."

The bird landed on the counter and pointed her beak at the treasures she found.

"You are such a good bird."

The Raven pecked at the silver whistle.

"It's close, but I'm afraid it's not the one." She scrolled through her phone to find a selfie of herself wearing the gold and ruby necklace. It was the selfie her aunt took of them after she'd given the whistle to her right before her aunt passed away. "This is what it looks like."

Gwendolyn tilted her head when she looked at the picture.

Pepper unhooked the clasp of the necklace she was wearing. It was a silver pawprint pendant that she'd purchased at a fundraiser. She placed it next to the bird. "Here's a present for you. Thank you for gathering all these whistles."

The raven picked up the necklace in her beak. She strutted around the counter holding it in her mouth.

"Uh, oh. You realize you made a friend for life. Gwen's on a mission now. I hope the magic in your whistle isn't dangerous," Tabitha said. "Can I see the picture?"

Pepper's stomach flipped. Could the magic in the whistle harm familiars? She handed her phone to Tabitha.

Her new friend placed a hand over her mouth and gasped. "I know what this is."

Pepper looked around the shop to make sure Vulture hadn't snuck in the back door. He routinely patrolled the outside.

"You do?"

Tabitha nodded. In an almost whispered voice she said, "You're a caretaker of the Hellhounds. I'm honored."

Pride filled Pepper as she pulled back her phone. "You've heard about this?"

"I studied MO's in college."

"MOs?" Her heirloom was a MO, whatever that was.

"Magical objects. How did you lose it?"

A huge twinge, more like a twang of guilt pelted her chest. "The Hellhounds snatched it from my neck when I set the rascals free. I saw Jeb wearing it the other night."

"The Hellhounds stole the MO? Are they still lose?" Tabitha asked.

"Yes, they truly are hellions." No more treats for them. At least for a while. She couldn't really blame them for not wanting to go back to hell.

"This isn't good. I wonder what the consequences will be? Life is like a pendulum. For every action, there's a reaction." Tabitha's concern was etched on her face.

Pepper had wondered what would happen if they didn't return the day after Halloween. Right now, it seemed the hounds were unruly big dogs getting into trouble. But what if they were out there marking more people than they should? Could hell get overpopulated?

Tabitha placed her hand over Pepper's. "Don't worry. We'll help you get the whistle back."

Gwendolyn hopped onto Pepper's shoulder and made some clucking noises in agreement.

"Thank you. I can use all the help I can get. Please make me a promise that you won't tell a soul."

"I promise." She hugged Pepper.

A warm snuggly feeling expanded from her heart and filled her chest. Intuition told her she could trust Tabitha.

"I have a couple questions. If you don't want to answer, no problem."

Pepper nodded.

"Why were you two trying to do a banishment spell?"

Abby entered the pet shop as if on cue. "Hello, you two."

"I think that's a story for Abby to tell." She waved Abby over.

"What story?" Abby asked.

Pepper filled Abby in on how Tabitha knew about the whistle and had asked about the previous spell they'd worked with her mother's help. She wasn't sure if Abby wanted her to spill the deets.

"We were trying to banish the tampon Genie. He cursed me to become the Jersey Devil every time I got my period," Abby said it like it was an everyday occurrence.

"Get out. I've heard those Jinn have a twisted sense of humor." Tabitha was taking the news like it was no big deal. Having a witch on their side could be a good thing. It seemed Acme Witchcraft Academy really was a credible school.

"Well, we ended up using a spell from my deceased grandmother. I have her journals at home. We were able to trap the evil Genie for good." Abby grinned a triumphant smile.

"Okay, I have to ask, who are those hot hunks of men always surrounding you?"

"They are secret government agents that hunt mythical beasts," Pepper said.

"I get a predatory vibe from them, especially from the Ottar guy." Tabitha protectively stroked Gwendolyn's feathers.

"They don't know about the hounds and I want to keep it that way."

"The reason my locating spell didn't work was because the MO is very powerful. When you mix magics, spells sometimes backfire," Tabitha said.

"Weird stuff always happens around us." Abby giggled.

"Why are they here then? The agents?"

"Because they're hunting for Jackalopes." Pepper figured she might as well let Tabitha in on all the secrets.

"Those are nasty creatures. They suck the blood out of their victims." Tabitha was up to speed on her beasts. Should she be worried about her? Maybe Tabitha was responsible for the Jackalopes? She pushed that idea from her mind. Tabitha didn't seem like the type to cause harm to people.

"We found out how vicious they can be," Abby chimed in.

Ottar and the others clearly didn't like witches. "You need to watch out, Tabitha. What if they hunt you?"

Tabitha waved her hand in front of her face. "We aren't magical beings. We practice magic like doctors practice medicine. We channel the power of the earth around us for spells. I doubt they would hunt us. Besides, we have protection from the government after that whole Salem witch hunt scandal."

Tabitha's explanation soothed her fears a bit. She still couldn't help worrying. Those men were dead set on ridding the world of Cryptids and other mythical creatures.

"I've got to run. My coven is having a bake sale to fundraise for their cat rescue. That's the reason I came by. Would you like to donate some of your dog cookies?"

A smile grew across Pepper's lips. "Of course. I'm always happy to donate for a good cause." Animal rescue budgets were tight. There was always vet bills, food, and other supplies to buy. "I can also donate some organic cat toys. I have some over here."

They followed her to the cat aisle. She pulled several catnip toys off the peg. She placed the stuffed mice and a bunch of her individually wrapped cookies in a paper sack. "If you want, bring some flyers of the cats available for our adoption bulletin board. She pointed at the board loaded with pictures of animals.

"Most of our cats are unadoptable. They're old familiars who were rejected or their witches have passed on. They tend to live extra-long lives. We have several that are over fifty years old."

"Fifty? Oh my gosh." Usually, cats don't live much past twenty. What if she could practice magic and make all her dogs familiars? They would live longer lives.

"Yeah, we think it's because familiars are conduits for magic and they absorb some of the power. The really old ones can practice magic, and they get into a lot of trouble. Think of senior citizen magical ornery cats. I've got to run. Thanks so much for all the goodies." Tabitha motioned to the raven and it hopped onto her shoulder.

"Bye, Pepper and Abby," Gwendolyn said.

Vulture walked through the door in time to watch Tabitha leave. "That bird talked."

"Yes, ravens are super smart and can talk like other birds." She had a feeling Gwendolyn could do a lot of things.

Ottar followed Vulture inside, his neck and face bright red. "I thought I told you to stay away from the witch."

Chapter 27

What the hell was that witch doing here? Ottar couldn't believe Pepper was messing around with magic again. Blood pumped to his temple, causing it to throb.

"The crow talked, Boss," Vulture said. He shook his head with a disbelieving look smeared across his face.

"I told you. Ravens can speak. What's the big deal?" Pepper's cheeks pinkened.

"I've never heard a Raven talk." Vulture frowned and walked out of the shop.

Ottar waited until the door closed behind his transporter. "Stay away from the witch." Reports from the past indicated witches were responsible for all kinds of disturbing events. There was even talk that they'd conjured up some of the Cryptids in the past. Though there was no concrete proof to that allegation, Ottar didn't want her taking any chances.

"Oh. My. Gosh. She stopped by to see if I wanted to donate some dog cookies for their cat rescue bake sale. Besides, Tabitha wouldn't hurt a soul, so get used to her. She's one of us now. The third musketeer." Pepper grabbed Abby's hand and pulled it to her.

Just what he needed. Another troublemaker. He'd thought two were enough. Now, a magical one had been added to the mix. He didn't trust witches, especially ones that zapped him with lightning. "How much do you know about her? You said you only recently met her."

"I know enough to know that she's a good person." Pepper's frown deepened. "How much do I know about you?"

He flinched. She'd made love to him. Sure, he hadn't told her much about himself or his past. Right now he was dealing with all kinds of nutty things—like his dreams. How much did he know about himself? If only he could recall the block of time missing in his brain's archives.

All he knew about Pepper was she was as sexy as hell. She didn't eat meat because of the cruelty the industry inflicted on the animals. But most of all, she loved. Loved animals and people. She took care of her friends and put them first. She'd stuck by Abby when she turned into a horrible beast. Crikey, he was warming up to the woman.

"I'm going. I have a scheduled call with the caterers. You guys play nice." Abby winked at Pepper. Did Pepper tell her about their rowdy monkey sex in the woods?

"Bye, Abby-tastic." Pepper walked her to the door and hugged her goodbye.

He could use a hug right now. Where the hell did that come from? This veggie lovin' woman boggled his mind. "We need to talk about what happened in the woods."

"Why? It was a spur of the moment endeavor. Don't worry, I don't expect a repeat or a proposal." She pulled out a box cutter and sliced open a medium sized box, her attention focused on the merchandise inside instead of on him where it should be.

No repeat? *Ouch.* "Don't worry. I'm not going to propose. I want to make sure we feel the same about this."

"Same egg and same carton." She pulled out blue and pink dog collars from the box and sorted them into piles on the counter.

How could she be so nonchalant about the mind-blowing sex they'd shared? If they went at it again, would it be just as awesome? He craved her in his arms right now.

"Has River arrested the person running the dogfighting ring? I think it should be his main priority. You know those nasty people bring drugs and crime into the area? Let alone, those poor dogs are suffering." Pepper looked up and her blue eyes flared.

"River has a lot on his plate right now." A niggle of guilt hit his stomach for dropping the Abby-is-lying-to-you bomb on him earlier this morning. River had the right to know though. He was going to make life-long vows to her. It was his duty to make sure his friend was fully informed. At least that's what he kept telling himself.

She scanned his body. "You're getting bigger."

He shrugged. His shirt was tighter than usual today. "Maybe my shirt shrank the last time I washed it?"

"Nope. Your biceps are as big as my thigh. Something is changing you." She studied him while tilting her head and tapping her finger on her lower lip.

"You're imagining it." He certainly shouldn't be having this convo with Pepper. It had to be because of the lightning strike. He'd research it when he had a spare moment. Right now, he had more than enough to keep him busy.

Shaking her head, Pepper gathered her piles of collars and placed them on the end of the aisle display. She took pride in her little pet shop empire that she'd created. The store was spotless and well stocked. The Haber Cove residents seemed to enjoy shopping there.

River stormed into the store like he had a hornet's nest stuffed in his boxer shorts. "Pepper. We need to talk. Now."

~ ~ ~

Pepper swallowed hard. In the past, when River wore that expression, nothing good came of it. He had the same look on his face when he'd found out Abby was the Jersey Devil.

"Ottar can you give us a few minutes?" He aimed a glare that said *don't disobey me* to the Aussie.

Pepper's heart bounced around in her chest, beating tenfold.

Ottar slammed his hands into his front cargo pants pockets and stormed out the door.

"I know you are up to something and Abby is probably involved in whatever it is. What I can't figure out is why you would risk her happiness and ask her to lie to me?"

Whelp, there you had it. River didn't pussy-foot around the tulips. He aimed for the jugular on her ever-so-guilty neck of shame.

She'd have to play dumb to see how much he knew. "What are you talking about?"

"Don't worry, Abby hasn't said a word. She's as loyal as a friend could be. I'm not going to make her choose between you and me."

Good to know. He really did love and understand Abby.

He raked his hand through his blond curls, clearly in turmoil. "Do you know why Ottar is here?"

She relaxed her lips enough to speak and scratched her cheek. "He said he had to tie up some loose ends, and then the Jackalope thingy happened." Did Ottar lie to her? If so, why did she feel so betrayed right now? She'd lied to him repeatedly about the Hellhounds since he arrived.

River clenched his teeth and shook his head. "He's here because of the heat signature. The one that shows up on your property every Halloween."

Holy hellions. L.A.M.P.S. was spying on her? Oh, my God, she had a heat signature on her property. What the heck was a heat signature? "What are you talking about?"

He paced around in front of her. "Ottar said that every Halloween there's a huge heat signature that flares up right after dusk and then before dawn. That it shows up silver on our heat sensitive satellites, which happens to be the hottest the signature goes. You and Abby were on your property Halloween night. You two have been sneaking around—

more than usual. Since this happened on your farm, I figure, it's you who instigated this. Why did you have to drag Abby along for the adventure? Don't you realize what a difficult position you've put her in?"

Double crap crap. She *had* put Abby in a horrible situation. She'd asked her friend to risk her marriage for her. Her throat tightened, making it hard for her to suck in a breath. How could she be so selfish? "I'm sorry, River. Please don't take this out on Abby. It's all my fault." Gosh, she was a rotten friend. Talk about feeling like dirt. Shoot, she felt like maggot puke.

"Don't worry. I knew what I was getting into when I asked her to marry me. What upsets me the most is that she's keeping secrets from me. I want her to trust me." His eyes pleaded with her to spill the truth.

"I shouldn't have put her in this situation." She should have known better than to include Abby in the Hellhound's escapades.

"Can you fill me in on what's going on? Is Abby in any danger?" The crease in his forehead deepened and his voice softened. He truly worried about Abby, which sent warm zoomies through Pepper's heart.

Could she trust him not to bring the Aussie in on this? Probably not. "All I can say is this is a family tradition passed down from generations. It's not a curse like Abby had, but more of an obligation. It would have been over November first, but we hit a snag. Abby has been kind enough to help me."

He studied her with a stern face.

Ottar banged on the glass door to the pet shop.

"Please don't let him in yet." She wasn't ready to be ganged up on by two L.A.M.P.S. hunters.

He shook his head at the barbarian and waved him to go away. "Is there anything I can do?"

"I'm afraid you can't help. But I *will* figure this out. And no one will get hurt." At least she hoped not. She still didn't know what the consequences were for the Hellhounds not returning to hell on time.

"How do I know this won't happen every year? How do I know you won't drive a wedge between me and Abby in the future? Married people don't keep secrets from each other."

After she caught the hounds, there would be no repeat. She'd learned her lesson with the hellions. "If I don't have this wrapped up by the time you guys are married, I'll tell you what's going on. I give you my word. But you have to promise me that you won't cancel the wedding because of this."

"I'm not going to backout of the wedding. She means the world to me and I can't live without her. I don't want her putting herself in danger. Now something tells me that the person who's trying to kill you has something to do with the heat signature. Am I right? Did you summon a demon or something?"

"It's not a demon." Shoot, he was getting close, but then he was oh-so-far from her Hellhounds.

"What on Earth is so important that you would risk your life and possibly your best friend's life for?"

Wow. She didn't think she could feel worse—but now she did. "All I can tell you is that I have an important duty and if I don't perform my family obligation, really bad things could happen to the universe. Please don't ask me any more questions."

River nodded once. "You'll tell me if it's not wrapped up on my wedding day?"

"I promise." She crossed her heart with her finger.

He pulled her into a big hug. "I have faith in you, Pepper. I love you like a sister. Please realize we can help you and you don't have to carry this burden alone." He squeezed her tighter.

"I know, you big galoot. Thank you." She trusted River, it was the big Aussie Tarzan and his ruthless organization she didn't trust. "Hey, I do have a few things that I think you should know."

He pulled back, his face still laced with concern. "I'm listening."

"Okay, so ever since Ottar was zapped by lightning, which we totally had nothing to do with, he's been acting weird. It's like he has superpowers. He moves super-fast. He smells things that I don't smell, and my sense of smell is pretty good. And, he's been bulking up, like his muscles are getting bigger than usual. He also growled. I swear it's the weirdest thing."

"Are you sure you're not imagining it?"

She shook her head really fast. Of course, she wasn't imagining it. "No, he even mentioned something about it when he tackled me last night while we were being shot at."

"I'll look into it. Anything else?" He raised his eyebrows.

"Yes, I know that this is low on your list of priorities, but you need to catch whoever is running that dogfighting ring. They are horrible people, and crime in this town will explode if you don't nip this in the tail right away."

"You don't need to tell me about it. After I leave, I'm going to check an abandoned warehouse. Someone called in with the lead."

"If you find the dogs, don't kill them. There are special rescues that have great rehabilitation programs for fighter dogs. They have a good chance of leading happy normal lives." There. She'd said her peace. Most people would write off these poor babies, but more and more specialized rescues were working with them. She wasn't trained for this kind of rescue, but she knew people who were. She often donated cookies and toys to the organizations to help soften the financial blow.

"I'll keep that in mind. Thank you." He placed his hat on his head and turned for the door. "I'm glad I talked to you instead of Abby. I know her nerves are kind of frazzled with the wedding and all. I didn't want to alarm her."

"I really appreciate it. Thank you." She hugged around her middle.

River opened the door and Ottar shot back inside. He was wearing a T-shirt and shorts. It was November for heaven's sake and he didn't look the least bit cold.

"I have to check out a warehouse in about an hour. I can use some backup. You in?" River asked Ottar.

Ottar sized up both her and River. He had to be dying to find out what their little pow-wow was about. "Hell, yes. Text me the address. I'll meet you there."

River left the store.

Ottar strolled over by Pepper. "You look like someone pissed in your kibble. What's up?"

She rolled her shoulders, but it didn't relieve the tension in her upper back. Maybe she'd stop by Heavenly Fingers and get a massage. She loved the masseuse Brandon because he'd paid extra attention to her upper back. Whenever she left the spa, she felt like she could take on whatever was troubling her soul. "I have a lot on my mind. Have you found out who's trying to kill me?"

"Nope. It's like they're a ghost."

Chapter 28

Ottar had paced outside while River talked to Pepper. It'd killed him not to know what they were talking about. He'd strained to hear their conversation, but couldn't hear anything, even with his enhanced hearing. When River opened the door, he'd bolted inside.

"Abby's bachelorette party is tonight." Pepper nibbled on her thumbnail.

"Yeah, you're going to have to call it off. It's hard enough watching you at home, let alone in a bar packed with people." Maybe he should handcuff her to himself? Or his bed? In just her bra and panties.

She closed her mouth and slammed another box onto the counter. "I'll talk to Abby."

Well, that went okay. Was she finally figuring out how serious of a threat this was?

The bell dinged and Charlotte walked in. Her fur coat hung open, revealing her cleavage. He tried not to look, but her jugglies were out in the open. They were too large and didn't compare to Pepper's perfect breasts.

"Charlotte," Pepper acknowledged her. She continued unpacking the box.

The widow ignored Pepper. "Oh, Ottar. I'm so glad to see you." She took tiny steps on her high heels, closing in on him.

Her perfume smelled like rubbing alcohol. His nostrils burned with each inhale. "G'day Charlotte."

Pepper shot him a you've-got-to-be-kidding look. One side of her lip curled. Was she jealous?

"I have a roast in the oven. Want to come over and help me eat it?" Charlotte batted her eyes at him. Her fake lashes looked like wolf spiders mating on her lids.

Nope. "I have to work tonight."

She pouted her bright red lips. "Aw, but it'd be so nice to catch up with you." She rubbed her cold palm against his chest.

"Sorry, but duty calls." Moving her hand from him, he stepped back. He didn't want to be her next dead lover. Hmm. Charlotte wasn't on the list of suspects. He'd have to add her. But the shooter smelled distinctly male.

Pepper tightened her lips some more. She was indeed, jealous.

He chuckled. Pepper did like him. Maybe they would have another go-around of hot sex before this mission was over.

The large front window blew in and glass shattered across the floor. The women jumped.

Charlotte screamed.

"Get down!" He shoved the widow to the ground.

Pepper disappeared behind her counter.

He sprinted to the front and looked out. A black sedan with tinted windows peeled down the street. There was no license plate on the vehicle. He rushed back inside to see if anyone was hurt.

"It's clear," he said.

Charlotte's legs were sprawled on the white tile floor. Maybe he pushed her a little too hard? He latched onto her arm and helped her to her feet.

She pulled her skirt down and adjusted her coat. "This place is a madhouse. I'm so glad you were here to save us." She patted her fairy floss hairdo.

Pepper rose from behind the counter, rolling her eyes. "Did you see anything."

He shook his head. A large bullet hole punctured the wall just over Pepper's shoulder. He looked away, so he didn't alarm them. "Charlotte, why don't you go home."

"Fine. I don't know why you hang around *her* anyway. She's crazy and probably paid someone to shoot out her window." She tottered out of the store.

Pepper nibbled her bottom lip.

"That was a close call. They missed you only by a few inches. This is getting serious. I should throw you in jail to protect your arse." Or maybe he should take her home and protect her sweet arse in bed.

"Jail? No way. I'm the victim. Why don't you hop into your big government-issued SUV and chase him down?"

"He's long gone. There was no license plate to go on, but I know the make and model of the vehicle. I'll have one of our data people find out who purchased one in the area. In the meantime, I need to meet River as soon as Vulture arrives."

This little town was like a circus and Pepper and Abby were the main attraction. Poor River was going to age fast around these two.

~ ~ ~

Later that evening, Pepper plopped down on her worn gold sofa in her living room. She sucked in the familiar soft scent of the vanilla candles, burning in the kitchen.

Vulture ran around the house, checked all the windows, and shut the curtains when they arrived. He took her pups outside to do their business, plus fed the horses.

Her heart pounded a million times a minute. She was tired of this whole lets-shoot-Pepper game. Now, she'd have to cancel on Abby's bachelorette party. Which didn't want to do. Why should she have to suffer because someone was trying to kill her? Actually, the killer wasn't very good at killing. They'd had plenty of opportunities to nail her but kept missing. At least she had that going for her.

She climbed the stairs to her bedroom and picked up her phone to tell her friend the bad news. "Abby."

"Hey, Pepper."

"I'm so sorry but I can't go tonight."

"What? Why not? You have to come tonight."

"Because someone shot at me again. I can't risk your life. You might get caught in the crossfire."

"It's not going to be the same without you. Holly had to leave to clean up another site. It's only going to be me and Tabitha. Can't you figure out a way to come? Please?"

She blinked a few times. There had to be a way she could go. She couldn't bring them to her house, but maybe, if she went incognito, she wouldn't risk their lives. If only she could get away from Vulture and sneak out.

"There may be a way. I'll text you if I figure it out. Oh, and Vulture won't be stripping tonight. He's on Pepper watch." Vulture was a hottie, but for some reason, she wasn't disappointed. Now if Ottar had been the one stripping . . .

"That's okay. I'll make River do a striptease just for me when I get home," Abby said.

Pepper ran up the steep stairs to the attic. Dust swirled in front of the solitary window. She opened the cedar chest where she stored her old Halloween costumes. After finding her black wig and padded pregnancy stomach getup, she ran back down the stairs to her second story bedroom.

Screams sounded from the living room. Good, Vulture was still watching his horror movie. He'd be busy for a while.

She didn't have much time. Abby was probably waiting down the street already. Stuffing her hair under the long black curly wig, she pulled on her pregnancy pad, and then an oversized black dress. Hopefully, she'd fit through the window.

Not long after she escaped from the house, Pepper joined Abby in her car. The brisk November breeze chilled her to the bones, even with the extra padding.

"Woo who! I love your disguise. I don't think anyone will recognize you unless they'd seen your pregnant nun costume a few years ago."

Shoot. She'd forgotten it was that recent. Would someone spot her? "So, are we picking up Tabitha?"

"Nope, she's meeting us a Your Alibi." Your Alibi was the local bar in town. It was small and always packed. But they sold cold beer, played great music, and had a dance floor.

"Did River get home from investigating the warehouse?" She adjusted her dark sunglasses.

Abby pulled into the parking spot, then turned to face her. "No. What are you talking about?"

"He received a tip on the dogfighting ring. They can be dangerous."

"I'll text him to see if he's all right." Abby pulled out her phone, a worried expression tugging her smile to a frown.

Pepper pushed Abby's hand holding the phone down. "You can't do that. He'll know I'm with you, and then he'll tell Ottar. I had to sneak out, remember?"

Abby parallel parked across the street from the bar. They passed about fifteen motorcycles lined up in front. "I can't believe these guys still ride in this cold weather."

"They bundle up and wear a helmet." Pepper shivered thinking about it.

Tabitha ran up to them. "Hello, ladies. Are you ready to party? Pepper? Is that really you?" She laughed and circled around her. "I love it. I almost didn't recognize you."

Pepper let out a breath of relief.

"Why the goddess are you dressed up? Halloween is over." Tabitha held the door open for them as they entered the bar.

The beat of deep base music ricocheted off the walls and the drums pounded in her chest.

"Remember, someone is trying to kill her, and she didn't want to put us in harm's way. She also doesn't want to end up dead. Someone shot out the windows in her pet store today," Abby said.

Pepper nodded. Thankfully she was able to call the glass guys, and they replaced the windows before she left. "I'm sorry but Vulture won't be stripping tonight. He's busy." She chuckled to herself thinking about him spending the night watching horror flicks while she was here partying.

"I hope no one recognizes you," Abby said.

"Stop worrying. What could possibly go wrong?"

Chapter 29

Ottar and River made their way through the dark abandoned warehouse. Ottar shined his flashlight along the walls. Muted weak barks in the distance broke the silence. The ammonia stench of dog waste saturated and stung his nose. "Let's split up."

River gave him a nod.

They circled around the large space, staying close to the gray steel walls. *Where the bloody hell were the dogs?* When they met up on the other side, River flicked on the lights overhead.

Ottar blinked a few times to let his eyes adjust.

Large granite headstones and marble Greek god statues littered the large space. Spiderwebs connected a few head busts which sat upon carved columns. Plumes of dust hovered around the bases, giving a fog effect.

"Looks like no one has used this place in a while," Ottar said. Flying powder particles latched onto his tongue, coating his mouth.

"I checked into the property records before we left. The owner died about six months ago and his family hasn't cleared anything out yet. It's kind of cool but also creepy in here." River pointed to a cloaked figure holding a scythe, sitting on a bench. The large hood concealed the faceless marble Grim Reaper as if he was waiting for them.

A slight shiver scurried down the back of Ottar's neck.

The barking grew louder and almost frantic. "Look for a door."

They both weaved around the statues, careful not to bump one.

"I found something." River pointed to a steel door behind a curtain and drew his weapon.

They stood on each side of the door. Ottar placed his hand on the doorknob, held up one finger, then two, and then three. He swung the door open.

River turned on the light switch next to him and illuminated a set of stairs leading down to a basement.

"I hate basements," Ottar said under his breath. He followed River down the set of stairs.

Fifteen crates filled with dogs lined the room.

The dogs barked, bouncing in their small cages. Most were medium sized. They spun around, growing more excited, and Ottar hated this place. The odor burned the inside of his nose. A large pen sat in the corner, probably where they held practice fights. Bloodstains smeared the wall and floor around the ring.

Something inside him pinged his chest with a stab. These dogs were forced to attack each other for sport. They were cooped up here with no ventilation, in filthy cages, without as much as food or water. He was glad Pepper wasn't here to see this. It would have broken her heart. "Looks like you've found the dog stash. Good on ya, mate."

River made a call to animal control. He talked to a woman and mentioned Pepper's name.

Ottar scratched his head as he looked from dog to dog. A mother with pups lay in a cage without any blankets. Crikey, no wonder Pepper was so upset about this. He took off his shirt and opened the cage. The mother cowered in the far corner of her tiny prison, her pups tucked safely beneath her. Carefully, he spread his shirt on the bottom and closed the door. The dog circled around three times and laid down. He could have sworn he saw a tear in her eye as her babies snuggled in to suckle.

River shot him a what-the-hell look.

"What? It's cold in here and the pups have nothing to lay on." She needed it more than he did, and he had another shirt in the SUV. No big deal.

"Animal control is on their way. They must hold the dogs until a court date. Then, they'll contact rescues who can rehabilitate them."

"A hearing could take months. These dogs will have to live in cages for a while longer." Surely the animal rights people could do something to help the dogs.

"Yeah, it doesn't seem fair, but that's the law. At least the cages will be bigger, and they'll be well fed and warm."

Ottar walked to a crate where a large white and brown dog sat. His face had a long scar running from one eye down across his nose. One ear was missing and the other had a huge chunk taken out of it. The dog wagged his tail. "Hey, mate." The animal placed his nose through the bars for attention. He scratched the dog's nose. This wasn't fair at all. Somehow, he could imagine how they felt. "It's not fun being locked up. We're getting you help. Hang in there, bud."

Ottar's phone rang. Vulture's number appeared. The dogs barked again. "I'll be right back." He hit the answer button and ran up the stairs. "What's going on?"

"There's a weird siren going off. Pepper isn't answering when I call her."

Damn, he'd forgotten to tell Vulture about the alarms he rigged on the windows. Was she crazy enough to leave? "That's the window alarm. Pepper escaped."

He could hear Vulture running around, swearing under his breath. "She's gone. Her window is open."

"Do you see her?"

"Negative. It's been about ten minutes since the alarm first sounded."

Damn. He should have warned him she might try to sneak out the window. He really didn't think she'd want to leave after someone targeted her earlier today, but he'd underestimated her yet again. He ran back down the stairs. River was writing notes on a pad of paper.

"Where's Abby's bachelorette party?"

He shrugged. "Probably *Your Alibi*. It's the only decent place to go that serves alcohol around here."

Footsteps sounded above them. "River? Is it safe to come down?" A deep male voice asked.

"Yes," River called up. Then he looked at Ottar. "That's animal control."

Relieved his friend wouldn't be alone, he said, "Pepper's missing. I'm going to find them."

~ ~ ~

A large disco ball spun above Pepper, shining little flashy lights twinkled across the walls. Abby and Tabitha grooved on the dance floor next to her. The music filled her soul with freedom as she danced.

A large guy with a handlebar mustache and spiky hair asked to dance with her. She spun to face him and gave him a nod. The song faded and they waited to see what kind of song would play next.

"I haven't seen you around here." He grabbed her left hand and placed a kiss on her ring finger. "Not married?" he asked while raising a brow.

He wasn't her type, but a dance was a dance. No harm done as long as he kept his hands to himself. She pulled her hand away from his mouth. "Nope."

"Let me introduce myself, I'm Chester."

"Pleased to meet you." She purposely didn't give her name and rolled her eyes behind her sunglasses. She knew Chester Roper, who everyone nick-named Roper the Groper. He was a mailman, and when he handed packages to women the back of his hand would "accidentally" rub against their boob. He ran a different route than her pet store, so she never had to fend him off.

Abby danced her way to Pepper. "I'm thirsty. Let's go back to the table."

"Bye, Chester." She nodded and followed her friend across the bar. "Oh, my gosh, thanks for the interruption."

"Anytime." Abby sat in the red vinyl covered booth seat.

Pepper lifted her beer and took a long drink. Something niggled at the nape of her neck. She couldn't place her finger on what, but it seemed someone or something was watching her.

Tabitha came back to the table with a frown. "Hey, girls, I have this weird feeling something bad is going to happen."

Yeah, she did too.

The door swung open, in walked Ottar, and he headed straight for them. He narrowed his eyes at her and clenched his jaw tight.

She gulped and let out a squeak. *Uh oh.*

He strode in like a man on a mission. He slammed his hands on the table.

Their beers bounced and her friends winced.

The music stopped. Everyone looked at them.

He pointed at her. "Outside now." He gripped her wrist and pulled her toward the door.

Oh boy, she'd pissed him off good this time.

When they reached outside, he let go of her. "I can't believe you snuck out."

"No one recognized me. Not even Chester Roper the Groper."

He shook his head and squinted like he didn't know what the heck she was talking about. "I picked you out right away. By the way, the sunnies"—he pointed to her sunglasses—"And a prego pad isn't going to disguise you."

A few men came out of the bar and stood behind Pepper. A man with a long beard and a bandana covering his head, wearing a leather jacket, said, "Ma'am, is this man bothering you?"

Oh, she could have fun with this. Those guys could tear Ottar a new butthole. There was five of them and only one of him. River was nowhere in sight. She took a deep breath debating. She wasn't that mean and turned her sunny smile on them. "No, it's a misunderstanding. My *brother* was just leaving." She narrowed her eyes at Ottar.

"No, I wasn't leaving." He turned to the men and balled his fists. "You wanna' 'avago with me, mate?" His eyes were all nutso-like, big and bulging. He was going to blow a gasket in his brain.

She needed to defuse the situation and fast. Turning to the guy, she said. "He's fine. Just a little hot-headed. Please, you don't have to do this."

The man held up his palms, looking straight at Ottar. "We don't want any problems, we only want to make sure the little lady is okay." They moved about fifteen feet away against the brick building.

Pepper backed him up closer to the street by the motorcycles, so they wouldn't hear her. Pointing her finger at him, she said in a low voice, "You need to cool down."

"Cool down? Your life is in danger, and you're running about like a kangaroo on holiday."

She looked over at the men, and while their backs were turned, occasionally they would sneak a peek over their shoulder. "I don't like being cooped up all the time." Out of the corner of her eye, she caught a glimpse of Jethro in his small form standing behind Ottar. She hiccupped.

"Let's go, or I'm going to put you in jail." Ottar grabbed her arm. The men turned around.

A deep Hellhound bark sounded. Oh, heck, this could turn nasty. If Jethro thought for a second Ottar was a threat to her, he might do something crazy.

"Jethro," Pepper yelled.

Out of nowhere, something invisible grabbed Ottar and body-slammed him into a motorcycle. The bike fell sideways into the next, and the rest of the bikes dropped to the asphalt like a train of dominoes.

Chapter 30

What the blue balls attacked him? The thick odor of sulfur filled Ottar's breath. His hip hurt where something had picked him up like yesterday's rubbish and slammed him into the bikes. Whatever it was, it was invisible and big. Very big. And Pepper knew what it was.

Wedged between a set of motorcycle handlebars and a spoked wheel, he kicked his legs and stood.

The men gathered in front of their motorcycles with their arms crossed and frowned. The motorcycle guys looked like they were going to shred him to bits.

Pepper ran over and stood in front of him.

"I'm calling the cops. That was so uncool," bandana man said. He held a phone to his ear. The others snapped pictures of their toppled bikes.

Bloody oath, now he had to deal with this shit. "I am the cops." He pulled his temporary deputy badge out of his pocket and held it up. "River hired me. He's busy investigating something else and sent me here to arrest this woman." He pointed to Pepper. "Are you hindering an arrest? Because I can arrest you, too."

They backed away with their palms up. "What about our bikes?"

He looked over his shoulder at the bikes piled on the ground. Houston was going to be as mad as a cut snake. *What the hell, he'll live.* "Send me the repair bills." He shoved the badge into his pocket, almost tearing his pants. Pepper had a lot of explaining to do. Whatever had attacked him was protecting her. She didn't even seem surprised. In fact, she called out its name. *Jethro.*

Her eyes were as wide as a cow's arse. She scratched the back of her wig.

"You're coming with me, now." He checked up and down the quiet street for anything that could pass for whatever attacked him. Nothing was there.

He placed his hand on the back of her neck and guided her toward his SUV down the street.

Pepper sat in the front seat, arms crossed. She pulled off her wig and wiggled out of her pregnant pad.

"Stop with the lies and fess up," Ottar demanded.

She squirmed in her seat and looked up the side window while pressing her lips together. She was so beautiful even when she rebelled against him. He could hardly catch a breath.

"You know what tackled me. What is a Jethro?" If she didn't talk soon, he would lock her up, for her own good—and his sanity.

She shifted in her seat and aimed her gaze at him. Her teeth scraped across her bottom lip. "Where are we going?" she asked in an innocent voice full of deceit.

"I'm taking you home." For now. He pulled onto the street and turned the corner.

"You wrecked Abby's party. I hope you're happy."

No, he wasn't happy, especially with her. "Was a party worth risking your life for? What would have happened if whoever is trying to kill you showed up there? What if he missed you and hurts the others? What if Abby got shot?"

She slumped in her seat. "Why haven't you and River caught him?"

Fair question. "Maybe because several things are going on all at once? You're not making this easy."

He pulled into her driveway. Damn, he should have told Vulture to leave some of the lights on in her house.

Everything was dark. "Stay here while I check the house. After I make sure the house is secure, you're going to spill your secret on what the hell attacked me."

~ ~ ~

Pepper didn't like Ottar ordering her around. In fact, she didn't like his possessiveness at all. He had a lot of nerve trying to take over her life. She'd done a darn good job taking care of herself since she was a little girl. She'd made sure she was safe and had lived twenty-five years so far. Even when she was seven years old, her mother would sometimes leave for days on her drug-induced binges. Pepper was able to feed and tuck herself in bed. Those days were dark and lonely. She'd never have to endure that again now that she had her friends and her animals. Still, something was missing.

And even though the big Aussie drove her bat-shit crazy, she had to admit she felt better when he was around.

After Jethro attacked Ottar, he looked like he was going to shoot flames from his ears. How could she possibly explain her family obligation to him? He'd only want to capture them for his precious secret organization. She was not a traitor to her Hellhounds and would protect them at all costs, even if it meant giving up the pleasure she received with Ottar. It wasn't only physical. He stimulated her mind with playfulness. It was almost as if he'd absorbed some kind of animal instincts.

She looked over at her barn. In the dark, you couldn't tell it needed another paint job. Only this morning she'd noticed the brown paint peeling. She squinted her eyes. Was the door ajar? Darn it. Vulture must have left it open.

One of the horses whinnied. Then another.

What had disturbed them?

Her stomach rolled into a ball. What if one of those Jackalopes was in the barn?

She got out of the SUV and traipsed through the grass. The tingling of beetles dancing on her spine made her pull her shoulders to her ears. She readjusted them before pulling the door open and flicking on the lights.

Fred and Wilma were in their stalls safe and sound. Her body relaxed. She pivoted to leave.

A large hand closed around her mouth.

She ground out a "Mmmm," noise. She jammed her elbow backward as hard as she could but only hit air. Her heart beat a gazillion times a minute.

"Now what do we have here?" A tight voice asked.

She knew that voice. It wasn't possible.

"If you make a sound, the horses get a bullet to the head," his tone cold as a blizzard in Antarctica.

She stopped still. No way would she let the bastard hurt her horses. She gave a nod.

The pressure on her mouth let up. Turning, she looked into Keith's dark brown eyes. They reminded her of a shark's gaze, with no soul, and no emotion. "Why are you doing this? Is it because I mushroomed your yard?" That was a pretty lame excuse for trying to kill someone if you asked her. Some people were so sensitive.

"No, I had this in the plans long before that." He pointed his gun at her.

She backed away until she hit the wall. "What do you want?"

"I want those Hellhounds." His eyes were glazed but still aimed at hers.

"I don't know what you're talking about." How the heck did he find out about them? Where was Ottar? She moved one step at a time, away from her horses.

"Charlotte told me about your family's obligation. Funny how you never knew she was your cousin. She said her mother was exiled from the family before she was born."

Was Charlotte her cousin? No way. She knew there was another aunt, but this? This was insane. She couldn't be related to Charlotte.

"She said that you're the caretaker of the Hellhounds. Me, being the genius entrepreneur I am, decided to open a dogfighting business just for them. I can't tell you how much money is involved in betting. But the trusty sheriff recently confiscated all my dogs. I don't need them anymore though, because you're going to give over your control of the Hellhounds to me. Those beasts will champion my dogfighting ring. They'll make me millions." Spittle gathered at the corner of his mouth. The guy was insane with greed.

Her poor hellish babies. They weren't cut out to fight. She'd have to protect them and her horses. She glanced around the barn, looking for a weapon. But there was nothing. *Think. Think.*

He held out his free hand, the other still pointing his pistol at her. "Give me that magic whistle, now. Or I'll shoot one of your horses."

"I don't have the whistle. Why do you think I've been searching for them?" Charlotte knew about the whistle, too? That conniving bitch!

"Wrong answer." He pointed the gun at Fred and pulled back the clicky thing.

Her heart stopped. "Wait."

His sneer turned into a full out smile and he lowered his gun. "I thought you'd protect your precious horses. If you give me the whistle without any trouble, I'll spare your animals. Either way, you're going to die." Those dark evil eyes said he was telling the truth.

"You won't kill me." She said it more to reassure herself than to convince him. Still, it didn't help much. How the heck was she going to get away?

"I have no problem killing. I've done it before, and I'll do it again. Especially with this much money on the line."

Boy, she knew how to pick them. First Thomas, the mommy's boy kidnapper, now Keith—the stone-cold killer. Maybe it was time for her to give up men forever. She looked at the door. Where the hell was Ottar? What was taking him so long? She needed to stall or find something to take him down.

Keith laughed. "Your bodyguard isn't coming. Charlotte has a surprise for him in your house."

Her mouth dried and the room spun. Had she put Ottar in danger? Surely, he would best whatever Charlotte had in store for him.

Chapter 31

Ottar walked into Pepper's house and flicked on the light switch. Nothing. Someone must have cut the power. The dogs bounded up to him. "Hey, mates. I'm glad you're okay," he said in a low voice. He couldn't imagine if one of Pepper's beloved pets was hurt. She loved her animals with all her heart. He was starting to take a liking to them, too.

After researching her background, and he did a lot of digging, he found out her mom had been a drug addict. She passed away when Pepper was in the eighth grade and Pepper moved in with her kooky eccentric aunt. From everything he'd read in the file L.A.M.P.S. had on her, her aunt loved and provided for her. But Pepper must have needed something more emotionally and took to caring for and loving animals to fill in the gap. She seemed to feed off the unconditional love she received from them.

Pulling out his flashlight, he crept through the hallway into the kitchen. A floorboard creaked when his weight pressed on it. He tried the light switch on the wall. It also didn't work. He texted River to back him. There was no reply. After investigating the kitchen and deeming the space clear, he searched the rest of the house.

Pepper's bedroom was empty, along with the other upstairs bedrooms, and the attic. He bounded down the stairs and checked the guest room. Nothing.

He peeked out the window and saw the barn light was on. Damn, Pepper must have left the SUV. Adrenalin pulsed through his nerves. The killer must have been outside.

He bolted to the door, his hand almost on the knob when Charlotte stepped in front of him.

"Hiya, Ottar." She batted her thick artificial lashes.

What the devil? "Charlotte, you need to leave. You might get hurt."

She was wearing a black lacy bodice and fishnet stockings, with strappy things to hold them up. Why was she here in Pepper's house, half naked? Was she crazy?

"Ottar, I know you want me." She rubbed her hands down the sides of her briefly covered body. "I'm here, ready to pleasure you." Her sultry voice was laced with sexual need.

Yep, she was nuts. "I don't have time for this right now. Put some clothes on."

She laid her fingers on the front of his pants and stroked them across his shaft. He tensed.

"You're not happy to see me." She puffed out her bottom lip. Charlotte was a beautiful woman and there was a time he wouldn't have turned her down but that time was long gone. Her nose was sharper than Pepper's, her hips wider, and she was a little shorter. He didn't know why he compared her to Pepper, but he did. Maybe because Pepper was the only woman he thought about lately? Or wanted. Hell, he compared all other women to her now, and no one else stacked up.

"Get out of my way." He pushed her to the side and jerked open the door, then ran down the steps.

A shot sounded from behind him, a stab of pain hit him in the back, and his knees buckled. The side of his face hit the cold ground.

A burning flared in his back. He rolled over to try to douse the flames.

Charlotte pointed a forty-five at him. Where the devil had she hidden the gun in her ensemble?

He swallowed hard, moving his hand slowly to his weapon. No gun. He looked to the left where it laid inches out of his reach.

"Was turning me down worth your life?" Charlotte's frown deepened then she pulled the trigger again.

The bullet slammed into his chest and the warmth of his blood soaked his shirt. Damn, the bitch shot him a second time. Sucking in another breath, a squeaky noise wheezed from his lungs. *Not good.* Pepper was in danger and he couldn't do one damn thing about it.

Charlotte nudged him with her toe. Probably to see if he would get up. This wasn't the movies. Once you take a bullet to the chest, you usually stayed down. As things spun out of control and his vision swirled, his one prayer was that River would arrive in time to save Pepper.

Charlotte stalked off toward the barn.

~ ~ ~

A shot rang out, and Pepper ducked.

"Looks like Ottar didn't take the bait. Too bad." Keith stood to the side of the barn door and peeked out the crack. "Charlotte took care of him for me. He's never coming for you now. You're all mine." His attention returned to her. "Now let's see, where were we? Ah, yes, the whistle, Pepper." His eyes revealed something evil and malicious behind them.

Took care of Ottar? Charlotte shot her huge barbarian? Tears rolled down her cheeks. Even though Ottar sported his savageness at times, he'd tried to protect her. She gave him nothing but sass and made it almost impossible for him to guard her. This was her fault. How could she be so selfish? She had no spunk to fight back. As if the events from the last week had finally taken their toll on her.

"Aww. You cared for your boyfriend of the week. Would you have cried for me if the roles were reversed?" He winked at her.

Eww, yuck.

Another shot rang out. Hope surged through her. Did Ottar shoot Charlotte? Or maybe River arrived and shot her?

With the gun still pointed at her, Keith peered out the door again. "Poor, Pepper. Your boyfriend is having a bad day."

Charlotte popped through the door a moment later. "I'm out of here. I did my part. I expect the funds you promised to be transferred to my account immediately." *Charlotte and Keith?* That bitch! She'd known Charlotte was a bad egg, but this pissed her off to no end.

"How can you do this?" Pepper asked her.

Charlotte turned to her. "Shut up. You never deserved to have the caretaker role. My mother was supposed to have it, then me. Our stupid aunt blamed your mother's drug addiction on my mother." Charlotte stopped, put her hand on her temple, and said, "Who cares who gave your mom the drugs? Our grandmother tossed my mother out of the family. My mother laid in bed, bawling while my dad raised me. Finally, she took her own life."

Charlotte's mother gave her mother drugs? Her mom committed suicide? No wonder she was so messed up. Still, Pepper felt sorry for her.

Pepper cleared her throat. "I'm sorry about your mom, but why did you shoot Ottar? He did nothing to you."

Charlotte waved her hand in the no-big-deal-way. "I gave him a chance to live." She looked down at her sleazy ensemble. "Too bad he passed on my offer."

Ottar had more sense than she thought. Maybe he *did* care for her?

Barking came from the corner. Ellie Mae and Granny, in their little dog forms, spun in circles. Her heart beat fast.

"Leave now, he's going to hurt you," Pepper said to her hounds. Her chest squeezed so hard it took the wind out of her.

Jethro joined them. He farted a small flame at Granny. They must have hit the Mexican Restaurant's dumpster again.

"These are the notorious Hellhounds?" Keith pointed to the small black Pomeranians with red eyes. "They're tiny fluffy lap dogs. How the hell are they going to win in a dogfight?" He turned back to Charlotte. "You get nothing."

He raised his gun and pulled the trigger.

Charlotte's head snapped back and she collapsed. A round hole in the center of her forehead dripped blood onto the floor.

"You killed her." Oh no, no, no. She couldn't deal with this. First Ottar then Charlotte.

"No, you did. Or at least everyone will think so. I'll stage it to look like you came home and found Charlotte and Ottar in your bed. You shot them and then killed yourself."

Pepper's blood boiled through her arteries, and she launched at him.

Keith swung his gun and smacked her upside the head. She collapsed on the floor, her temple pulsing with pain.

Jeb materialized in his rhinoceros-sized body. He jumped on Keith and a shot rang out. Jeb faded to invisible.

"Oh, Jeb." Tears broke through her barriers and streamed down her face. Her heart pumped louder. The tears kept coming though, and her breaths were short and uncontrollable.

Keith was on his hands and knees now, the gun still in his hand.

He turned to face her. A hologram of a flame appeared, burning on his forehead. Pepper's mouth dropped open. *It must be the mark the hounds gave out to those with souls damned to hell.*

Served the bastard right.

"Now, it's your turn." He pointed the gun at her.

Chapter 32

Beads of sweat dripped down the side of Ottar's face. He fisted his hands. If only he could get up and save Pepper. His gaze shot up to the full moon. His pulse raced, pumping a strong flow of blood through his body. *Great, now I'm going to bleed to death faster.* His eyes grew heavy, his breaths short. He laid his head back and closed his eyes.

He sniffed the ground. Running on four paws? A fearful kangaroo hopped away from him. A full moon lit the clouds in the darkened sky. A wolf with a gray muzzle strolled up next to him. He chuffed and then let out a low growl. With his nose, the wolf nudged Ottar toward the Aborigine's village. The rich smell of roasted flying foxes and iguana filled the air. His stomach rumbled. They padded through the bush. He caught the putrid scent of Drop Bears. The two of them took off toward the village, barking.

He had to make it in time. Needed to save the village. The women and children couldn't defend themselves from the vicious Cryptids. Faster. Faster. He ran through the thistle. The pack of Drop Bears would decimate the village. His grandfather barked behind him, encouraging him to hurry.

Three Drop Bears the size of Grizzlies ransacked the timber homes of the tribe. Two other Drop Bears slashed sharp claws at the tribesmen, while they jabbed at them with sharp spears. Over ten men had fallen dead on the ground. The bears were winning.

A Drop Bear, with a child lodged in its mouth, lumbered out of a house. Ottar sprang on its back, sinking his canine teeth into the beast's tough neck. It released the child and shook him off. He lunged again at the monster, and ripped into its chest, chomping down on the thick fur. Coppery-rich red blood ran down his chin as he locked his jaws. He shook his head to tear the flesh from the bones. The huge beast raked its claws along his back. Pain erupted, which propelled him to take another bite.

His ears twitched at the screams of the tribe. He had to kill these beasts before they finished off his friends.

A yelp sounded from his left. His Granddad? He turned to see a Drop Bear sink its fangs into the old wolf's chest.

Ottar jumped and snapped his mouth on the neck of the Bear he fought. He tore at the fur and tough skin until the Drop Bear fell. He turned and ran to the beast butchering his Granddad, but he was too late. The monster fed from his grandfather's remains.

Ottar's chest ached with grief. He raised his head and let out a sorrowful howl.

He looked around the land—men, women, and children lay on the ground. His heart broke and throbbed. Not one of the tribe moved. Not one. They were all dead, lost to the Cryptids he was supposed to stop.

He howled again, a long mournful sound.

Men in uniforms stormed the village with their motorized vehicles. They pointed their guns and loud shots rang through the air. A sharp pain stabbed his chest, another in his hindquarters. He got up and ran until his legs were unable to carry him. He fell to the ground. Everything darkened until there was nothing but black.

Ottar's eyes jerked open. He couldn't take his eyes off the moon. He struggled to sit up. He had to reach Pepper before the stupid bitch Charlotte shot her, too.

He let out a deafening growl. His muscles contracted. His bones popped and moved. The moon blurred. Maybe it wasn't a mere dream. Maybe somewhere deep inside he was indeed a wolf.

His arms itched, and his nails stung. He glanced at his hand. Claws grew from his fingers and fur sprouted over his arm. His body convulsed, shaking his brain.

Another shot from a gun captured his attention. This time the sound came from the barn.

Must. Save. Mate.

A wiggling sensation cascaded in his chest and a bullet rolled off his body.

What the hell?

He flipped over and pushed up on his hands and knees. His back arched.

Another shot.

Pepper.

His body shook, and bones cracked. His snout grew. His legs shortened. He let out a fierce bloodthirsty howl.

Pepper screamed from inside the barn. Rational thought left him. He swung his massive head toward her call.

He took off on four legs, running swift and fast. He panted letting the crisp air roll over his tongue.

Bounding toward the door, he saw Keith pointing a gun at Pepper.

~ ~ ~

Pepper sucked in one last breath. She knew her time ended. The bastard was going to kill her regardless of whether she gave him the whistle or not. Her thoughts went to her animals. She prayed Abby would take care of them and love them as much as she did.

She lifted her gaze to Keith's. The burning hell mark flamed wildly on his forehead. A calming warm feeling blanketed her. At least he would be brought to hell this year. His soul had no chance to redeem itself now. A small chuckle escaped her lips.

"You think it's funny that you're going to die? Laugh on this bitch." His finger tightened on the trigger.

A gigantic brown wolf bounded through the open barn door and launched through the air at Keith. Its large teeth sunk into Keith's gun hand. The wolf shook his head and crunched through bones.

Keith screamed. His knees collapsed. Terror etched across the jerk's face.

Pepper couldn't move. Her breathing picked up. She needed to get out of here.

All five of her Hellhounds, transformed into their larger forms, surrounded her. Jeb stood in front with Mr. Drysdale to her left and Jethro to her right. Granny and Ellie Mae sat behind her. The animal packed barn left hardly any room to move.

Her horses whinnied and clip-clopped to the back corner of their stalls, their tails twitching in defiance.

The wolf poised on Keith's chest with his severed hand in its mouth. It swiped a large paw across the jerk's face and knocked him out. The wolf hopped off and dropped the hand, then coughed up a mouthful of blood. *Eww.*

Pepper sucked in a breath. Her trusty Hellhounds refused to move, guarding her, protecting her. They whined in question, sat on their haunches studying the beast, probably trying to figure out if it was friend or foe. Pepper looked from the hounds to the wolf.

The wolf licked its lips and strolled over to them at a cautious pace. He cocked his head as he studied the hounds. Finally, he laid down on his belly, his tail wiggling his hindquarters. *Smart wolf.*

Everyone stayed still for a few minutes, which seemed like hours. Unable to sit and do nothing, while Ottar probably lay outside dying, she decided to make her move. Maybe she could still save him somehow?

"Nice puppy," she said, edging away from the wolf.

The wolf rolled its eyes.

Really?

"I'm going to check on my friend who's hurt outside. I'll bring you back one of my doggy cookies if you stay put." She moved one foot, then another, and gauged the distance to the barn door.

The wolf watched her.

Her hounds shifted out of her way but stood guard between her and the wolf. Somehow, she didn't think the wolf would hurt her. His body language didn't show any aggression toward her whatsoever.

She stepped around Charlotte, who lay dead with blank eyes, a round bloody hole in her forehead. "Oh, Charlotte, why the heck did you have to be so bitter? I tried to friend you. I'm sorry you lost your mother, too." The more she thought about it, she couldn't blame Charlotte's mother for her own mother's drug addiction. Her mother had a choice. She chose wrong.

She peered out the door but didn't see anyone. "Ottar," she called out. Her heartbeat quickened. Maybe he was okay? Maybe the bullet only grazed him.

A wresting noise behind her caught her attention, and she looked over her shoulder.

The wolf shook on the floor. Its fur shuddered and crawled around on its body.

The hounds stepped closer to the wolf, inspecting him, but kept their distance.

The wolf howled and wriggled.

Her heart thumped and bumped in her chest. She hated to see any animal in agony. She just couldn't take it.

She patted her pocket for her phone. Darn, she'd left it in her truck.

The wolf shimmered, its bones cracking. Oh, my god, the wolf was in pain. Keith's blood must have been tainted or poisoned. Stepping closer, she wished there was something she could do for the poor animal.

Its hind legs lengthened, and the fur dissolved. It was changing into something. Holy cow, the wolf was shifting, like Abby did when she turned into the Jersey Devil. Her mouth dropped open.

Once the transformation completed, Ottar lay naked on her barn floor.

~ ~ ~

Ottar peered up to see Pepper's eyes saucer wide and her mouth open big enough to catch blowflies. He should have waited until she went outside to change back. More of his locked-up memories returned. The microchip had some way to control his inner beast and muck up his memories. *Damn Houston.*

Pepper rushed over to a stall, grabbed a blanket, and tossed it over him.

"Nothing you haven't seen before, lovey," he said.

"You. You? You're a werewolf!" She backed up. Her hounds circled around her. "Don't hurt me."

He wrapped the blanket around his waist. "Crikey, I'm not going to hurt you, Pepper!"

Bending over Charlotte's body, he felt for a pulse. Nothing. *Damn.* He kicked Keith in the ribs, but he didn't move.

Giant-sized Pomeranians with glowing red eyes stared back at him. So these dandies were what Pepper had been hiding.

She sucked in her lips.

"What the blazing balls are these animals?" He pointed at the demon dogs.

"These are the notorious Hellhounds. I'm the caretaker." She looked to the animals with love in her eyes, and she wrapped her arm around one of them.

"The caretaker?" Since when did they need a babysitter? Didn't demons take care of themselves?

"My family has been taking care of them for decades. Meet Granny, Jeb, Mr. Drysdale, Ellie Mae, and Jethro." The dogs straighten when she pointed and called each of their names.

Weird names for dogs. "Why were Charlotte and Keith trying to kill you?" This whole thing didn't make any sense.

Pepper explained everything that happened.

"Why didn't your hounds kill Keith?"

"They can't harm humans. They can only mark them. See the flame on Keith's forehead?"

He didn't see anything on the gobber's forehead, except some blood. "Nope."

"Hmm. Maybe only caretakers can see the mark? Oh my gosh, you turned into a werewolf." She was back to that. "I thought they only existed in romance novels and teen movies. How can you be a L.A.M.P.S. agent when you're something you're supposed to be hunting?"

"When you and your friends cast that spell, the lightning fried a microchip implanted in my wrist. Houston installed the chip to block my shift. The bastard took away my memories, too." He vaguely remembered his boss giving him the choice to have the chip implanted or to be incarcerated for the rest of his life.

The hounds shrunk down into small balls of black fluff. They blew flames from their arse and chased each other. "What are they doing now?"

"They keep eating from the Mexican Restaurant's dumpster, and it gives them really bad gas. I need to grab the whistle from them. They're going to start my barn on fire." She lunged at one of them, but they disappeared out of sight.

"Where the bloody hell did they go?" Ottar ran to where they were, but the only thing left was the stench of sulfur and bean gas. He waved his hand in front of his nose to dissipate the stench. They were indeed hounds from Hell.

Pepper raked her hand over the top of her hair. "They can go invisible. Now we're going to have a hard time finding them. You must have scared them."

His brows snapped down. *Yeah. Right.* "Why don't you call River while I put some clothes on? Oh, and can you keep quiet about the shifting thing? Just until I can figure out how to break it to him?"

She gave one nod. "Same with my hounds. What about him?" She pointed to Keith.

Ottar tore a piece of material from the blanket and wrapped it around Keith's bloody stump. "He'll live." He grabbed a rope hanging from the barn wall and hog-tied the bastard so he couldn't get away.

After a quick shower, he pulled on fresh clothes. He'd have to come clean to River right away. It wasn't fair for him to hide this from his best friend on the night before his wedding. He still had no idea what he was going to do about Pepper and her freaky hillbilly hounds. Strooge! He'd made a total mess of things. Houston would chuck a wobbly.

As soon as he walked out the door, River pulled up in his squad car, with Abby's small car right behind him.

Pepper and Abby squealed and hugged.

Ottar's chest ached. All he wanted to do was to wrap his arms around Pepper and tell her everything was going to be all right. Happy that Abby was there to comfort her while he and River could sort the whole mess out, he scratched his head.

Crikey. He'd have to confide in his friend and hope River would keep the secret from Houston. Although Houston probably knew he'd shift sooner or later. His boss had blown up his phone with calls and texts all day long. Ottar let out an exhausted sigh. His stomach growled. Shifting took a lot out of him and made him hungry.

River cleared his throat. "What the hell happened? What ripped Keith's hand off?"

Yep, he'd have to come clean. He didn't want to blame it on Pepper's hounds. "We'll need to call Holly and Vulture. Keith needs medical attention."

Abby pulled Pepper aside. Her bottom lip quivered as she asked, "Did the hounds do this?"

Pepper shot a glance at Ottar. It stung enough for him to wince. Would she keep this from her best friend? The two women had been through a lot. They'd taken the news of beasties like professionals, even fought them. No wonder River fell in love with the small one.

River shifted his stance. "What are you not telling me?"

"Keith and Charlotte worked together on the dogfighting ring. They targeted Pepper for some reason. Keith decided he didn't need Charlotte anymore, so he shot her in the head. After she shot me. *Twice.*"

"Why aren't you bleeding? What the hell happened to Keith's hand?"

"I need to know I can trust you." He waited for River's reply.

River cocked his head. "Look, bro, we've been through a lot together. What's going on?"

Ottar explained about the microchip, about the time he was incarcerated at L.A.M.P.S. headquarters, about being caught while the Drop Bears killed his grandfather and the village, and about the deal Houston gave him. He added how he'd taken the L.A.M.P.S. gig so he could stay out of the Australian prison.

River let out a whistle. "Wow, that's some freaky shit. Are you aware of everything when you're a wolf? You realize you harmed a human. L.A.M.P.S. is within their rights to lock you up."

Chapter 33

Pepper overheard Ottar spilling his guts to River, and he'd kept his word by not blabbing about her Hellhounds. Here it was, the eve of River and Abby's wedding, and her life interfered with them getting a much-needed night of sleep before their big day. She felt like a maggot on dog poop.

She wrapped her arms around her sweet friend and kissed her on the head. Abby took the news about Ottar being a werewolf without saying a single word. Surprisingly Ottar told River in front of them.

"River," Pepper said.

He turned to her.

"That's not exactly everything. Charlotte was my cousin. I didn't know it, long story. Anyways, she told Keith about my family's secret. That's why he wanted to kill me. Ottar saved my life."

River waited for her to say more.

May as well just come out and say it. "I'm the caretaker of the Hellhounds. I let them out every Halloween so they can mark the souls of the damned. I usually call them back at dawn. Only this year, the little devils stole my whistle." Wow, it felt good to finally unload the secret. "They still have it, and they're running amok."

"That's the reason you and Abby were sneaking around?" River asked.

She nodded to him.

River shifted his hat on his head. "This is a total mess."

Yep. A hot mess with sprinkles. She raised her brow at River, waiting for him to lay into her.

Instead, he turned to Ottar. "You realize Houston is going to lock you up again? He's not going to take the chance of you going wolfy and killing someone. Christ, he may order termination, and I'm not talking about firing you."

Pepper's throat tightened as if a huge anaconda coiled its scaly body around her neck and squeezed. Would L.A.M.P.S. kill Ottar because he was different? Even after all the work he'd done for them? She'd never met this Houston, but she already didn't like him. More than anything she wanted to punch him in the nose.

"If you run, he'll have every hunter on the payroll searching for you. He was asking weird questions yesterday. I knew something was up." River paced. Pepper didn't want to be in his, or Ottar's, place right now.

"Ottar were you bitten, or were you born a werewolf?" Abby asked. Great question. Pepper wished she'd thought of asking it.

"Yes, Ottar, we want to know all the deets. I didn't know they had wolves in Australia," Pepper said.

"My family were born werewolves. My ancestors were from England. One of them was arrested and sent to Australia way back when they sent prisoners to the Down Under."

So he grew up as a werewolf. Which explained a lot. It explained why he liked outdoors so much, and why he was so barbaric, feral. Then the thought hit her. "Did your mother have litters of wolf cubs?" Holy furbabies. She'd always joked she'd wanted puppies instead of babies. She and Ottar had unprotected sex. What if she was pregnant and had a litter of eight cubs growing inside her? Her stomach dropped to her feet. "Will I turn into a wolf?"

"My mother was human. She gave birth to one child at a time. It's not a virus like all the legends say. It's in our DNA." He gave her a smile, probably to try to set her at ease. Which didn't work.

"I'm taking Pepper inside to clean her up. We'll be back in a few," Abby said to the guys.

She walked with Abby to the door. Every muscle in her body was screaming. The evening's events sent spasms from her lower back to the top of her neck. She wasn't used to all this stress.

"What do you think they'll do about the Hellhounds?" Her pulse thumped in her temple.

"I don't know." Abby sat and patted the couch cushion next to her. "Charlotte was your cousin?"

Pepper plopped down next to her. Her body mimicked her deflated mood. "She said her mother was the reason my mom got hooked on drugs. She was kicked out of the family. I can't believe how bitter Charlotte was." She wished she would have known. Maybe she could have done something to ease Charlotte's pain?

"It wasn't your fault." Abby laid her hand on Pepper's knee.

"I was lucky my aunt Emily took me in after my mom died. Charlotte said her mom killed herself." It must have been awful for her.

"Let's go back to Ottar. It's clear he cares for you. How do you feel about him?" Was that a hint of protectiveness in Abby's voice?

"I really don't know. He gets on my nerves. He eats my bunnies. Now he's part canine. But, sometimes he's sweet. He tried to protect me even when I was being unreasonable. And that stupid smile of his makes me want to jump his bones."

Abby raised a brow. "Really? Tell me more."

No, she wasn't going to appease her friend's curiosity with a play-by-play review. "Look, I'm worried about him. What if they kill him for helping me out?"

"I have a feeling he knew what was at stake when he shifted and harmed Keith."

Did he?

Ottar surprised her in many ways. For him to forfeit his freedom for her life touched her heart. Her knight in furry armor.

Abby zeroed in on her. "Okay, did you and Ottar do it? You don't have to tell me, but from that look you gave him, I'm betting he didn't keep the wallaby in his pants." Her friend knew all her telltale signs.

She nodded, having a hard time finding her voice. Everything hit her at full force. "Ottar turned into a wolf. He tore Keith's hand right off his arm."

"Yes, and he did it to save your butt. He risked his freedom to save your life."

Maybe she did mean something to Tarzan?

"Do you know what I think?" Abby asked.

She shook her head.

"I think you're more afraid of Ottar's feelings toward you than the fact that he turned into a wolf. You push people away from you before you form a bond with them."

"I do not." Not really. Did she?

"You do, too. Think about it. You only go on two or three dates with guys before you dump them. It's like you get rid of them before you can develop a relationship with them."

"That's not . . ."

Abby interrupted her. "It's true. I'm your only close friend. Sure, you have a lot of acquaintances you call friends, but you're not really close with them. Heaven knows it took forever for you to totally trust me. I think you're afraid." She raised her chin.

"That's silly. I'm not afraid."

"Don't take this the wrong way. You know I love you like a sister, but I think you're frightened everyone will leave you like your mother did. You have abandonment issues. It's like you're scared they'll get close to you, they'll find out who you really are, and take off."

Pepper winced. Did she really do that?

"I'm sorry I had to be blunt with you, but I don't want you to blow this while I'm away on my honeymoon. Sometimes to find something worthwhile, like a relationship, you have to take chances."

"But there's a good chance Ottar *will* go away. You heard River. He said they might lock him up or even kill him."

"Yeah, they might. Or maybe things will work out. But if you don't take a chance, you'll be alone with your animals the rest of your life."

Her animals loved her unconditionally and she loved them. "That wouldn't be so bad, would it?"

Abby sighed. "Once I start a family, I won't be around as often. You need to find your true love, that special person to share your life. I think Ottar may be that guy. But, you'll never know unless you try. All I'm asking is for you to think about what I said." Abby nudged Pepper's shoulder with her fist.

Wow, Abby usually wasn't so blunt. Did she really push people away from her before she cared too deeply for them? She had some soul searching to do tonight.

She turned to see her bestie swaying in her seat, her eyes half closed. "You need to go home. You're going to have dark circles around your eyes for your wedding photos."

"I'm glad you told River about the Hounds. That takes a huge burden off my chest." Her friend rose from the sofa, her movements slow. "Are you sure you're going to be okay? I could spend the night with you."

"I appreciate that, but you'll sleep better in your own bed." She gave her friend a hug and walked her to the door.

Holly was outside talking to the guys. Pepper liked the cleaner and had a feeling she'd take care of the Charlotte and Keith mess. Ottar and River carried Keith, with an IV hooked up to his arm, to the SUV.

After her shower, she lay in bed, staring at the ceiling. *What a night.* Charlotte had turned out to be her cousin. Too bad Keith killed her. Would they have had a meaningful relationship if Charlotte had let her in?

Werewolves were real, and Ottar was one of them. Did she really push people away from her? Yes, she did. Her friend knew her better than she did. Should she take the risk and let Ottar in?

Would her heart survive if she decided to love Ottar, only to have L.A.M.P.S. kill him?

~ ~ ~

Ottar stood next to Pepper's bed. Her long golden locks fanned across the pillow. She reminded him of an angel. He shifted from foot to foot, waiting for the courage he needed to get into the bed without an invitation.

She rolled over on her back and the covers dropped below her bare breasts. Her taut nipples called to him. This was his sign. Why else would she sleep naked?

He pulled off his clothes. With shaking hands, he lifted the cover and slid next to her. Her breath caught, only for a second, then went back to the steady pattern.

His hand hovered over her. He debated whether or not to touch her. Was he afraid she'd wake up and kick his freaky, furry changing ass out of her bed? More than anything he wanted to be close to her, to soak in her warmth, and feel her love.

He gazed at her soft pink cheeks, almost frozen with her deep slumber. Reaching over, he cupped her jaw in his large hand. Her face seemed so delicate in his palm. With his calloused thumb, he brushed her velvet lips with a yearning to kiss them, one he couldn't justify.

He didn't deserve her love or her acceptance. She was pure and good. A true warrior in the world of cruelty to those that couldn't protect themselves. This woman devoted her life to protect the animals that had no say in their future. Was he one in that category? Right now, his future was damn uncertain.

If only he could have her one more time, feeling her full love and attention.

Her breathing picked up and she rolled into his arms. He squeezed tight around her waist, sniffing her clean silky hair. "Can I stay with you for a little while?" Shit he sounded needy.

Her eyes fluttered open. She propped her head on her hand, her elbow still on the pillow. "Are you going to blame me for turning you into a werewolf?" She raised her sexy thin brow. A strand of hair fell onto her face.

He pushed the stray lock behind her ear, and his hand lingered. She should've kicked him out of her bed. He'd torn off Keith's hand with his jaws. "Na, I was a wolf all my life. Your *hocus pocus* fried the chip that blocked my shifting. I guess I should be thankful. I would have died if I didn't shift and heal the bullet wounds."

She nibbled on her pink lip and gazed into his eyes with those deep baby blues. "I'm sorry you had to hurt someone because of me. I'm sorry that L.A.M.P.S. put a chip in you." She paused as if to say something else but didn't.

"I'm getting my memory back. I can't tell you how frustrating it was not to be able to recall a block of time." Hell, it was more aggravating because he thought he was going insane.

"Thank you for coming to my rescue." She walked her fingers over his bare shoulder.

"I'd do it again." Hell, that sounded stupid. "I meant if you were in trouble, that is."

"Now I have a question for you."

He nodded for her to ask.

"About my Hellhounds? Do you think they're going to try to lock them up? It'll disrupt the whole good versus evil and all that." She narrowed her eyes.

True, if the most horrible souls weren't claimed by hell, what would happen? When they died, would their spirit walk the Earth for eternity? If so, what kind of evil would they unleash on the living? More stuff to think about. Like he didn't have enough to torment his mind.

"I have to report to Houston tomorrow. I have no idea what he will do. I do know that they've given pardons to other Crytpids, but after I hurt Keith, they might not be so lenient with me."

"And you're hoping they pardon you." She didn't ask it as a question.

"Yes. I don't want to be locked up or have my memory erased again. River is talking to Houston to see if he could get a feel for what's going to happen."

She lay her head back on the pillow and exhaled. "I hope they don't do that to you."

He leaned over her chest and kissed her. Her lips were soft and sweet.

She returned his kiss with unbridled passion. First, her kisses were short almost pecking his mouth. As she continued they grew stronger, longer, and more frenzied.

He rolled onto her, pinning her underneath his body, so she couldn't escape his touch. She wiggled beneath him, and her nipples brushed against his chest.

"You think of me as prey, Wolfman?" A small giggle escaped her.

Good, she was enjoying this. Like he was. An instinct rose inside him. A feeling he couldn't deny. "I need to claim you."

Her squirming stopped. "Oh my God, don't tell me this is about mating for life. I read about that in one of Abby's romance novels. You're not going to bite me, are you?"

"Rubbish. We don't *need* to bite you. We do mate for life, though. You see it's hard to get close to someone without the werewolf secret being exposed." That was the main reason why he never held on to a woman very long. "As far as biting goes, sometimes we can't help it. There's a thin line between our human and wolf form. Between the full moon and hot throws of passion, it can happen. I promise it won't hurt." He flashed her a smile to put her at ease. "You might like it."

She snapped her lips together with a nod. He'd give almost anything to know what was going on in her mind.

"You sure you don't want some meat tonight?" He gave her a wink to let her know he was joking.

She laughed. "Remember, I'm a vegan."

The smoldering flame in her eyes urged him on. "Not tonight, love." His lips brushed against hers. He lingered while enjoying her scent and taste. Everything was amplified now that he'd shifted. His senses were hyper aware. He wanted her more now than ever. "You're mine." Just then he realized she hadn't spelled him, his wolf wanted her as a mate.

He closed his palm over her soft breast and caressed her. She let out a soft moan through her lips.

She was his mate. His perfect match.

~ ~ ~

Pepper relaxed under Ottar's body. Her flesh tingled under his touch. Her nerves ignited, and she maneuvered her hand from his back to caress his bare chest. She ran her fingers along his smooth skin, and suddenly she wasn't satisfied with touching. She traced her tongue along his sectioned stomach. His skin was hot and salty.

His breathing accelerated to short staccato breaths. "You drive me wild," he said.

"Good." She didn't fight the smile that spread across her face. Oh yeah, she was totally in the mood for some Ottar.

He pulled her up and his mouth covered hers again, his hands slowly caressing her breasts. He broke off the kiss and she let out a disappointed moan. Her lips cooled, wet from his.

He sunk down to her breasts and circled her nipple with his tongue.

She gasped when he tugged it between his teeth with a gentle pull.

He lifted his head and winked at her.

"Don't stop." She groaned and hungered for more of him.

"Oh, possum. We've only begun." He trailed his lips down the side of her neck and hovered over her pulse, his breath tingling on her neck. He moved to her shoulder, then down her side—taking his time with each kiss on her skin. He continued southbound and over her hip bone then between her legs. Each stroke set her ablaze.

"Daaaamn," she said in a breathy voice.

"I need to be inside you."

She couldn't agree with him more. He moved up and nibbled her neck while shimmying his muscular hips into position.

He hesitated briefly and brought his eyes to hers. His gaze was raw but tender. "You're the most beautiful woman I've ever laid eyes on."

Her heart fluttered in her chest.

He eased inside her, filling her with his shaft. She grasped his hard ass and pulled him in deeper. The strokes started slow, then grew rapid. With each pump, she rose up to meet him. Her teeth sunk into his shoulder, making muffled noises, while she moved with his rhythm, their bodies in complete sync with each other. A throbbing pressure built inside of her and after two more thrusts, she screamed. Waves of pleasure exploded through her, sending a quivering straight to her core.

Ottar arched and moaned with a hard thrust.

She squeezed him inside of her.

He dropped on top of her and she melted into him. Never, had she imagined sex with a barbarian could be so intimate.

A new rush of adrenaline sent her heart racing. Second thoughts crowded bliss from her mind. What if she never saw him after tomorrow?

Chapter 34

Pepper rolled out of bed and looked at the clock. *Shoot.* She jumped into her sweat pants and threw on a knit sweater. The party equipment people would arrive any minute. She rushed down the stairs and skidded around the corner to the kitchen.

A shirtless Ottar sat at the table staring out the window, a cup of coffee in his hands. Was he thinking about the awesome lovemaking sessions last night?

She grabbed his coffee mug and took a sip. "Thanks for making the coffee. Whatcha looking at?"

"Those guys trying to set up that tent." He took his cup back and looked down at it. "You drank all my coffee, possum."

She gave him her mischievous smirk. "What's wrong with the guys setting up?" Four men maneuvered a flat large white tent. They kept spinning it like they were trying to decide which way it should go. "They'll figure it out. They're professionals."

"They're bloody idiots. They've been working on it for the past twenty minutes." He snorted and shook his head like he couldn't believe it.

Funny how not even twelve hours ago he was on all fours and biting someone's hand off. Now they seemed like they were playing house. And to top it off, she was comfortable with it. It felt good to talk to him in the morning and steal his coffee. Abby was right. She'd never taken the time before. She'd never had a reason before, but with Ottar, it was different. She poured a cup of her own and topped his up.

"Today's the big day. I hope everything goes smoothly with the wedding," Ottar said.

She felt like albatrosses floundered inside her stomach, bouncing off the lining. This day had to be perfect for Abby. Her friend counted on her.

Still, she couldn't help worrying about Ottar. Houston would attend the ceremony and there was a darn good chance he'd haul Ottar away. What could she possibly do to stop him?

He gripped her hand and looked at her with deep brown eyes. She used to think they were harsh and savage. Now, they'd turned warm and caring. "I've been thinking how we could corral the hounds."

"How?" They weren't like catching normal stray dogs. They didn't come around when she set out treats near the storm shelter.

"We'll set a trap with a cage. I'll pretend I'm hurting you since they seem very protective, then I'll hit the trap door." His face lit up while he explained the plan to her.

She shook her head. "Nope, I'm not going to chance it. They could mark you like they did Keith. He won't see the pearly gates in his afterlife. I couldn't live with myself if they damned you to hell because of me."

Ottar stood and enveloped her in his arms. She rested her face against his strong warm chest. In a low voice, he said, "Hun, they didn't mark him because of you, they marked him because he was a murderer. So don't you worry that pretty head of yours." He raised her chin with his finger and kissed her with comforting lips. "I'm not going anywhere."

She couldn't help the smile that spread across her face. "Do you have a suit for the ceremony?" Funny how she never thought to ask him before now. He didn't seem the type to carry around a tux in the cargo area of his SUV.

"River set me up with the rental place."

She couldn't wait to see him all spiffied up. "Great. I need to get things rolling here. Why don't you go help River get ready?"

Ottar's phone rang.

She busied herself washing out the coffee cups and straightening up the kitchen. She thought about the love they made last night. It wasn't like the wild mind-blowing sex they had the other day. No, last night was tender and sweet. She wanted more of that, more of Ottar, more of the love they'd conjured up together.

Ottar hung up the phone. He bent and gave her a kiss, his stubble scratching her cheek. "Got to run, love. There's been another murder."

Her heart raced at the thought of another person murdered in their small town. When would the Jackalope nightmare end?

Ottar paused at the doorway.

"What's the matter?" she asked.

"I want you to know, you're beautiful, Pepper. And you're my mate."

"Mate?" She'd heard him use the term mate as in friend. But why would he call her that now? Unless . . .

"Mate, as in mate for life." He grinned his goofy lopsided grin. "You're stuck with me. If you'll have me." He walked out the door with his shoulders thrown back and his chin held high. He carried himself as if he knew she wouldn't turn him down.

Her heart raced so hard and fast she had to sit down. The room began to spin.

Chapter 35

Ottar slammed his hand on the top of his SUV. "I can't believe those wankers struck again. Now they're just taunting us."

River took pictures of the body to put in a file at L.A.M.P.S. These Jackalopes were getting damn creative. A hunter was propped against a tree, his body drained of blood, with a large hole in his chest from a gunshot. How the hell did they manage to shoot a gun? Then the bloody Jackalopes had the nerve to stick two branches in his knit hat to make it look like he had antlers.

"No wonder we can't find these guys. They're smarter than we thought," Ottar said.

"You're going to be busy chasing Jackalopes while I'm on my honeymoon." River laid on a smile. Sure, he was happy because after the wedding he was on his way to Maui.

"Don't crack a stiffy yet. You haven't walked down the aisle." He hoped the best for his buddy, but still, he couldn't help teasing him.

"What's with you and Pepper? She seemed okay with the whole wolf bit."

Pepper was Pepper. She wouldn't turn away an animal in need, even if it was an Aussie who turned into a hand stealing wolf. Just one of the things he loved about her. She didn't judge, and she had a huge heart. But how did she take the news about her being his fated mate? He didn't stick around long enough to witness her reaction. Honestly, he'd chickened out. "She's fine. I think."

"Can you wrap up this site?" River asked. "I have a meeting with Houston in less than an hour."

Wow, Houston didn't waste any time. Was his fate already decided? He didn't like the bloke one bit, especially after remembering all the pain he'd put him through in captivity. Now he may end up there again, without his mate.

"Holly is on her way to clean up this mess." Ottar wasn't going to ask if the meeting was about him. "Don't worry. Whatever happens, happens. Go to your meeting and then get ready for the wedding."

After River left for his meeting, Ottar roped off the site around the dead hunter. Holly would arrive any minute.

All morning he'd been fighting the urge to tear off his clothes and run through the forest as his wolf and experience the freedom one more time. Houston might lock him up, and if he didn't, his superiors sure would. Houston's boss wouldn't allow him to stay free after taking a limb from a human. Even if the said human was an evil murderer. He still tasted Keith's nasty, tainted blood on his tongue.

He sprinted in the opposite direction. When he was sure he was far enough away from the murder site, he pulled off his clothes. Waves of ripples crawled across his body. His feet and hands turned to paws, and his nose lengthened.

The crisp clean air filled his lungs. His paws pumped through dirt and he ran through the woods on all fours. Ottar sniffed the ground, smelling the decaying soil, squirrels, and an occasional toad. Finally, he caught the odor of the Jackalopes. The scent trail of the nasty buggers was stale. Sometimes he had to double back because the wankers split up. They had circled trees and ran through bushes.

The odor grew stronger. The Jackalopes were close.

He crept silently, one paw after the other, into a small cave. The retched Jackalope droppings and urine singed his nose. Without a sound, he padded deeper into the cavern. He passed a dead Jackalope—the carcass was cold but hadn't started to decompose. Off to his right, lay five more. Dead. Their black beady eyes stared up at the ceiling. He pushed on one with his nose. It didn't move. Bite marks riddled their necks. Some had been partially eaten. His stomach growled. The wolf in him wanted to chow down.

He sniffed it again. Hellhounds. Definitely Hellhounds. Ottar strolled deeper into the cave, his ears turning back and forth on top of his head, trying to catch a sound. Any sound. Nothing. *Damn.*

He let out a long huff. Enough time wasted, he'd be late to River and Abby's wedding.

Houston was probably waiting for him with handcuffs or pawcuffs. He whined a winsome sound. Maybe they'd let him say goodbye to Pepper. A powerful urge slammed into his gut.

He should run away.

~ ~ ~

Pepper placed the last birdseed ornament on a nearby tree. She breathed in the crisp clean scent of cool November air. While she gazed over her barn, paddock, and finally her Dinosaur statue, she noticed it. Both glass eyes reflected the brilliant sunlight. Ottar had finished repairing her dinosaur.

She circled her brachiosaurus, taking in the textured resin and blended gray coloring around the eye that matched its face. He did a great job and even repaired the bullet hole in the leg. A weird flutter tickled her chest. She was his mate, whatever that meant. Shaking her head to clear her mind, she didn't have the time or energy to ponder on the meaning.

Inside the large tent, the party rental company had set up folding chairs facing an arbor with white mums and blue daisies intertwined in the lattice. On the other side of the tent sat four round tables covered in linens. White covers draped over the chairs with light blue ribbons tied around the backs, and she placed a mirrored plate with a candle on each table.

Abby pulled up in her car and honked. Pepper ran out of the tent to greet her. She couldn't wait to help her best friend prepare for her special day.

"Hey bride-to-be, how's things going?" She pulled Abby's dress out of the car. The dress was encased in a large white plastic garment bag with a zipper down the middle. Abby's mother exited from the passenger door. Her gray eyes matched Abby's. In fact, Abby looked like her younger clone. Both had their brown curls piled on their heads in goddess hairdos.

"Hello, Mrs. Fitzpatrick. You look lovely today."

"Can you believe my baby is getting married?" The older woman looked down at Abby with such pride.

A ping hit Pepper's heart. How she wished for a mother who was proud of her. Today was Abby's day. Not let's-all-feel-sorry-for-Pepper day. She had a job to do, and her mission was getting her best friend to complete her vows, without a hitch. "Let's get you guys ready."

They piled into Pepper's bedroom. They hung up their gowns and worked on each other's makeup. The dogs' tails banged Pepper's legs while they paced around the room.

"How's Ottar doing?" Abby asked in a teasing tone with a smirk on her face.

Which really meant, how was Ottar handling his new furry duo. She really didn't know. Last night, he'd seemed kind of resolved, and almost defeated. But this morning he acted as if they had a future together, a permanent one. "I think he's doing as well as expected." She didn't want to go into any more details with Abby's mother right there. Surely Abby didn't let the wolf out of the bag.

Abby's stomach let out a long, loud growl. "Oh my gosh, I forgot to eat this morning. I'm starved." She rubbed her tummy.

"I made some finger sandwiches and a veggie platter for

us to munch on before the ceremony. I used vegan cream cheese and vegan mayo."

Abby and her mother flinched. Why did everyone freak out at the mere mention of the word vegan? Didn't they realize eating vegan was usually healthier than a normal diet?

Pepper let out a sigh. "Don't worry, you won't be able to tell the difference." She had made cucumber sandwiches and cut them into tiny pieces earlier that morning.

She wanted to check on the venue set up anyway. Inside, the tent heaters made the space nice and toasty. She adjusted the mums and carnations, forming a circle around the candle centerpieces. Soon the cake and the food would be delivered. She straightened the tablecloth on the buffet table. Everyone would choose what they wanted to eat. Chicken, beef, and lots of different vegetable options. Satisfied that everything was going smooth, she retrieved her munchies from her kitchen for Abby and her mother.

"These are so good," Abby said with her mouth full. "You're right, I can't tell these are vegan."

Pepper took a bite. The tangy Italian dressing, creamy vegan cheese, and crisp cucumber blended together for a perfect combination.

They finished their snack and dressed. Abby's white dress hem hit right below the knee. The delicately laced skirt gave it an elegant look. A wide white ribbon tied around her waist to become a large bow in the back. "You make a beautiful bride, Abby-poo. River's the luckiest guy in the world."

Pepper intertwined baby's breath flowers through Abby's hair. She looked like a princess straight from a fairytale. Her heart filled with warmth when she stood back to look at her.

She was happy her best friend had found someone to fill her dreams and live happily ever after with. River would make the perfect husband.

Her thoughts went to Ottar. Had she found her Prince Charming? She didn't know if she could live with someone twenty-four-seven no matter how well they got along. Men were messy, especially Ottar. But the "mate" mother bomb he'd dropped before he'd left seemed to say he wanted a relationship. He may not be around at all after Houston found out he turned wolfy and had attacked Keith.

Ottar seemed pretty positive he was going to be locked up for a very long time. Her chest ached thinking about him in a cage. Oh gosh, why the heck was she thinking about the long-term with the big oaf? It must be that curse of wedding ceremonies which put all females into relationship mode. She shook her head, hoping to remove the thought.

Abby stood in front of the full-length mirror. Her friend looked perfect.

Pepper dressed in her bridesmaid taffeta dress. The baby blue pencil skirt and strapless white bodice hugged her curves. A matching half jacket topped off her outfit. She pinned up her hair into a partial bun.

"Ready to do this?" she asked her friend.

"It's either now or never," Abby replied.

Pepper had a niggling this would be a wedding no one would ever forget.

~ ~ ~

Ottar showered at River's house and changed into the tuxedo his friend had rented for him. The monkey suit fit fine, but still felt confining. Preferring his cargos and T-shirt, he pulled on his starched collar. His neck itched like a hundred fire ants nipped at him.

"You look very uncomfortable." River had the biggest grin plastered on his face.

He was happy for his friend. "Mate, why did you have to go so formal? I feel like I'm in a straightjacket." As soon as he said it he'd wished he hadn't. Surely, L.A.M.P.S. wouldn't make him wear one.

River slapped him between his shoulder blades. "Come on, it's not going to hurt you to wear a tux for a few hours. Pepper's going to think you look hot."

Would Pepper like this get-up? The thought made his gut flip with anticipation. He looked at himself in the mirror and readjusted his shirt cuffs. This might be the last time he saw her. Following River to his SUV, the thought that this very well could be his walk to death crawled through him.

Crikey, he wasn't ready to die. The wolf inside him urged him to run.

They drove to Pepper's house and got out of the vehicle. At least the rental guys finally figured out how to set up the tent.

"We only invited a few L.A.M.P.S. employees and Abby's mom. Abby wanted to keep it small," River said.

Leif, Holly, and her brothers arrived in their L.A.M.P.S. issued SUV. Holly's wide grin made her eyes sparkle. Surprisingly, Houston had made an exception to allow Holly and Leif to work together. Who would have thought Houston would have some compassion? It did help that Holly's brothers banded together and threatened to quit if he fired her and Leif. The McClure brothers carried a lot of pull in the organization because their father was one of the founders of L.A.M.P.S.

Ottar didn't have any family connections. He had a bad feeling there would be no exceptions when it came to his situation. The agency would bring him down and probably enjoy doing it. They'd demanded his loyalty only to stab him in the back in the end.

Dickheads.

He swallowed, trying to remove the large lump of rage forming in his throat.

Several other agents filed into the venue, one by one. River greeted them and showed them to their seats. Over twenty agents and other L.A.M.P.S. personnel decided to join them today.

Tabitha entered with a large Raven on her shoulder. The freaky bird had a string of pearls around its neck and a little pink hat with a bow strapped to the top of her head. River escorted her over to the front row and showed her to a seat. Ottar still didn't trust the witch, or any witch, for that matter. He didn't understand their magic, and the bird gave him the creeps. There was something very suspicious about the raven.

He'd heard familiars had powers, and L.A.M.P.S. would need to investigate this one. There he went again, still thinking about his job. He wouldn't have to worry about familiars or any other creatures in the future. Like any other bloke, his job defined him. He was damn good at hunting Cryptids. He fisted his hands. Damn, he was gonna miss all this.

A few empty chairs remained after everyone was seated. Houston and Vulture were missing.

River looked at his watch.

"Don't worry. Abby is inside Pepper's house. Her car is here." Ottar placed his arm around River's shoulders. The poor bloke was excited about being chained to a walking trouble magnet. He smiled. Life would never be boring for River with Abby at his side. He wondered what a life would be like with Pepper.

"Thank you for being my best man. I know this wasn't on the top of your fun things to do list. In fact, I thought you'd be long gone by now."

Yeah, he had thought about running. Adrenalin swirled around inside him, waiting to burst through his limbs. The only thing that kept him from taking off was his mate, Pepper. He didn't want to leave her after the escapade with Keith and Charlotte.

Besides, she would need help corralling her Hellhounds. And last night was one of the best nights of his life. They'd made love most of the evening. She fit into his arms as if she was made for him. He loved her and every bit of her kookiness.

The wedding march music started. Pepper stepped inside the tent. Her hair was partially up with waves of golden silk running down her back. What he wouldn't give to run his fingers through those waves one more time. Her big blue eyes were outlined in black and her high cheekbones highlighted in pink. The light fabric of her dress clung to her curves.

He sucked in a deep breath, and his heart raced. She was his.

Pepper walked down the aisle in time to the music. She held her chin up, and she wrapped her fingers around a bunch of flowers. She stepped next to the minister and pivoted to take her place across from him. His gaze followed her perfect arse with each step. More than anything, he wanted to throw her over his shoulder and take her behind the tent to have his way with her. Yes, she wouldn't be wearing that dress very long if he had his say. His pants grew tighter in the groin area. *This will be a long ceremony.*

The music grew louder, and everyone stood. Abby stepped through the doorway, her brown curls piled up on top of her head.

River straightened his body and threw back his shoulders. Yeah, the man was whipped. He didn't seem to mind it at all, though. In fact, it looked good on him.

Abby almost sprinted down the white walkway. She stood across from River, smiling while they waited for the music to catch up. She blew a kiss at him. *Bloody oath, could this get any cheesier?*

The minister peered over the book in his hands at the couple and cleared his throat. He started his mumbo jumbo. Ottar tuned out the talk.

He watched Pepper sway from foot-to-foot, her tear-filled eyes on Abby and River. She nibbled her luscious bottom lip.

The minister blah blah'd on and on.

Vulture tiptoed into the back of the tent while clutching a canvas backpack. He took his seat and the chair let out a loud squeak.

River dipped Abby and placed a long, wet kiss on her lips. The music played, and everyone stood.

The happy couple clasped hands and strolled down the middle aisle grinning like horny kangaroos.

Pepper met him in the middle and he locked arms with her. She clung to his arm as they walked together.

"You are . . ." He couldn't put the sentence together without sounding sappy. "Beautiful."

She arched those sexy brows he loved so much. "Thank you. So are you."

They stood in the line and greeted all the guests. All twenty-five of them.

Abby and River looked happy.

A wave of tension crawled across his skin.

Something was wrong. Very wrong.

Chapter 36

Relief filled Pepper. For once, everything was going according to plan. After about twenty minutes of pictures, caterers brought in the trays of food and placed them on the buffet. The guests sat down with their drinks at the round tables in the back of the tent.

Abby's mom and Tabitha sat next to each other, with Holly, Leif, and Vulture. Vulture wore a leather jacket and black jeans. The fairy lights reflected off his bald head.

She turned on the stereo and started Abby's playlist for the guests. She'd chosen poppy eighties tunes. Leave it to her friend to pick the coolest music.

Everyone mingled and made pleasant conversation. That's when she spotted the tent doorway ripple.

A brow furry rabbit with antlers hopped in. Then another, and another.

The Jackalopes stormed into the wedding reception. No, no, no. They were not going to ruin her best friend's wedding.

Darting past the tables, she ran to intercept them. Ottar beat her to the beasts. He pulled a tablecloth off a nearby table. Glasses crashed to the ground splintering everywhere.

What the heck? Abby would lose her deposit on the rented dinnerware.

He tossed the tablecloth over one of the little rascals. Everyone stood, scattering their dishes off the tables. Two more horned rabbits burrowed under the side of the tent, while others filed in through the door opening. They flashed their sharp fangs and hissed at the guests. *This was not happening.* The tent filled up with Jackalopes!

Armed L.A.M.P.S. agents darted around, chasing the little brown and white bunnies. There were so many pint-sized monsters they'd never get control of them.

And when she thought it couldn't get much worse, in bounded her black Hellhounds in their small, fluffy forms.

"Jeb. Jethro. Come back here." Pepper chased Jeb. Her heart raced like a greyhound. If the agents caught them, they'd turn them in to L.A.M.P.S. She couldn't let that happen.

The hounds ran under tables after the Jackalopes, barking their little heads off, their tiny legs a furry blur. The bunnies scrambled under chairs, and up the sides of the tent. Several swung from the fairy lights, their horns tangled in the strands. A large one with a broken antler jumped onto the food table. Pepper ran across to them, only to be beaten by Granny and Mr. Drysdale. The Pomeranians hopped onto the long table, and the platters filled with Teriyaki Beef and Chicken Picatta smashed to the ground. Creamed gravy with olive-colored capers splashed against the side of the tent. *Oh no, not the food.*

Abby screamed while River held her.

Bang. Bang. Bang. Ottar sprinted around shooting the little monsters with his gun, wearing his lopsided grin.

"Don't shoot my hounds," she called out to him. She didn't know if they could be hurt by the bullets and she didn't want to find out.

"I'm not bloody shooting at the pups," he yelled back. "I'm after the horny vampire rabbits!"

The other agents opened fire on the Jackalopes.

Roman, Holly's older brother, held three dead ones by the antlers in one hand, and carried a gigantic hunting knife in the other.

Leif swiped at them with an ax, chopping at them, while they bared their fangs at his throat.

Holly's wild red curls fanned around her as she spun and slashed at the little beasts with a machete.

Matt and James, Holly's other brothers, shot at the monsters with automatic weapons. Bullets splintered tables and exploded glasses. Surprisingly, they hadn't killed anyone. All the agents grinned as they hunted.

Pepper's pulse spiked and thrummed in her temples. "Don't shoot the dogs!" she yelled out at the top of her lungs.

Abby's mom stood there with her mouth gaped open, her face paper-white. Oh, poor dear. They'd have a lot of explaining to do to her later.

Tabitha's raven launched from her shoulder, and Gwendolyn divebombed a smaller Jackalope.

Jeb jumped over a chair and landed on a tiny beast. The Jackalope was on its back, beating Jeb's muzzle with its hind feet. Jeb grew to the size of a large pig and bit down on its neck.

The other Hellhounds shifted to the same size as Jeb. More tables overturned, and the sound of destruction was deafening.

Pepper rushed over by the three-tiered wedding cake and lifted it from the table. Granny crashed into her legs. She scrambled, trying to keep the cake upright before she fell backward.

She moaned before she hit the ground. The cake smashed against the front of her beautiful blue gown. Cool whipped cream covered her body. All five Hellhounds swarmed her, their warm tongues tickling her as they lapped the icing off her arms. "Stop it you guys," she said trying to keep her laughter inside.

Jeb circled her and barked, the golden whistle still hanging from his neck.

Gwendolyn the raven swooped down and snatched the whistle from Jeb. The dog sprung up to catch the bird but missed.

Gwendolyn flew to Pepper's shoulder. She reached over and wrapped her hand around the whistle.

"Ah ha. I got it." She held up the prized whistle. "Thanks so much, Gwendolyn. You're such a good friend."

Abby and Ottar ran to her. She looked around at the total destruction of what should have been Abby's happiest day.

"I'm sorry about your wedding," she said to Abby.

Abby laughed. "Yeah well, I kind of expected something would happen. We tend to draw weird things. I'm not surprised at all. Besides, everyone looks like they're having fun."

"I think we've got all the Jackalopes," Ottar said, a victorious smile plastered across his face.

Pepper's heart ached when she saw all the tiny carcasses lying on the grassy floor of the tent. Their tiny bodies were littered with teeth marks and bullet holes. A few were in small wire cages that Holly had brought in. They gnashed their sharp teeth on the wire bars.

What a freaking nightmare.

~ ~ ~

As pleased as Ottar was with the sight of all the dead and captured Jackalopes, he really didn't feel all that satisfied. Abby and River's wedding was ruined. Pepper was covered in cake, and her head bowed. They could blame it on him. He should have had this case closed by now.

He glanced at Pepper, who fingered a golden whistle hanging around her neck. His shoulders relaxed. She would be able to call those Hellhounds back to hell now. Mission complete.

Why did those pesky Jackalopes decide to attack the wedding? He searched the messed-up tent to find a reason but didn't see anything. Tabitha and Abby's mother were the only people who weren't L.A.M.P.S. personnel, besides Pepper and Abby. Abby's mother was sitting on a chair, an expression of shock and disbelief veiling her face, as the bride and groom squatted next to her. Abby's hand rested on the woman's knee, comforting her. Tabitha talked to the raven sitting on her shoulder, stroking her blue-black feathers.

"Hey." Vulture came up next to him carrying his large black backpack. "I'll never forget this wedding."

Ottar nodded while he continued to look around.

"I brought you something." Vulture pulled up his backpack and unzipped it. He reached in and pulled out a dead Jackalope by the horns. "I landed the chopper on this guy."

Ah ha. "The Jackalopes were avenging the one you killed." No wonder they came in full force. "Actually, you did us a favor. I think every Jackalope showed up."

Pepper's pack of Hellhounds were back to their rat-dog size. They sat along the side of the tent, with their red eyes glowing. If they weren't such troublemakers, he'd swear they were kind of cute.

Houston strutted over toward him. Funny, he hadn't seen the wanker enter the tent.

"We need to talk." Houston used his authoritative voice on him.

For years the L.A.M.P.S. bastards kept him locked up, did unspeakable experiments on him, then chipped him to make him forget the whole thing. No wonder he'd felt like he was living a life that didn't belong to him. "I'm not going to be locked up again. And, I'm not letting you chip me." He wasn't going down without a fight.

"Let's go outside where we can have some privacy." Houston nodded toward the tent opening. It was amazing the tent was still standing.

They exited. Fresh air filled Ottar's lungs and more than anything he wanted to shift into his wolf and go for a run.

"I've been thinking about how long you've been with us," Houston said.

Yeah, he'd given them fifteen years of his life, and he'd lost the freedom of his wolf for all that time. He missed padding through the outback, and how he and his grandfather used to keep the peace.

"I've talked to the authorities, and we've decided that we're not going to chip you again." Houston stared him down probably waiting for a reaction.

"You may as well kill me, because I'm not going to be your guinea pig, or locked up for that matter." He could shift right now and take off. It could take them years to find him.

"No. You may be able to track the Cryptids better while in your shifted form. It seems we have an epidemic of creatures running around. We don't have the time or the patience to train more hunters."

Ottar nodded. "This past year alone we've had five times as many Cryptids on the loose."

Haber Cove was kind of a hub for magic and mayhem. "Also, we want you to keep an eye on the Hellhounds. We feel if we capture them, and keep them from their duties, it might disrupt things." Houston tugged on his collar. Oh, boy, he looked uncomfortable.

"I agree. I can keep watch on the little devils." A flow of relief washed over him. If L.A.M.P.S. had gone the other way and decided to capture the hounds, it would have crushed Pepper.

"I have intelligence that the Peterson woman saw you shift. We'll have to wipe it from her memory. We're also going to wipe *you* from her memory."

Ottar's stomach crashed and burned into his spine. Could he walk away from his mate? Na, that wouldn't be possible.

"You'd have to wipe me from Abby's mind, too. I don't think River will stand for that." Chew on that, suit man.

"We'll see. You'd be surprised what we can accomplish." Houston studied his face. "I see you have feelings for Pepper."

"I've been staying at her house. Of course, I've grown fond of her." He couldn't let Houston see his true feelings. The bastard might use her against him.

"Losing her is a small sacrifice for your freedom." Houston turned and walked away.

Chapter 37

Since all the catering ended up splattered on the ground, Pepper ordered pizza. It wasn't the best wedding food, but it was warm and filling for their guests. The guys set the tables back up, and everyone sat eating pizza and drinking beer.

Ottar locked his gaze onto hers from across the room. His intense stare showed a sadness behind his eyes. The sorrow over possibly losing him made her chest feel like it weighed a hundred pounds.

Abby nudged her with her elbow. "This is the best wedding ever. Thanks so much for having it here." Her eyes glittered with happiness.

"Aw Abby-nator, you did most of the work. This will truly be the wedding no one will ever forget." She let out a little snicker.

The wedding guest's chatter filled the area. Holly and Leif had cleaned up the Jackalope carcasses. No one would have guessed a slaughter had taken place. She hated to see all those creatures lose their lives, but they were killers, and they had to go.

Ottar bowed his head and walked over to River. *What could they be talking about?*

Abby nudged her with her elbow. "I'm glad everyone will remember my wedding." She finger-waved to River.

Oh yes, everyone one would remember this fiasco, and they'd most likely tell the tales to new L.A.M.P.S. agents. This wedding would go down in history in their handbooks. If they had handbooks.

"I'm going to call the hounds back to their hidey-hole. Would you mind if I left for a little while? I don't want the L.A.M.P.S. agents to get too familiar with them. They might figure out a weakness in the pups, and I don't trust them one bit." She also didn't trust the hounds not to steal the whistle back. They'd enjoyed their extra days of freedom. The hounds proved to be most devilish.

"I agree. Though, I think Granny has taken a liking to Holly."

Granny sat on Holly's lap, back in her lapdog-sized body, her red eyes glowing. Smoke rings puffed out of her nostrils. Every once in a while she lapped at Holly's face with her purple tongue. Holly grinned and slipped her a pepperoni.

"Yeah, all I need is for one them to fart and the whole tent will go up in flames."

Abby made the "shoo" gesture. "Go. And hurry back. We'll be leaving soon for the honeymoon."

Pepper zigzagged through the guests, and almost bumped into Roman before she made her way out of the tent. Relief washed over her when she finally reached the storm shelter. She caressed the cool golden whistle hanging around her neck. Still, unease niggled at her gut. Would they come to her now? She'd sure miss the little guys.

She blew the whistle, but it was silent to human ears. It was tuned to a doggy frequency, and only the hounds could hear it.

Jeb, Jethro, Ellie Mae, and Mr. Drysdale bounded through the doorway in their five-pound forms and rushed down the stairs of the shelter. She reached over to the box of vegan doggie treats on a shelf and gave them each one shaped like a heart.

While waiting for Granny, she scratched them behind the ears. Their plumed tails blurred while they wagged. They took turns sitting for a treat.

"Ready to go home? You guys had quite the adventure this year." They all responded with happy barks.

Ellie Mae danced on her back feet and pirouetted. Her tongue hung out the side of her mouth.

A woof came from the doorway. Granny stood at the top of the stairs.

"Come on, Granny. It's time to go home," Pepper urged.

The dog stamped her front foot. Smoke puffed out from her nose. What was she doing?

"I'm not joking around. You need to get down here this minute."

The stubborn old gal wouldn't move. She probably was the ringleader for stealing the whistle.

"Stop being so difficult. I'll blow the whistle again." She frowned at the older hound, bringing it to her lips.

Granny took her time coming down the stairs, and on every step, she turned and looked back to the entrance.

"Urgh, hurry up. I need to get back to the wedding." Pepper held up a doggie cookie.

Slowly, Granny walked to the gates leading to the underworld. She kept looking like she was debating making a run for it.

She didn't blame the hounds one bit. Who would want to live in hell?

Each one filed through the entrance with sad puppy faces.

"I'll come and visit every week. Just like I've done in the past. Stop looking so sad." From now on, she'd leave her whistle locked up until the proper time to use it. A hollowness seeped through her. She'd miss the little hoodlums.

She closed the gate and waited until she heard the click of the lock. The hounds pushed their tiny red-eyed faces through the fence. She placed a kiss on each of their hot sulfur stinking noses.

"See you next week. I'll bring you a treat."

They trotted down the hallway and disappeared.

"So this is the notorious gate to hell?" Ottar said from behind her. She'd been so busy with the pups she hadn't heard him come down the stairs. He leaned against the wall with his arms crossed.

"Yes. You found it. Please don't try to capture them. The balance of the universe will be disrupted."

He tilted his head. "I think L.A.M.P.S. got the gist of that." He reached out and wrapped his calloused fingers around her hand.

Warmth soaked into her skin. Damn, he was gorgeous in a suit. The material accentuated his well-honed muscles. His wide shoulders tapered down to a flat stomach, and the sight of him made her heart race. She wished she could jump right back into bed with him and continue the sex-a-thon from last night.

He cracked his famous smile, but it didn't reach his eyes. "We need to talk." His voice softer than usual, and that worried her.

She gave him a nod. Her tummy filled with squirrely feelings. "We do, but not right now. I want to see Abby before she leaves."

He grabbed her around the waist and pulled her close to him. He kissed her, hard. His lips were hot, plump, and wet. His tongue sent shivers of ecstasy down to her girly parts.

She returned the kiss and didn't hold back. His large hands rubbed up her back with strong fingertips tracing her spine.

His warm breath tasted minty. His scent engulfed her with hints of the forest, pines, and woods.

She pulled back, knowing what kind of kiss this was. "Why are you kissing me like this is our last kiss?"

"I'm not. I . . ."

Then it hit her like a freight train. "Either you're leaving for good, or Houston's going to take my memory." A hot fury rushed from her gut and ignited through her veins. Like hell. She'd never let L.A.M.P.S. take Ottar from her without a fight.

~ ~ ~

Ottar wanted one more kiss. It pained him that the memory of their time together would be wiped away. L.A.M.P.S. had a code of silence, and they didn't care about fallout. *But he did.* His mate wouldn't remember him, she wouldn't remember their time together, she wouldn't remember how he shot her dinosaur or got on her nerves. She wouldn't remember she cared for him.

Damn, Houston. And damned L.A.M.P.S. How could he go on without her?

He gazed into Pepper's deep blue eyes. She'd changed his life, and accepted him, wolf and all. He couldn't imagine not being able to make love to her again.

When Houston told him he intended to wipe her memory, Ottar vowed to keep the cameras going in her yard, so he could keep tabs on her. Pepper tended to attract Cryptids and all kinds of critters. What would happen if a monster attacked her? She welcomed all kinds of buggers with open arms. The woman had no sense when it came to vicious Cryptids. He remembered how she reacted to the Jackalope in her garden. The beast would have killed her if he hadn't intervened.

He had to figure out a way to stay with her. She needed protection. His protection. He didn't trust anyone else to do the job. Crikey. Who was he kidding? He'd fallen in love with the crazy tree hugging, animal loving, plant-eating woman.

"I'm right, right? You guys are going to wipe my memories. Don't I have a say in this?" Pepper asked.

He shook his head once. He felt like a dirtbag. This was all his fault. He knew better than to get involved with anyone. Hell, he constantly preached that principle to all the hunters.

"Are they going to imprison you?" The caring look in her eyes tore at his heart.

"No."

Her frown softened. "At least that's one good thing." She kicked a small stone with her shoe.

He pulled her in for another kiss. He wanted to feel her soft lips against his. He wanted to cuddle her body and inhale her scent, just one more time.

Chapter 38

Pepper and Ottar walked back to the tent together. Pepper couldn't be happier for Abby. Her friend was embarking on a new journey with her love. Soon they would start planning a family. Mini curly headed Abbys and Rivers would be chasing their dogs, Hercules and Kazoo, around in their backyard.

Her heart filled to the brim with love for her bestie and her hubby. The bride and groom waved to everyone as they jumped into the black limo, which everyone had decorated in classic wedding style. The car pulled about ten feet down the driveway and stopped. Abby hopped out and ran toward Pepper. She met her half-way.

"I almost forgot." She pulled Pepper aside by her arm. "Thank you for everything. I couldn't have asked for a better wedding. I'm also lucky to have you as a friend." Abby pulled her in for a big hug.

Pepper's broken heart warmed. She didn't want to break the news to Abby about the mind wipe before she left. Would she even remember Abby when she got back home? "Have fun on that honeymoon. And take lots of pictures."

Abby laughed. "I don't think we plan on leaving the room."

Too much information. "Um, then maybe don't take pictures?"

"I have a feeling you'll get your happy ending too. I hate to leave you right now." Abby's smile faded.

Pepper plastered on her fake grin. She didn't want her friend thinking something was wrong. She turned Abby by the shoulders back toward the car. "Go. Have fun with River and don't worry about me."

She'd heard tales of L.A.M.P.S. brain swipes going bad from River. Most the time everything turned out okay. But every once in a while, the person ended up like a vegetable, which wouldn't work for her. She wondered why Ottar had a chip instead of the mind alteration. Maybe it was because of his shifting and healing ability?

The newlyweds pulled away in their vehicle with cans clanking behind them.

The guests said their goodbyes and piled into their black SUV's. Pepper walked back into the tent to start cleaning up.

"Hey lady, need any help?" Tabitha asked, joining Pepper. Gwendolyn was perched on her shoulder. The bird had some feathers sticking up on her back from the Jackalope fiasco.

She smiled at Tabitha and Gwen. "That would be wonderful."

They gathered the plates and placed them in a plastic bin.

A man dressed in a black suit and buzzed hair barged through the tent opening with his gaze zeroed in on her. She had a good inkling he was the notorious Houston.

Her breath caught, and her blood roared through her veins. *This was it.* He would take her away and preform the lobotomy on her brain. Looking from left to right, she figured there was no way out of the tent. She picked up a large, heavy serving spoon from the table next to her. If he got too rough, she'd bean him in the head with the utensil. She'd have to face the consequences. If this was the only way to keep Ottar from being locked in a cage, she'd pony up. She'd do it for him.

Standing firm, she squared her shoulders and faced him. He was not going to intimidate her. Nope, she wouldn't give him the satisfaction.

"Pepper Peterson, you need to come with me." Houston signaled her over to him.

She squared her shoulders. "I'm not ready. I need to arrange for someone to watch over my store and take care of my animals. We need to wait until Abby and River get back." This was ridiculous. Why did they have to do this right now? Why the rush, anyway?

"No, we do this today. I'll have someone from L.A.M.P.S. take care of your personal obligations." He tapped his foot impatiently.

Egads. What the heck was his problem? He acted like he'd had a hot stick rammed up his butt. His beady little eyes shifted back and forth.

She pointed the spoon at him. "I'm not leaving until I get to talk to that person. They need instructions. It's not easy to run a store and take care of all my animals."

"You can brief them in the car." He looked over her shoulder to Tabitha. "We're going to need to take the witch and her familiar also."

Gwendolyn flapped her wings and cawed, "I'd like to see you try."

Pepper flinched. She'd dragged Tabitha into this, too. "What? Tabitha is fine. She won't say a word." She stepped in front of her. The jerk would have to get past her first.

Tabitha held the cake knife in her hand. She wasn't going to be a willing participant either. Gwendolyn sat on her shoulder and squawked.

Roman, Holly's older brother, burst into the tent and strode over to Houston. He towered at least six inches over his boss, and something about Roman's body language signaled to Pepper he was in charge. "The women are staying. We need to talk."

Ottar burst through the opening. "What's going on?"

"I've been working with internal affairs the past month,

investigating the Cryptid trafficking. It seems Houston here has been a busy guy." Roman pulled out a pair of handcuffs.

Houston jerked away, narrowed his eyes at Roman, and scowled. "No one informed me you were reassigned."

"That's because you were a suspect," Roman said to him.

Houston lunged and yanked Pepper in front of him. He placed a knife against her neck.

Her eyes widened and a haze blurred her vision. She couldn't breathe.

Ottar sprouted fur and shifted into his big brown wolf. He sprang at Houston.

Houston's arm tightened around her midsection and a sharp pain blazed on her neck. The damn bastard nicked her.

Ottar clamped his wolfy jaws onto Houston's arm.

Houston yelled, and the knife fell to the ground. The two of them scuffled.

Bang. A loud shot echoed through the tent.

Everyone's eyes widened as they looked around, almost frozen in place.

Ottar fell to the ground, panting. His tongue lolled out of the side of his mouth.

Pepper screamed. *No no no, not Ottar.*

Roman pulled out his gun and aimed at Houston. "Drop your weapon."

Pepper glanced to Houston. He lifted his pistol and this time, he aimed it at her. "You need to die, bitch."

Anger, fury, and rage boiled in her veins. How dare he hurt Ottar. How dare he try to steal her happiness. She tightened her grip on the serving spoon and before she realized what she was about to do, she beaned him in the head with as much force as she could muster. The spoon vibrated in her hand. A cracking noise sounded.

Houston's expression turned to surprise before he dropped to the floor.

Roman secured Houston's weapon and rolled him to his stomach. He placed handcuffs around Houston's wrists. His eyelids flickered, his cheek resting on the ground.

Pepper knelt next to Ottar. Still, in his wolf form, he panted, a puddle of blood under his muzzle and chest.

"Someone call an ambulance." She looked to all the other agents who had filed back into the tent. She hadn't noticed them before now. "Please, someone help him." Her heart raced in her chest.

"He should have started healing himself by now," Roman said, frowning. His expression made Pepper suck in a tight breath.

Small gurgle noises sounded from the wolf's chest. "What's wrong with him?" She ran jerky fingers through his fur, trying to rouse him, trying to get him to come around.

Houston laughed, a hideous sound. He lay on the floor, his hands cuffed behind his back. "I shot him with liquid silver."

Had he planned to kill Ottar all along?

Pepper sneered at him, tears streaming down her face. "Please. Someone help him." She gently petted her wolf's head. She finally found someone who would love her for all her little quirks, someone who would stay with her, and now Houston had stolen that from her. "Please."

The agents were silent. All wore worried frowns on their face.

Roman felt for Ottar's pulse and probed the gunshot wound. A silver liquid drained from the hole. "Someone grab a syringe. Maybe I can draw enough of the silver out."

"It won't work. It only takes a small amount to kill a Werewolf," Houston sing-songed from the floor, his evil smile broad and malicious.

She grasped Roman's arm. "No. No. You can't let him die," Pepper pleaded, swinging her head around, searching for someone in the room to help them. "This can't be the end. No way. He was supposed to be my happily ever after. He's my mate."

"I can try," Tabitha said. She stepped closer to them.

The crowd whispered.

"Please," Pepper said, her voice barely audible. "Do something."

Tabitha knelt next to her with Gwendolyn on her shoulder. The raven's eyes started to glow a golden color.

Tabitha chanted soft words. Over and over she repeated those words, so softly Pepper couldn't make out what she was saying.

Nothing was happening. Sweat beaded up on Tabitha's brow, but she kept chanting.

The agents now quiet, watched with hopeful expressions.

Holly sobbed.

Tabitha paused and then a bright gold light shot from her fingertips into the wolf's chest.

Pepper sucked in a breath and her heart pounded louder and faster.

A metallic liquid slowly streamed out of the bullet hole and floated in the air. Tendrils of silver wrapped into a ball suspended above the wolf. She kept up the chanting. The silvery orb grew to the size of a marble.

It's working.

The silver streamed from his body, slowed into wisps until there was nothing.

Tabitha rubbed her arm across her wet forehead. "I think I removed all of it."

Ottar's wolf coughed. His paws moved. The wound on his chest mended together. His big brown eyes fluttered open.

A boulder of heaviness disappeared from Pepper's chest. She could breathe again.

The brown wolf rolled up onto all four paws. He shook his head with a dazed look still in his eyes. His fur shimmered, and bones crunched until Ottar crouched in front of her, naked.

Pepper grabbed a tablecloth and handed it to him as he stood.

Ottar wrapped it around his waist.

Pepper hugged his neck and pressed her lips to his. She kissed his cheek, then the other one, before she kissed his lips again.

Roman approached them. "I'm glad to see you pulled through."

Ottar raised an eyebrow and cleared his throat. "Are you? Or are you going to lock me up?"

"No. I'm the commander of L.A.M.P.S. now." He strolled over to Houston and lifted him to his feet with one hand. "One of the lab people noticed several of the Jackalopes missing a couple months ago. So when the Jackalopes showed back up on the radar, we knew it was an inside job."

Houston strained against his cuffs.

"Why the bloody hell would someone intentionally free dangerous Cryptids? And why the hell did he shoot me?" Ottar demanded. He looked baffled and pissed at the same time. His face turned ten shades redder and if his heart pumped any more blood to his face, his head might explode. He curled his fists by his sides.

Pepper keyed in on his every move.

Houston looked to the tent opening then back at Roman and Ottar.

Was Houston going to run for it? Surely the agents would stop him.

"What about the Goochies and Gnome?" Ottar asked. "Was that him too?"

"We were missing two Goochies, a male, and female. At first, we thought they were eaten by the others. They do that sometimes. We don't have any idea how he got his hands on the Gnome." Roman grabbed the back of Houston's neck and hung on to him. The bastard's throat muscles strained under Roman's fingers.

"People died. He almost killed me! Why the hell would he do this?" Ottar yelled.

Roman shrugged. "Maybe to make his region look good? Who knows what motivated this sick asshole. We intend to find out."

Pepper looked over at Tabitha who looked exhausted. "Thank you for saving him."

The witch smiled.

"Yes, thank you," Ottar said to Tabitha. "For a witch, you're not that bad." He gave her a grin.

Roman looked at her new friend. "Tabitha, on behalf of L.A.M.P.S., we thank you for your services. Ottar, as of today, you are the supervisor for the Eastern Region. Due to some unpleasant outcomes in recent mind swipes, we won't require the parties involved today to have their memories erased. They'll have to sign a non-disclosure statement." He looked at Pepper and Tabitha. Then he turned back to Ottar. "Also, you're permanently stationed here at Haber Cove, with River. You'll monitor and protect the Hellhounds with Pepper. We can't afford to have them get loose again. You'll also be in charge of training new Hunters and assigning them to different cases. You'll have Houston's position."

Pepper's tense shoulders relaxed. The numbness from Houston acting like a total prick wore off. "What about Ottar's chip? Are you going to reinstall one?" She imagined he loved his freedom from that thing.

Roman shook his head. "We're not replacing it. L.A.M.P.S. decided he's more useful to us without it, given his *talents*. Even though he'll work here at the hub, we'll call him in on the most severe and dangerous cases." He smiled at Ottar. "You okay with all that?"

"Bloody oath, mate." He cracked a wide-faced grin. "I thought you were going to take away the best part of the job."

Pepper wrapped her arms around her middle. Even though she was overjoyed that her mind wouldn't be swiped and Ottar would stay free, she couldn't help but think about what would happen to their relationship. What was required of being a Werewolf's mate?

~ ~ ~

This was the best news Ottar had heard since he'd joined L.A.M.P.S. He never liked Houston and disliked him more after the prick shot him. He curled his fingers into a fist and punched the bloody asswipe in the face.

Houston's head snapped back even with Roman's hand still on his neck.

"You done?" Roman asked.

He'd like to punch the dodgy wanker a few more times. "Yep, for now anyway."

"Very well. I'm taking him to the main headquarters in Area 51. You'll receive a contract with your new job description in your email. Do you have any questions?"

"How come you waited to arrest him until after the wedding?" It seemed like a lot of the drama could have been avoided if they'd nailed Houston a few days ago. Shit, he could have died.

"I searched his truck after the ceremony. I found a box of Snowbirds with a mailing label on it. That was the last evidence we needed to close the case." Roman steered Houston toward the exit and looked over his shoulder at Ottar. "Don't let us down."

"Not a chance." Ottar frowned. Snowbirds were the worst. The nasty things multiplied quickly and could strip a forest in no time at all. They also had a thirst for human flesh. What if Houston had already mailed some of the Cryptids out?

Chapter 39

Later that evening Pepper watched as Ottar darted around the yard. Bam Bam the golden retriever, ran away from him, carrying a tennis ball in his mouth. Dino the sheltie barked and chased after the both of them. Barney and Betty sat on the step next to her, panting.

She pulled her coat closed to keep the chill of the fall breeze from blasting her chest. Warm fuzzies filled her heart as she watched Ottar play with her furry babies.

So much had happened today and yet seeing Ottar alive and well brought her a happiness she didn't dare dream she deserved. He was everything she could have hoped for and a little more. Yeah, that more they'd have to work through, like his taste for bunnies. She had no doubt they'd figure out a compromise.

Ottar laughed and turned to her. His eyes sparkled with joy and love for her.

She waved at him.

He pulled off his shirt and kicked his pants off. A shimmer of magic covered his skin and replaced it with fur. He shifted into his wolf, raised his nose to the sky, and howled.

She didn't mind his furriness at all and loved both his shapes.

Barney and Betty jumped off the porch and ran to him. He took off, cutting right and left. He circled around Bam Bam and stole the tennis ball.

Bam Bam whined and then crashed into him, rolling him over on the ground.

She'd always wished for someone who would love her pups as much as she did. It seemed her dogs loved him too. Never had she imagined her boyfriend would end up being part canine.

Ottar played for another hour with her dogs. They tackled each other and rolled in the mud.

"C'mon guys, do you have to get so dirty?" Oh yeah, Ottar was going to help her bathe all of them before bed.

He howled another howl, shaking the dirt from his coat. The mud splattered the other dogs. They jumped and snapped their teeth at the dirty droplets in the air.

Later that evening, Ottar slid into bed with her. "We're going to need a bigger bed."

The dogs sat on the floor looking up at them. "They prefer their doggy beds. They get too hot up here."

He cocked an eyebrow at her.

She shifted the covers. "Are you saying you're going to stay a while." A girl could hope, right?

He pulled her close to him. "Possum, I'm here forever. You're my mate and we mate for life."

Pepper smiled to herself. "You're officially adopted, Wolf Man."

Also from **Soul Mate Publishing** and **Bonnie Gill:**

TEMPTING THE LIGHT

Bad luck magnet Abby Fitzpatrick gets fired, catches her boyfriend cheating with a mime, and is cursed by an evil genie who pops out of a tampon box. She's bound and determined to remove the spell and, as fate would have it, the hottest guy she's ever met is out to kill her.

River Stone, a Cryptid hunter for Legends and Myths Police Squad (L.A.M.P.S.), poses as sheriff for Abby's hometown of Haber Cove, New Jersey. He's out to find and capture a man-eating gnome and bag the legendary Jersey Devil monster. Little does he realize, the woman who catches his heart is the same creature that he was sent to destroy.

Tempting the Light is the first novel in the L.A.M.P.S. series that features hunky secret agents who find true love while hunting and slaying dangerous Cryptids.

Available on Amazon: <u>**TEMPTING THE LIGHT**</u>

PURSUING THE LIGHT

L.A.M.P.S. hunter Leif Gunther grew up as an only child. He has a system for keeping order in his life while hunting Cryptids. He enjoys the solitude and quiet the job provides. Until a chatty redhead is assigned to assist him in his quest for the pack of Goochies terrorizing West Virginia and his systemized life gets turned upside down.

Cleaning up after Cryptids is not Holly McClure's favorite job. She'd rather be hunting like her four brothers. Her boss pairs her with the same man who stole her hunter spot. Now she has an opportunity to show she's a better hunter. Not to mention she has to keep her fairy godmother, who just happens to be a Sheepsquatch, a secret from Leif.

Leif just has three rules. Keep quiet, stay out of my way, and don't touch my stuff. Too bad Holly can't help breaking them repeatedly. Drawn together by the chase, Leif and Holly find that if they work together they make a great hunting team and their passion grows as they pursue their prey.

Available on Amazon: **PURSUING THE LIGHT**

Bonnie Gill grew up in the suburbs right outside Chicago. As a child she loved making up ghost stories at night to scare her sisters and friends.

She writes Paranormal Romance with a twist of humor. When she isn't writing you can find her on a haunted tour, volunteering at pet rescues, or digging around in her fairy garden waiting for fairies to show.

She lives in Northern Illinois with her three rescue dogs and her ever-patient boyfriend who laughs at all her goofy jokes.

She loves to hear from her readers. Please visit her website www.Bonniegill.com.

Please sign up for Bonnie Gill's newsletter to get the latest information on new releases. http://bonniegill.us11.list-manage.com/subscribe?u=e57c26c42f7dac877ef168059&id=12c1872a1b

Bonnie's Facebook Page https://www.facebook.com/Bonnie-Gill-340592565963637/

Please like Bonnie's Amazon page https://www.amazon.com/Bonnie-Gill/e/B01E0NCJIS

Bonnie's Bookbub page https://www.bookbub.com/profile/bonnie-gill

For more fabulous romance reads check out http://www.soulmatepublishing.com/

Lightning Source UK Ltd.
Milton Keynes UK
UKHW020646220419
341411UK00010B/684/P

9 781682 918203